PROFILE
OF
FEAR

Book Four of the Profile Series

Alexa Grace

PROFILE OF FEAR

This novel is a work of fiction. Names, characters, places and incidents are products of the author's imagination or are used fictitiously. Any resemblance to actual events or locales or persons, living or dead, is entirely coincidental.

Copyright 2016 by Alexa Grace
ALL RIGHTS RESERVED.

ISBN-13: 978-1-533676-21-4
ISBN-10: 1-533676-21-6

Published in the United States of America.

Critical Acclaim for USA TODAY Best-Selling Author

Alexa Grace

"Grace delivers enough sizzle to raise the temperature, showcases her talent for sharp repartee and executes the action like an ace fighter pilot. With riveting suspense and commanding characters, this is one addicting, must-have summer read."
—Diane Morasco, Reviewer for *RT Book Reviews*

"…great chemistry, a great sexual tension, and enough drama to fill a corn field…really great mystery, with just a touch of horror in the form of a serial killer… I definitely recommend this if you are into romantic suspense novels!"
—Liz at Fictional Candy

"With engaging characters, witty banter, a sexy hero, a feisty heroine, murder, suspense, romance, a serial killer, what's not to enjoy in this fast-paced romantic suspense. If you enjoy Cherry Adair and Catherine Mann's writing, you'll enjoy Alexa Grace. What a strong debut!"
—MyBookAddictionReviews

"Up-and-coming author, Alexa Grace, captivates with her literary debut—the Deadly Trilogy, a romantic suspense police procedural series. Masterfully weaving current, past, and future characters throughout, readers are afforded the opportunity to not only attain and retain beloved relationships, but also intimately connect mentally to primary and secondary individuals through glimpses into—at times disturbingly dark—thought processes." Five Stars!
—TopList-BestFictionBooks.com

"Up-and-coming author, Alexa Grace, captivates with racy, yet tasteful, romance paired with intense, suspenseful investigations makes for a contagious, page-turning police procedural series."
—TopList-BestFictionBooks.com – Five Stars

"Alexa Grace is one of the most talented, upcoming authors. Her characters are believable and strong, her stories credible, her writing, fabulous. She has an easy-to-read style that provides enough details without being overtly graphic."
—Musing Maddy, Reviewer at Ravishing Romances

Also by Alexa Grace

DEADLY OFFERINGS

DEADLY DECEPTION

DEADLY RELATIONS

DEADLY HOLIDAY

PROFILE OF EVIL

PROFILE OF TERROR

PROFILE OF RETRIBUTION

PROFILE OF FEAR

This book is dedicated to my sister and best friend, Karen Golden-Dible. Thank you for your unconditional love and support.

It is also dedicated to Drs. Patrick Loehrer and Bryan Schneider, my cancer-fighting superheroes.

Acknowledgments

My sincere appreciation goes to Lt. Adrian Youngblood of the Seminole County Sheriff's Office, who generously gave his time to answer my questions and review the book for police procedural accuracy.
A warm thank you to my editor, Vicki Braun.

Much appreciation goes to the Beta Reader Team who devoted their personal time to review each page of this book: Gail Goodenough, Barrie MacLauchlin, Lisa Jackson, Tammy Richardson, Mona Kekstadt, Sylvia Smith, Carly Maitlen-Long, and Karen Golden-Dible.

Congratulations to Mary Hesselgesser-Wright, Sandy Galloway and Phoebe Weitzel who have characters named after them in this book by winning the "Name the Character" drawing.

Finally, I want to express my appreciation to my daughter, Melissa, my family, friends, readers, and street team. Without their encouragement and support, this book would not have been possible.

Chapter 1

Leaning against a tree, he adjusted his ball cap to better cover his face as he searched the crowd. He felt exposed in a farmer's market with so many people milling about, especially without a couple of his people standing guard. He had created a world of darkness, with many places to hide and conduct his illegal, but lucrative businesses. Being out in the open like this made him anxious, and he fingered the switchblade in his pocket like a child would a security blanket.

He almost lost it when he had to walk past a cop directing traffic at the entrance off the highway. Pressing his hand against the gun under his jacket, he hoped no one recognized him, because it would get ugly fast.

He'd returned to the United States fifty thousand dollars richer, leaving the safety of the Vega drug cartel in Mexico. He'd had his men looking for her for a long, long time with no luck. But her time and luck had run out, as he knew it would. She was his first priority, his mission.

He spotted a slender woman in a black tank top and a long, faded skirt pushing a baby in a stroller. She struggled to push the stroller on the bumpy surface of the field, the wheels periodically getting stuck. She'd stop, readjust, and then push on. Her focus was on the farmer's products at each booth, not on the people surrounding her—not on him. Her mistake.

Soon she stopped to inspect a box of ripe red tomatoes in the back of a farmer's pickup truck. Thin and sickly looking, she had dirty blond hair hanging down her back. If this was the woman he sought, she'd changed a lot in three years. Gone were the cornflower-blue streaks through her blond hair and the theatrical makeup she liked to wear, imitating her rock star idol of the moment.

In the next booth, he pretended to check out some mechanic tools on long wooden folding tables while she looked at homemade baby clothes under a canopy nearby. Careful to keep his space and not be noticed, he studied her and started to doubt himself. Was it really her, or was it wishful thinking on his part? He'd paid Diego a pound of meth for the information. If he'd been sent on a wild goose chase, he'd gut Diego like a deer in front of the others. Valuable lesson for all. No one messed with Juan Ortiz. No one.

He couldn't keep his eyes off her, but he wasn't absolutely certain she was the woman he'd been looking for. At least not yet. Pulling out a couple of dollar bills from her purse, she handed them to the merchant. She bent down to put the bag of tomatoes in the stroller, her tank riding up to expose a couple of inches of flesh. That's when he saw the tattoo on her hip. It was a small circle with his initials inside. He branded all his bitches with it. It *was* Donda. The icing on the cake—the baby was with her. *His* kid.

Feeling an old fury rise, he struggled to keep it in check. Losing control in this public place would only work against him. In the worst-case scenario, it could get him caught. The FBI would get a good laugh out of that one. One of America's most wanted captured in a backwoods farmer's market.

Hell, if she recognized him she'd scream, and bring unwanted attention. No, he couldn't make his move, at least not yet. Gritting his teeth, he watched her. Was she really so stupid to think she could run from him, and hide the fact she'd had his baby? Surely she'd had a clue about how important his possessions were to him. Those who stole from him went down in painfully creative ways. He'd made sure she witnessed several executions to keep her fearful and in line. He was incredulous when she escaped. He'd make her pay for it—with her life. Or maybe not. Death was instant. Making her suffer had more appeal.

Profile of Fear

Quietly, he shadowed her until she came to a booth with several baskets loaded with sweet corn. Parking the stroller, she moved under a canopy where an old woman handed her a plastic bag. Ignoring the baby, she sorted through the ears of corn, placing her selections in the bag.

He aimed his laser focus on the kid in the stroller, a little girl dressed in a soiled pink romper sucking on her two middle fingers, and staring at him with the same sparkling blue eyes his mother, Juanita, had. He blinked. It was uncanny how the kid had zeroed in on him, as if she recognized him. He flicked a picture of her with his cell phone.

An ear-piercing shriek shook his reverie, causing his body to jerk. He dropped his cell into his pocket and bumped against a man next to him, who shot him a what-the-hell glare and stepped away. Screaming and crying, his kid kicked her chubby, little legs and pointed directly at him, drawing the attention of shoppers in both booths. A woman nearby glanced at him accusingly, as if he'd done something to the child. A warning bell went off inside his head. Too much attention. Backing away, he shot out of the booth and disappeared in the crowd.

Dropping the ears of corn in her arms to the ground, Donda twisted her attention to the stroller where her baby screamed. It was a frightening sound and as she moved closer she saw the child hysterically pointing to a man in the next booth. He was tall with a slender build, and even though a ball cap covered most of his face, she recognized him. It was his eyes. His eyes were dead, dark, and evil. The monster was here. Brittle, jagged pieces of her personal nightmare sliced through her brain. Blood drained from her face and she trembled so hard she feared she'd collapse. Run! Why wouldn't her legs move?

An older woman in the booth stared at her as she picked up the ears of corn from the ground. "Are you all right? You look like you've just seen a ghost."

Sucking in a deep breath against the panic, she unbuckled her child from the stroller and kicked it aside. Hugging the little girl to her chest and dodging the other shoppers, she ran toward her car in the parking area, praying he would not be there waiting for them.

Juan reached his truck just in time to see Donda shove the kid inside an old Toyota before she jumped into the vehicle herself. Once she got the car started, she jammed the accelerator and flew out of the makeshift parking lot in the field, leaving a cloud of dust behind.

Pulling out his cell phone, he dialed Diego. "Where are you?"

"Convenience store about a half mile away."

"It's her. She's driving an old blue Toyota RAV4."

"I see it. She just passed me. What do you want me to do?"

"Follow the bitch and keep an eye on her and my kid. Don't let her out of your sight. She spotted me, so be ready. We may have to move fast. I want my kid unharmed and delivered to me. And don't kill Donda. *I* want that pleasure."

Tossing the cell phone onto the passenger seat, he slipped the key into the ignition, started the car, and exhaled a sigh of relief. He'd found the kid. Not that he wanted a fucking rug rat around. But his mother, that was another story. That kid was worth her weight in gold to him. He needed to get back in his mother's good graces, and the kid was the way to do it.

His mother had been harping about wanting a grandchild since he hit puberty. Which was surprising since Juanita Ortiz wasn't exactly Mother Teresa when it came to human kindness. If displeased, she'd been quick with a hard slap to Juan's face, and if that wasn't enough to get his attention, she'd get creative. There were times he winced with pain as he sat at his school desk, welts on his ass from his dad's belt, or a branch from the weeping willow tree in the backyard. When he was nine-years-old, she poured boiling water onto his back as a punishment for disobeying her. Neighbors heard his screams and soon Social Services came to visit. They put him in a foster home and charged her with child abuse. But in a year, they'd returned him to Juanita, believing her claims of finding God and changing her ways. That would have been believable if the beatings hadn't continued.

Through the years, Juanita Ortiz made sure her son was

useful. She started him out with shoplifting by the time he was three, delivering packets of cocaine as an adolescent, and helping her run a prostitution and drug ring in his teens. The sex and drug trade proved to be lucrative, so much so that she attracted unwanted attention from the Feds. So she packed up her things and fled to Mexico, leaving Juan behind to fend for himself. It was south of the border that she hooked up with Miguel Vega and the powerful Vega drug cartel.

Things were going fine for him, until he became the focus of an FBI undercover operation three years ago. Luckily, he was able to escape to Mexico and the protection of both his mother and the Vega cartel. Things went well until he and Miguel Vega had a misunderstanding about the drug and trafficking money Juan brought into the cartel. Miguel wanted ninety percent of the take. Juan disagreed and packed away $50,000 of Miguel's take. When Donda was found, he was determined to return to the United States to collect his kid.

Distance didn't impede his mother. Not once did she loosen her control over him. She was living in another country and things still went *her* way.

Her lover, Miguel, wanted kids. No longer able to have a child on her own, she wanted Juan's kid, her flesh-and-blood. It was Juan's job to bring his little girl to her. What his mother wanted, she got. And she wanted his kid badly.

Chapter 2

Noah Roberts gulped a swig of hot coffee, then twisted the cap back onto his thermos. He glanced at his father, Mason, who was driving the truck, and thought of his future—the day when he would take over the helm of Roberts Sanitation Company. His father wasn't getting any younger, and rheumatoid arthritis was kicking his ass.

The business had done well the past eleven years and they'd added ten sanitation trucks to their fleet. Just last night, they'd signed a contract to collect trash from each store in the Sycamore Mall, which had been built in the seventies but had new management. Lucky for the Roberts Sanitation Company. Not bad for a family, who not long ago, lived from paycheck to paycheck, with little left over.

They approached Sycamore Mall off Route 136 and began the ascent to the back of the mall. It was their first day to serve the mall and they knew the importance of first impressions, so they both wore crisp new uniforms and the truck was sparkling clean from the scrubbing it had gotten the night before.

When they reached the back of the complex, Noah noticed the stores' dumpsters lined up like toy soldiers. His father would stop the truck at each dumpster, and Noah jumped out to check inside every dumpster before it was loaded onto the truck.

A couple of years ago, a woman searching for aluminum cans in a trash bin was dumped into the back of one of their trash trucks; the driver emptied the bin without realizing the woman was inside. The truck driver was about to press the compacting button when he heard her screams. Noah's father now demanded that each dumpster be checked thoroughly before loading—no exception.

Mason Roberts pulled the truck near the first of several dumpsters outside the Macy's store, and Noah leaped from the truck. Immediately he was assailed by a smell so repugnant, it almost knocked him on his ass. Damn it. One of Shawnee County's residents had probably dumped their dead pet or road kill in the dumpster at Macy's. As he approached the dumpster, the stomach-churning odor hit him like a brick wall. Instinctively, he covered his nose and mouth with his hand and moved closer. There were actually three dumpsters sitting side-by-side with about a foot in-between. Searching for the source of the stench, he twisted his ankle on a rock, throwing him off-balance, and he fell to the pavement. As he picked himself up, he noticed something dark sandwiched between the first and second dumpster. It was a long, black, plastic garbage bag with its yellow tie fluttering in the breeze. He cursed again. Why couldn't people put their shit in the dumpster instead of leaving it for him to pick up?

As he pushed the first dumpster to the side, he noticed his father getting out of the truck and heading toward him. "What's going on?"

"There's a bag here that needs to go into the dumpster," Noah called out as his father pulled his undershirt up to cover the lower part of his face.

"Smells like something's dead."

Noah reached down to lift the bag. "Whatever it is, it's damn heavy."

"Probably a deer or something. I'll help you with it."

Noah untied the yellow plastic strip. A sickening odor rushed at him thick and pungent, and he felt bile rush to his throat. He struggled not to vomit. Opening the garbage bag to the sunlight, he looked inside into the face of a young woman who lay in the bag, wide-eyed, with her throat cut ear-to-ear.

Chapter 3

Deputy Gail Sawyer was the first to arrive on the scene with sirens screaming and lights flashing. A janitor smoking a cigarette lingered near a set of dumpsters sitting alongside the building. She parked alongside a garbage truck and then leaped from her vehicle. The distinct odor of death assailed her senses.

"Go back inside!" She barked at the janitor as she pointed at the door. "This is a crime scene. Unless you're a witness, get your ass out of here."

He went inside as a young man in a yellow uniform headed toward her. An older man in the same type of uniform sat on the ground on a slope facing the Wabash River, looking very pale and wiping his mouth with a white rag. Looking the younger man over, she saw "Roberts Sanitation Company" embroidered on his shirt.

"Did you call this in?"

"Yes. I'm Noah Roberts." He steered her attention to the ditch. "That's my dad, Mason, sitting over there. I found a body wrapped in plastic wedged between the first and second dumpster."

"Did you move or touch anything, Mr. Roberts?"

He shook his head. "Just touched the plastic to pick it up so I could toss it in the dumpster. It was too heavy, so I opened the bag to see what was inside. That's when I saw the girl." Pale and visibly trembling, he weaved a little and Gail grabbed his arm to steady him. Been there, done that. The first time she'd seen a dead body, she'd nearly passed out and couldn't eat for a week.

As the first uniformed officer to arrive on the scene, Gail realized the importance of her performance. Her ability to secure the scene and record events in her report could mean the difference between a successful prosecution, or a vicious criminal going free. She was working toward a detective badge. That meant no mistakes.

"Show me where the body is."

Noah led her to a set of three dumpsters. The body lay between the first and second dumpster. "If you don't need me, I want to go check on my dad."

"Sure. But don't leave the area. The detective in charge is on his way. He'll want to ask you some questions."

Gail had almost reached the plastic bag when she heard the skidding of tires close behind them. Her supervisor, Sgt. Cameron Chase, had arrived, with Deputy Larry Rice in a patrol car right behind him.

Cameron turned to Deputy Rice, who was getting out of his car. "Get your crime scene tape and secure the scene. No one gets inside the tape. Including other deputies. No one disturbs this scene. If the media arrives, make a barrier at the entrance road and keep them behind it."

Approaching Gail, he pointed to the two garbage men. "Who are they?"

"The younger one found the body."

Cameron slipped on a pair of latex gloves. "Anyone else around?"

"When I arrived there was a janitor, but he's inside the building now."

Cameron bent down and opened the bag to see the body inside. The young woman's face was a grotesque mask frozen in terror, her eyes and mouth gaping open.

"Gail, get the coroner and crime scene technicians out here pronto. I'm not putting any trace evidence in jeopardy by searching the bag for an I.D. We can get that later from the coroner or crime scene techs."

Carefully, Cameron walked around the dumpsters. Gail joined him after she made her calls.

"Is it odd to you that he'd dump the body in such a public place?" Gail asked.

"This is not where the murder occurred. The victim's throat is cut, which means a lot of blood, and I don't even see a drop. He chose this place to dump her body. It's almost as if he wanted it found. I mean, this county is filled with wooded areas and agricultural farms. He could have buried the body in a shallow grave and it might have taken us months or years to find it."

"Why would a killer want a body found quickly? It seems to me he'd want to buy time to get away. The sooner the body is found, the sooner we start investigating."

"Not sure. Maybe he wanted the body found to send a message to us. He thinks he's smarter than we are and doesn't think we'll connect the dots. He wouldn't be the first sociopath to make that mistake."

Gail retrieved her cell phone and began taking photos of the crime scene. "Did you recognize her?"

"Not sure. The body looks like it's in pretty bad shape. I did notice she was a teenager with brown hair, which could be any one of the young girls that's in my missing persons file."

Indicating a surveillance camera mounted near Macy's back door, Gail said. "Silent witness. We may get lucky and the crime was recorded."

Chapter 4

Dr. Bryan Pittman, Shawnee County Coroner, waited patiently in his autopsy room for Cameron to arrive. He stood over a stainless steel table where the body of the young woman found in the dumpster lay under a white sheet.

His job was done. He tried to keep his mind compartmentalized, focused on the work itself, and not on the dead body of a girl around the same age as Hailey Adams. Lord knows Hailey had given him fits since he started a relationship with her mother, Mollie, but he had grown to love her—teenaged angst and all. There was nothing he wanted more than to marry her mother and become Hailey's father.

Not that she wanted a dad. Mollie's first husband had died in an accident when Hailey was just a baby. The only man who had come close to fathering Hailey was Cameron Chase, who had dated Mollie. But that was in the past—before Bryan and Mollie had fallen in love. Sgt. Cameron Chase, head of the County Sheriff's Major Crimes Unit, was one of his best friends, and why Cam hadn't told him that he and Mollie were involved was a mystery that he hadn't solved. He kept waiting for the right time. But was there a right time to tell your friend that you were head-over-heels in love with his ex?

Bryan checked his watch and surveyed his surroundings. A walk-in refrigerated room was to his left, kept at a constant temperature near forty degrees Fahrenheit. His autopsy room was tiled for cleaning and disinfecting, and had a stainless steel operating table in the center. The scale for weighing body parts hung from the ceiling over the table. There were stainless steel trays, pans, scales, sinks, and tables, making cleanup easy. His staff did a good job keeping the room spotless, probably for self-preservation. The odors would be obnoxious if they didn't. Even with sterilization, the smell of human decay lingered in the room, but he'd developed the ability to ignore it and focus on the job at hand.

"Good morning, Dr. Pittman." Alvin Asher, one of his assistants, came into the room to deliver a set of sanitized instruments. Most of his staff considered Alvin a nerd, complete with black-rimmed glasses and an ever-present set of ballpoint pens in the pocket of his lab coat. He was a good-humored young man who deflected teasing from his co-workers with ease. What kind of cruel joke was it to name your kid 'Alvin,' especially in an era when 'Alvin and the Chipmunks' were popular? It couldn't have been easy for Alvin growing up, having to deal with constant jokes about something he couldn't change. Bryan had respect for Alvin, and had no doubt he would make an excellent coroner someday.

After Alvin left the room, Bryan took a quick glance at the instruments he'd delivered. There were a couple of Striker saws for ripping bone, suturing materials, saws, knives, and scalpels. Nearby was a tape recorder Bryan would use to dictate his findings during the next examination.

"Hey, hope I'm not late. In case I am, I brought a peace offering." Cameron walked into the room, holding up a white bakery bag and wearing a wide smile.

"Let me guess. Mollie's chocolate, chocolate-chip muffins. In that case, all is forgiven. Before we get started, were you able to view the tape from that surveillance camera at the mall?" Bryan watched as Cameron rubbed Vicks VapoRub under his nose.

"No chance. That camera is new and hadn't even been hooked up yet. I put a fire under their butts to get it installed before something else happens outside their store."

"That's too bad. Normally I would meet you in my office to discuss my findings, but there are a couple of things I want you to see as we talk. Our victim is a white teenaged female who weighs

110 pounds and is 65 inches tall. I estimate she is between fifteen- and seventeen-years-old. Her body is in the early stages of decomposition."

Cameron shuffled his feet impatiently. "Okay, Bryan. Don't start from the beginning. Let's go to good stuff that will help me put away the monster who did this to her."

"Manner of death is homicide. Cause of death is exsanguination from the throat wound. Aspiration of blood in her respiratory passage caused her to choke to death on her own blood. The throat cut was deep, and there were no signs of hesitation cuts or defensive wounds. She either didn't see it coming or was restrained. Judging from the bruising on her wrists and ankles, I vote she was restrained."

"Judging from the lack of blood at the scene, would you say the murder happened somewhere else, and the body was dumped behind the mall?"

"Good guess."

"Any identifying marks to help us identify her?"

"That's what I wanted to show you." Bryan lifted the sheet to expose the hip of the body and pointed to a circular mark. "She has a relatively fresh tattoo. It looks like a brand, like they put on cattle."

Cameron leaned closer, and then took out his cell to take a photo. "Yeah, I see that. Looks like the letters inside the circle are a 'J' and an 'O.'"

"I'm hoping it will help you identify her. I also took an x-ray of her teeth. The girl had good dental care. She's worn braces to straighten her teeth, and has a filling in one of her molars. We'll enter her DNA in the Missing Persons DNA Database, as well as the FBI's CODIS DNA databases. I'll let you know if we get a match."

"We've got three missing girls that match her description. I hope this is one of them so her family gets some kind of closure."

Three weeks later, Cameron was reading his email when his cell went off. Checking the display, he noticed it was Bryan Pittman.

"Hey, Bryan, what's up?"

"I've got an I.D. on your dumpster body."

"Good news. Who is it?"

"Brandy Murphy from Williamsport. She was sixteen and had been missing for six months. I was able to identify her by dental records and her DNA. When she went missing, her father, Benjamin, gave officers a copy of her dental records and one of her hairbrushes for DNA."

"She's one of the three missing girls I told you about. Brandy was last seen at Sycamore Mall getting into a newer model black van with tinted windows. We got the surveillance tape, but we couldn't identify the man with her, nor could we get a good look at the license plate. A hoodie covered his face. But she got into the vehicle willingly."

"Boyfriend?"

"The father says absolutely not. Brandy was not allowed to date. She'd just gotten her driver's license and it was her first trip to the mall. Brandy's body language and that of the man on the tape did not suggest she was on a date."

"Speaking of her father, Benjamin was just here and identified the body. I showed him the tattoo and he said he'd never seen it before. He said Brandy wanted to be a model and she thought a tattoo might hurt her chances of getting jobs. So she never would have gotten one on her own."

"If he's right, that means she got the tattoo while she was missing—with her permission or not."

Chapter 5

Waiting for Lt. Patrick Lair in his office made Sgt. Robynn Burton twitch with anxiety. Taking two weeks paid leave while Internal Affairs investigated her undercover operation-gone-wrong was bad enough. But waiting for the supervisor who had recently promoted her to sergeant in charge of the Criminal Investigation Division was excruciating. Would Lt. Lair fire her? Would he demote her? Both were possibilities she felt she probably deserved.

To distract herself, she looked at the photographs and basketball memorabilia lining Lair's office walls and filling his bookcases.

Lt. Patrick Lair was kind of a legend with the Indiana State Police. He grew up in Speedway, an only child of a facilities manager father, and a mother who was a librarian for the Indianapolis Public Library. Going to Indiana State University on an athletic scholarship, he soon became their star basketball player. After graduation he was recruited by the Indiana Pacers and was named their MVP for the last season he played, averaging twenty-eight points, eleven rebounds, eight assists, and three steals per game. In the Hoosier State, Lair was a basketball legend.

The media and basketball fanatics were in a frenzy when he retired to take a job with the Indiana State Police as a Trooper with a starting salary of $37,000 a year. Robynn's peers had bets that the millionaire basketball player wouldn't last six months once he got a taste of the long hours and hard work required of the job. They were wrong.

His professionalism and devotion to law enforcement made him a hero in Robynn's eyes. He mentored and believed in her as she moved up the ranks, which made her screwup even harder to swallow. Her mistake had cost one of her team members his life.

Her thoughts pulled her back to a memory that haunted her every day, asleep or awake. It should have been a simple bust. It was anything but.

Robynn remembered her early-morning meeting with Alex Easton, one of the rookie detectives she supervised. She was so used to seeing him in a dress shirt, tie, and khakis that she almost didn't recognize him. Unshaven, he wore a stained white tank with a pair of denim cutoffs. His unruly hair looked greasy, and he wore an earring in one ear.

She sat with him and reviewed how the buy would go down. Alex had looked a little anxious, but that was expected for a first assignment like this one. Once he was wired, he was ready to go. It was his first undercover assignment, and Alex was to make a buy of three rocks of crack cocaine worth $100.

They'd spent the last two weeks focusing on Leon Gary, a small-time dealer who was climbing the food chain of a gang that sold drugs on the north side of the county. They'd gotten his name from one of his dealers, who was stopped by a trooper on I-65 with a couple of kilos of marijuana in the trunk of his car. The guy had a pregnant wife at home and was desperate to trade information for his freedom. He seemed more afraid of her than the criminals he was ratting on. Without hesitation, he arranged the buy with a small-time dealer with connections, Leon Gary.

As it turned out, Leon Gary had a rap sheet five pages long, which included assault, domestic violence, shoplifting, selling of a controlled substance, and a host of other charges. Sure they wanted to get Leon off the street, but most importantly, their goal was to motivate him to spill some information about the gang leaders at the top.

Later that day, Robynn selected a space in the K-Mart parking lot so she had a visual on the unmarked white Mustang driven by her undercover detective, Alex Easton, and backed into a parking space near him.

Powering down her window, she watched as another detective on her team, Bruce James, parked his unmarked Dodge Charger five spaces over from Alex. Near the store entrance, former IMPD detective Wayne Griffin sat in his unmarked Ford Taurus. The plan was to swoop in and block the dealer's car with one of their own, to thwart his getaway, once the hand-to-hand transaction took place. On paper the plan sounded easy-peasy, but it wasn't.

Robynn's attention was drawn to an older woman pushing a cart full of boxes. She stopped near Alex's car and opened the trunk of her car. The last thing they needed was a civilian risking injury, not to mention scaring off their perp. Robynn ripped off her Indiana State Police jacket, and raced toward the woman's car.

"May I help you with those boxes?"

Eying her suspiciously before she spoke, the woman nodded. "That's very nice of you. Some of these boxes are heavy."

Robynn moved the boxes into the lady's trunk, slammed the lid down, and returned to her vehicle. As the woman drove out of the space, a man in a Lincoln SUV waited until she left and then pulled into her spot. He came to a stop and then powered his window down to talk to Alex. It was their perp.

In her earpiece, she could hear Alex make the buy, and then saw him hand an envelope of money to Leon Gary. He uttered the code word 'takedown.' That's when all hell broke loose.

Bruce James, lights flashing and siren screaming, squealed the wheels of his Dodge Charger in his haste to block Leon Gary's car.

Gary saw him and lifted a handgun, shooting Alex point-blank in the middle of his forehead. He then backed up and rammed the Dodge Charger, causing Bruce's airbag to deploy, slamming into his upper body.

After the crash, Gary sped off and thrusted head-on into the vehicle driven by Wayne Griffin. After that crash, Leon Gary raced through the parking lot, pursued by Bruce James, who recovered from the air bag deployment.

Robynn rushed to Alex's car and called for backup and an ambulance. But it was too late. Alex was dead.

In the meantime, Leon Gary's car jumped a concrete-and-grass-covered median. He leaped from the car, with Bruce James and Wayne Griffin in hot pursuit. Using a flying tackle, Bruce knocked Gary to the ground and struggled to hold on to him, until Wayne immobilized him with his stun gun.

Patrick Lair entered the room, softly patted Robynn on the back, and sat behind his desk. "Sorry. Hope you haven't been waiting long. I had to run home. My two kids are raising alpacas for 4-H and one of them got loose. An alpaca got loose—not one of my children. I found him grazing on my neighbor's newly landscaped yard. And no, she isn't happy." Grinning, he filtered through a stack of files on his desk, found the folder he was seeking, and pulled it out.

"I just got here," she lied and folded her hands on her lap to keep them from shaking.

Leaning back in his chair, his dark eyes studied her. The calm in his stare was more frightening than if he'd shouted at her. She couldn't meet his gaze and defensively locked her arms across her chest.

Lair finally asked. "Are you okay?"

"Yes, sir."

"You don't look okay. You look like you haven't slept in a month. In fact, you look like crap."

"I'm holding up. The past few weeks weren't exactly a vacation in paradise. The funeral, shrink visits, and stifling boredom are not exactly my idea of fun. I'm a cop. I should have been on the job."

Ignoring her statement, he said, "Internal Affairs has completed their investigation and you've been cleared of any wrongdoing."

That information should have made her feel better, but it didn't. With a mixture of gratitude and guilt, she replied, "I screwed up."

"Haven't we all?"

"I was his supervisor. He was on *my* team. My responsibility. How can the others trust me to have their back when I obviously didn't have his?"

"How were you supposed to know it was going to go down as it did? There are no sure things in undercover work. Too many moving targets."

"I should have had Alex meet him in an open space, like a park. We could have prevented Leon from using his gun."

"You don't know that, and you need to get past this. I need you back on the job with your full focus on some cases I need you to work on."

"What about Leon Gary?"

"He's the prosecutor's problem now. Not yours." He pushed the file folder in front of him across his desk to Robynn. "This is the case I want you to work on."

Robynn nodded and opened the file while Lt. Lair briefed her on the case.

"Shirley Metz was reported missing by her parents when the twenty-one-year-old didn't return home. The town and county police had a good start looking for her, with no results. The State Police got invited to the party about two months after she disappeared. She'd been missing for a year when her body was found by hikers near the Handley Dairy Farm just off State Road 341."

"What was she doing before she disappeared?"

"Her parents said she'd met two friends the night before at a local bar in Hillsboro about a mile from their house. The victim meets these women for drinks on a regular basis, so the parents weren't concerned about her safety. About 2:00 a.m., the friends say Metz got into her Toyota Camry and told them she was heading home. Somewhere between the bar and her parent's house, she disappeared. No trace of her, her clothing, or her car. No action on her credit cards. Gone. Metz had her purse with her, but she'd accidentally left her cell phone at the bar."

"Runaway?"

"Her parents say no. Metz had a nine-month-old baby she adored. She worked as a hairdresser at Sycamore Mall to support her baby and herself. Her father says she's not the type to run away. He says she has a baby, a job, and a life she wouldn't walk away from. I agree with him. Shirley Metz did not leave the area on her own volition."

He pointed to the file folder in front of Robynn, who opened it to see the gruesome autopsy photo on the first page. "Her throat was slit from ear-to-ear, with no signs of hesitation cuts or defensive wounds. She had bruising on her wrists and ankles that suggest she was restrained. No DNA or trace evidence. Her body had been scrubbed with bleach."

"Any new developments I should know about?"

"Last night, I read the autopsy report of a young girl found near a mall dumpster in Shawnee County. There were too many similarities to ignore. The girl's throat was slit, no defensive wounds, signs she was restrained. Most importantly, no DNA or trace evidence. The case belongs to Sgt. Cameron Chase. I want you to study Metz's case file and meet with him. My gut tells me these two cases are related. Talk to Chase about them. We have money in the budget to hire that profiler, Carly Stone, to do an analysis to help us narrow our focus. See if he thinks that would be a good idea."

Chapter 6

Robynn stepped onto the marble tile in the foyer of Giovanni's, a new Italian restaurant near the mall, and looked around. Italian landscape oil paintings graced the walls, while dark wooden floors contrasted with the elegant, crisp, white tablecloths. Lighting was muted; the tables and chairs ornate. She mentally kicked herself for not checking the restaurant out before arranging to meet Sgt. Cameron Chase about cases that may or may not be similar. There was only one word that would describe this place: Romantic. Which was absolutely the last message she wanted to send to Cameron Chase.

She'd hadn't seen Cameron since they worked together the year before. What was work-related quickly turned personal when he captured her mouth in a delicious kiss that made her head spin. He'd kissed her with his entire body, hard and so hot she thought her bones would melt. Soon, despite her reservations, she was kissing him right back, pulling him closer so she could feel his powerful body pressed against her.

When the kiss ended, Cameron told her that he was worth the risk, and she was jolted back to reality. The risk was great, and Robynn had too much to lose. She'd worked hard to climb the ranks with the Indiana State Police, and she couldn't jeopardize her career by getting involved with another law enforcement officer. It was different for female officers. The gossip about their relationship could derail her effectiveness in supervising the men on her team; she needed to collaborate as an equal to get her job done.

Could she afford to invest herself in feelings that would only lead to career disaster? Robynn did not want to jeopardize her job. As a single parent, her three-and-a-half-year-old daughter, Ellie, depended on her for financial support.

It had taken all the strength she had to push Cameron away and run to her car, ignoring his pleas for her to come back. In the weeks to follow, she'd ignored his calls, deleted his voice mails, and avoided him at meetings, but she hadn't forgotten him and the way he made her feel.

And how she was going to handle this meeting with him, and keep things professional, was anyone's guess.

The waiter led her to a private table toward the back of the room where relatively few diners sat. She hoped none of them would overhear their appetite-destroying discussion of autopsies and murders.

Soon she saw Cameron Chase enter the restaurant wearing snug jeans, a navy blazer, and a white silk T-shirt that fit his athletic body like a second skin. Usually clean-shaven, a few days growth darkened his sculpted jaw. With dark brown hair and eyes the color of espresso, he had a face that was blatantly masculine and too handsome for his own good. A spike of heat caught low in her gut. A pang of longing shot through her like a bullet. Though hard to admit, she missed being kissed and touched and held in a man's strong arms. And no man had affected her like Cameron Chase.

Conscious that she was staring, she dragged her gaze back to his face as he reached her table and met his knowing glance. It was as if he could read her mind. She felt her cheeks burn with embarrassment. Robynn renewed her determination not to let him see a chink in her reinforced wall.

Chapter 7

Cameron's first thought when he entered Giovanni's Italian restaurant was that it was quite a romantic place for a business meeting. Should he be encouraged that Robynn Burton had chosen this place?

Across the restaurant, he noticed her sitting at a table in the back. She usually wore her dark hair tied away from her face in a French braid. Tonight, she wore her hair down, a tangle of glossy hair spilling over her shoulders like a cloud of dark silk.

Average wasn't a word that could ever be used to describe Robynn. She had a face that was a delicate sculpture of high cheekbones with full sensuous lips, and a body that pushed all his buttons in a very big way. Not that he planned to act on any of those feelings tonight. There was a line between pursuing a woman and stalking her, so he willed himself to back off. Certainly that was her message, loud and clear, when she'd ignored his calls and voice mails. If she wanted to discuss their cases, that's what they'd do and he'd control himself, no matter how hard that would be. However, the way her eyes were undressing him as he moved toward her just might suggest she had other ideas. A guy could hope.

Reaching the table, Cameron pulled out the chair across from Robynn and sat down. "Good to see you, Robynn. Nice place." He couldn't help but notice she was blushing, and a smile slowly tipped up one corner of his mouth.

When the waiter placed menus before them, Cameron glanced at Robynn. "So what's good here?"

"I don't know. This is my first visit."

That response might explain the romantic atmosphere. She hadn't known about it.

The waiter returned and they each ordered an Alfredo dish with sautéed shrimp on angel hair pasta, and a glass of wine since they were both off-duty.

They quietly sipped their wine until Cameron broke the silence. "I'm sorry about Alex Easton. I know he was one of your detectives. Tough break." Instantly, he regretted bringing it up because Robynn's eyes filled with pain.

"He will be missed." Quickly changing the subject, she said, "My boss—"

"Patrick Lair, right? Former basketball player."

"Yes, Lt. Lair noticed some similarities in your Brandy Murphy murder case to our Shirley Metz murder. He asked that we compare notes to see if the women could have been murdered by the same killer."

"What similarities are you talking about?"

"Both women were young and went missing without a trace. Metz had been missing a year when she was found."

"Murphy was only sixteen-years-old and had been missing six months when we found her body wrapped in garbage bags and dumped behind the mall like trash. We'd tried like hell to find her, but it was as if she walked off the face of the earth. No clues except a grainy surveillance tape the night she was abducted."

"There was a surveillance tape?"

Cameron nodded. "Murphy was last seen at Sycamore Mall getting into a newer model black Escalade with tinted windows. We couldn't identify the man with her. A dark hoodie covered his face. No hits on the car either. My theory is that the guy made Murphy a tempting offer she couldn't refuse. She wasn't the kind of girl to go off with a stranger. Not without good reason."

Robynn captured the information on her notepad. "According to her family, Shirley Metz was twenty-one, but she wouldn't have left without telling her parents where she would be. She had a nine-month-old baby, a job, and a life she wouldn't walk away from. She worked as a hairdresser at Sycamore Mall. They're convinced she was abducted. I'm inclined to agree with them, but there's no evidence to support the notion."

Their food arrived and they made small talk while they ate, each carefully avoiding topics that were personal. Once the waiter cleared their table, Cameron asked, "Tell me more about your victim. What was she doing the night she disappeared?"

"Her parents said she'd met two girlfriends at a local bar in Hillsboro about a mile from their house. Not unusual. Shirley meets these women for drinks on a regular basis, so the parents weren't concerned about her safety. The friends said Shirley got into her Toyota Camry around 2:00 a.m., and told them she was heading home. Somewhere between the bar and her parent's house, only a mile away, she disappeared. No trace of her, her clothing, or her car. No action on her credit cards. Shirley had her purse with her, but she'd accidentally left her cell phone at the bar."

Cameron rubbed the bridge of his nose thoughtfully. "Sorry, Robynn. I don't see where these two cases equal one killer."

Slipping two manila folders out of her briefcase, she handed one of them to Cameron. "This is a copy of the case file for Shirley Metz."

Cameron opened the folder and glanced at the photo of Shirley Metz lying on an autopsy table, and then flipped to the coroner's report. "Talk to me about her autopsy results."

"Her throat was slit from ear-to-ear, with no signs of hesitation cuts or defensive wounds. She had bruising on her wrists and ankles that suggest she was restrained. No DNA or trace evidence. Her body had been scrubbed with bleach. Just early signs of decomposition, so she'd been living somewhere for the twelve months she was missing."

"Brandy Murphy's throat was also slit. Also with early signs of decomposition, she had no defensive wounds, and there were signs she was restrained. In addition, she'd been scrubbed with bleach and there was no DNA or trace evidence."

"Wait a minute. I'm not seeing the leap to this being one killer." Cameron scanned the coroner's report. "There's no mention of identifying marks on Shirley's body by your coroner. On Brandy's hip, we found a circular tattoo with the letters 'J' and an 'O' within the circle." He pulled out his cell phone, found the photo he'd taken of Brandy's tattoo, and handed his cell to Robynn.

"It looks like a brand like they put on cattle."

Cameron agreed. "We thought so, too."

Robynn opened her file to review the photos of Shirley Metz's body taken by the coroner. Extracting one of the pictures, she studied it carefully before handing it to Cameron.

"Our coroner missed it! There it is on her hip, the same circular tattoo. That's the link."

Cameron inclined his head in agreement. "You're right. Now we need to touch base with her parents and friends to see if she had the tattoo before she went missing. If she didn't, we may have a serial killer on our hands."

"What are your thoughts on using Carly Stone to create a profile based on what we know about the two cases? It would help us narrow our focus, steer us in the right direction. My lieutenant says we have money in our budget to hire her as a consultant."

Cameron retrieved a card from his wallet and handed it to Robynn. "It's Carly Stone-Chase now. Here's her business card. Let's get her started on a profile before this bastard kills again."

Chapter 8

They drove on State Road 341 until they reached an extensive wooded area. When Cameron stopped the car, Carly Stone-Chase got out and the sweltering summer heat hit her like a bus. Eighty-nine degrees and it wasn't even nine o'clock in the morning. By the time Sgt. Cameron Chase and Robynn Burton reached her on the other side of the car, their skin was flushed and they'd begun peeling off their blazers and rolling up their sleeves.

"Damn, Carly. Did you have to choose the hottest day of the year to see the spot where Shirley Metz's body was dumped?" Cameron complained as he pushed up his sleeves, a large patch of sweat already pooling under his arms.

Carly would have liked to have visit the original crime scenes, but thanks to the killer dumping both bodies elsewhere, that was not to be. So she focused on what she had: forensic photographs, police reports, autopsy reports, family member statements, and crime scene notes and sketches. But she still had questions about the dump sites and had to see each in person to focus on behavioral clues, thinking as the killer did—viewing things from his perspective. Besides, there was always a chance, however remote, that the crime scene techs missed something. Wouldn't hurt to look around.

Carly bent to re-tie her Nike's shoelaces. "I already told you, Cam. I need to see the original crime scenes. Since that's not possible for either murder, it's important I see where their bodies were dumped."

"Didn't you see the photographs in the file?" Robynn asked as she unbuttoned the top two buttons of her cotton blouse.

Carly sighed. They were tapping her limited patience. "Where a killer dumps his victim's body tells a lot about his behavior."

"It's there." Robynn interrupted as she pointed to the sharp turn in the road ahead.

They walked the hot pavement until they reached a hair-pin curve in the road. Robynn stopped and pointed to a drainage ditch, and then a thicket of trees. "She was right there, under that large oak tree."

Scrambling down the embankment, Carly leaped over the rainwater-clogged ditch and waded through clumps of switchgrass, with the two investigators close behind. Clouds of mosquitoes burst from the tall grass with each step, stinging any exposed flesh on their arms, necks, and faces. Swatting wildly, they quickened their pace as if they could outrun the pests.

Finally, Carly braced herself against the tree, slapping at a mosquito that had targeted her cheek.

Swatting a bug on her arm, Robynn pointed to the ground beneath the tree. "Shirley's body was found in a sitting position to the right of where you're standing."

Looking toward the road, Carly said, "Her body could be seen from a vehicle. In fact, she's dumped at the point of the curve where you could see it, no matter which direction you were driving."

Brushing a path of plant seeds and insects from his jeans, Cameron straightened and directed his attention to the road. "That's true. We wondered why a passerby didn't report it, but she was found by a couple of hikers."

Carly wiped the sweat dripping into her eyes with the back of her hand. "It bothers me that the bodies were dumped in two different locales."

"Why?"

"Brandy's body was found in a very public place, a busy mall. Yet Shirley's body is dumped here in a relatively remote, agricultural area. On paper, it seemed the killer had two different motivations for disposing of the bodies." Wading through some tall grass, she reached the oak tree and looked back toward the road. "But now that I'm here, I can see that he dumped both bodies in a place where they'd be discovered sooner than later. He wants them to be found. Besides communicating his contempt for the victims, he wants law enforcement to know he's here."

"Oh, yeah? Well, we know he's here, and his ass is grass," spat Cameron, a crest of anger filling his voice.

"Does he *want* to get caught?" asked Robynn.

Carly swiped another mosquito off her arm. "No, quite the opposite. He feels superior, bulletproof. He thinks there's no chance he'll be caught, so he's playing a kind of sick game with us."

Buzzing sounded above her head. By the time Carly noticed the honeycombed, papery bag hanging in the tree above her head, it was too late. The wasps fired out of the nest like fighter pilots, diving in to sting, regrouping, and coming back for a second run, then a third. Like getting stabbed repeatedly with a small needle, Carly felt her skin burning, as if salt were being rubbed into a paper cut. Panting, she couldn't get to the vehicle fast enough.

With angry wasps sticking to her clothing and stinging exposed areas of her skin, Robynn screamed, her arms waving wildly as she ran past Carly. Her foot became entangled with a tree root and she tumbled down, twisting her ankle. She hit the ground hard, knocking the wind out of her. Cameron swooped in and pulled her up by her arm. He swiped away the insects on her, firmly wrapped his arm around her waist, and helped Robynn to the car.

Once Cameron started the car, he adjusted the air conditioner to high and pulled a small first aid kit from the glove box.

"There's a café in Hillsboro not far from here. Let's assess the damage and talk there."

By the time they reached the café, Robynn had slicked her hair back into a ponytail, rubbed her bites with alcohol pads, and rolled up the sleeves of her white cotton blouse. She chastised herself for not dressing more appropriately when she'd known ahead of time the projected sweltering temperature, as well as the inevitable trek through the weeds to see the dump site. Worst of all, she'd let the heat get to her and aimed her annoyance onto the profiler who might enable them to catch the killer before more young women died. Not her smartest move.

At the restaurant, a familiar face greeted her. A poster for Shirley Metz was taped to the inside of the front picture window. Hillsboro was a small town, and people took it hard when one of their own went missing. They were even more devastated when her body was found. Robynn had been unable to stop thinking about the young mother since she received the case.

A waitress appeared and scrutinized the three of them. "Bees?"

"Wasps," Robynn replied. She fisted her hands so she wouldn't scratch at the bites, which were now large scarlet bumps that itched and hurt like a bitch.

"I'll go get our first aid kit. Meet you back at the restrooms." The waitress hightailed it back to the kitchen, retrieved a first aid kit, a stack of clean towels, and a bottle of antibacterial hand soap. She then rushed to the back of the restaurant where the three were waiting for her.

"Who wants to go first?"

Cameron nodded toward the two women. "I'll wait."

Robynn and Carly shouldered the door and entered the ladies room, which thankfully was clean. At the double sink, Robynn lay down the towels and Carly opened the first aid kit.

Ripping off her blouse, Robynn dampened a towel and poured on antibacterial soap, then carefully washed the throbbing bumps on her arms, chest, and legs. She noticed several stings on her face and lips. In fact, her lips were swollen twice their normal size.

"Turn around and let me see your back," said Carly, who then began washing the reddened welts near Robynn's spine. Carly then turned around and let Robynn do the same.

Robynn pressed a cold damp cloth to her lips. "This experience just strengthens my aversion to bugs in general, and wasps specifically."

"Totally agree. When we were kids, my brother, Blake, once trapped a bee under a Mason jar and asked if I wanted to see it. The second he lifted the jar, the bee dive-bombed me near my eye. It was swollen shut for a week."

"Ugh." Robynn found two cold packs in the first aid kit and handed one to Carly. They picked up the first aid kit, remaining clean towels and soap, then went into the hallway where Cameron was waiting.

"You don't look so good," said Carly.

"Thanks. Might I say you look like you have a monumental case of the measles?"

Carly grinned as the waitress appeared. "I've got a booth in the back open. It's pretty private. Want that one?"

Carly nodded in the affirmative and followed the waitress.

Robynn turned to Cameron. "Do I look like I have the measles, too?"

"Nope, but your lips look like Lisa Rinna's: sexy, plumped up, and made for kissing."

"Do you hear that?"

"Hear what?"

"That buzzing sound? That's the inappropriate-comment-alert going off."

Holding both hands in the air, he said, "You're right. Won't happen again. Sometimes I forget my filter and whatever I'm thinking just flies out of my mouth. Sorry."

Robynn handed the first aid kit and towels to Cameron. "Apology accepted. Just think of me as one of the guys."

He scanned her body appreciably. "Not going to happen."

Robynn chuckled and responded, "Cameron, you just did it again."

Cameron cheeks flushed and he dipped his head. "Then I guess you're just going to have to blindfold me."

She started to walk away, but he captured her arm. Startled, Robynn whirled around. "What are you doing?"

"I have wasp stings all over my back. I need your help."

"That is not a good—"

Her words were cut off as he pulled her into the small men's restroom and locked the door. "You can't be serious. This is a men's room."

"I'm in pain and serious as hell. You going to help me or not?"

Stripping off his shirt, Cameron turned around, revealing a deep gorge that gave rise to the thick walls of muscle on either side of his back. His arms were muscled, his stomach tapered, without an ounce of fat. Her body tingled with awareness.

As she gazed at the dozens of angry reddened welts on his back, a sense of guilt rushed through her. The stings must have happened when he was shielding her with his body as he helped her in the woods. Taking the towels from him, she moistened one with soap and water and gently cleansed the welts on Cameron's back.

"Feel better?" She asked.

With his eyes deep, dark, and mysterious, he turned to gaze down at her and huskily replied, "Infinitely."

"You're welcome." Robynn's eyes lingered on Cameron's full lips and he leaned in toward her. She wanted more than anything to feel his lips on hers again. Kissing her. Possessing her. The thought stoked the fire that kindled in her core. Realizing what was about to happen, Robynn pulled quickly away. She couldn't go there with him.

Once they settled in the booth, Carly on one side and Cameron sliding in next to Robynn on the other, they ordered a round of iced tea and tenderloin sandwiches. Cameron sat so close to her that she could feel the heat of his body next to hers. His woodsy, masculine scent surrounded her. Her self-control was circling around and around, slowly going down the drain. Damn Cameron Chase and his effect on her. Why couldn't he be an accountant or a teacher? Any occupation except law enforcement.

The waitress delivered the iced tea. Robynn thirstily attacked her drink, not setting it down on the table until it was empty. She'd never been a big fan of summer heat, and today was no exception. Inquisitively, she studied Carly. From all accounts the profiler was meticulous, working her way through the evidence until she came to a conclusion. She couldn't wait another second to hear Carly's thoughts about their killer.

Robynn's approach was head-on. "Carly, do you agree that we have one killer for both victims?"

"Yes." Carly sipped her tea and fingered the paper from her straw.

"What are your initial thoughts about who could have committed these murders?" Robynn asked.

"I think your suspect is an organized killer who planned both killings and moved the bodies from the original crime scene. In Brandy Murphy's case, he moved her body from the place where he killed her to a dumpster behind a busy shopping mall, thus denying law enforcement any trace evidence that may have been found at the original crime scene. A disorganized killer would have no interest in moving the body."

"What do you think moving the bodies signifies?"

"The transfer of the bodies indicates planning before and after the kill. Leaving the bodies in plain sight and within view of a surveillance camera may indicate your killer is advertising his presence to law enforcement. He's saying, "I'm here. What are you going to do about it?"

Robynn respected Carly's knowledge, but this theory bothered her. "So you're sure he does these things, but he *doesn't* want to get caught?"

"Like I said before, he thinks he's bulletproof, and there's no chance he'll get caught. He'll follow the cases in the media to make sure he's getting the attention he thinks he deserves."

"So we're not talking run-of-the-mill, dumber-than-dirt criminal?"

"Definitely not. He's smart enough to make sure evidence is destroyed by using latex gloves and cleansing the bodies with bleach. In addition, he is careful to take the weapon with him. He may not be book-smart, but he's street-smart."

The waitress returned to check if they needed more iced tea. Waiting until she was out of earshot, Cameron asked, "What are your thoughts on motive, besides the fact he's a sonofabitch who preys on women?"

"I think he is a full-blown sociopath whose motive is power or control, the ultimate possession of his victim. Complete domination is how he gets self-fulfillment. To the killer, the life-or-death power over his victims gives him tremendous emotional satisfaction."

"What makes you think that?"

"He didn't kill either of his victims immediately. With Brandy Murphy, it was six months after he abducted her. With Shirley Metz, it was a year."

Carly paused as the waitress delivered their plates of tenderloin sandwiches with fries. Dipping a french fry in ketchup, she gobbled it down before she continued.

"Because he held his victims over a period of time, instead of killing them right away, it's likely he intimidated them with violence to make them obey him. Fear is a powerful motivator. In fact, he uses restraints to render his victims helpless, and heighten each victim's fear. He needs to see their fear in order to get sexual satisfaction. The more hysterical they are and the more they struggle, the more he likes it. The cutting of the victims' throats while they are restrained is his signature, his preferred method of killing."

"Can you imagine the terror the women must have experienced as they watched him prepare to slice their throats?" Robynn's words were whispered and filled with empathy. She wished she didn't think of victims so much, but she did. The images in her brain of how their lives ended were haunting, and made her that much more determined to catch their killer.

With a look of distaste, Cameron offered, "He's one sick bastard, is what he is."

"What about the victims?" asked Robynn. "Do you think he had relationships with them?"

"No, he was a stranger to his victims. He targeted and may have stalked them. Both victims frequented Sycamore Mall. Shirley Metz worked in the Diva Hair Salon on the first floor, and Brandy Murphy liked to hang out there. The mall is his hunting ground."

After finishing his lunch, Cameron pushed his empty plate aside and glanced at Robynn. "We know from the surveillance tape that Brandy was last seen leaving the mall with a man driving a black Escalade. According to her father, Brandy didn't trust strangers. Leaving the mall with someone she didn't know was not in her makeup. We need to find out what kind of a lure or con he's using to convince a young, but careful young girl to leave the mall with him."

"What about Shirley Metz? How did she connect with her killer?" Robynn wondered aloud.

Waiting until the waitress cleared their table, Carly answered, "Shirley works in the mall as a hairdresser. The perp could have been a customer, or he could have approached her in the mall with his offer. Shirley does not fall for his con and it pisses him off. He follows her home after work and stalks her until the time is right to grab her.

"I know that your detectives have talked to both victims' significant others. I think it's important to talk to her co-workers to see if they noticed Shirley talking to a man in the mall. We might be able to get a suspect sketch. A second talk with Brandy's friends might help us identify her killer."

"Do you have any ideas as to what he's doing with these women as he holds them captive?"

"Which brings me to an important part of our discussion. Our killer may be interested more in profiting from his victims rather than killing them. It is very possible these women were victims of sex trafficking. They probably were murdered when they tried to get away. If there is one thing our killer craves, it's control and power. An escape attempt is a slap to his face, an affront to his power."

Cameron stared at Carly in surprise. "Sex trafficking? Seriously?"

"The tattoo is a red flag. Branding by tattoo or intentional scarring has become particularly common in the last few years by sex traffickers. The tattoo indicates ownership. It lets other pimps know that this individual is his property. The practice is not new. Slave owners used to brand their slaves to show ownership.

"If he's a trafficker, why would he commit the murders himself, instead of having one of his flunkies do the deed?"

"Both murders were the ultimate punishment for disobeying *his* rules. He would do them himself for a couple of reasons. First to satisfy his overwhelming need for power and control. In addition, he would have done it himself to instill more fear in his other victims. It's a possibility he had the others watch. As if to say, 'This is what happens when I am disobeyed.' However, having said that, he may not have been the suspect who dumped the bodies. Depending on where he is in the food chain, he could have a flunky do it. But the killings? He'd insist on doing those himself."

"Back to the tattoo. How can we link it to a suspect?" Robynn asked.

"The FBI has a relatively new database, Next Generation

Identification (NGI), which increases automated identification capabilities beyond fingerprints and palm prints. Although law enforcement has used photographs of scars, marks, and tattoos for several years to help identify or eliminate suspects, the NGI automates that process. Before I left the office, I sent NGI a query about our tattoo. Hopefully, the info is there when I return."

Chapter 9

It was four in the morning and the cloudless sky was pitch-black. The white clapboard farm house was illuminated by floodlights atop three deputy vehicles, parked side-by-side facing the structure.

The meth bust was in full swing. Slapping at a mosquito, Sgt. Cameron Chase watched as Deputy Ben Deacon, clad in protective yellow coveralls with an air mask over his face, hauled a man out of the house. Hello, Willie Hicks, methamphetamine cook and one of the most prolific dealers in Shawnee County, Indiana. It had taken three months to infiltrate his inner circle, and this bust was the cherry on top of their law enforcement sundae.

Deputy Deacon, a six-foot-two body builder, effortlessly gripped Willie's arm. The meth dealer flipped about like a fish out-of-water—an anorexic fish—especially compared to Deacon. Reaching the police cruiser, Deacon handed him over to another deputy, who shoved him in the back seat after reading Willie his rights.

Cameron moved closer to Deacon. "Anyone else inside?"

He removed his air mask and rubbed the back of his hand over his forehead. "Yeah, there's a woman and a child."

"The woman should be Willie's wife, Donda. Are you sure there's a child?"

"Yes, sir. Little girl. Looks to be around two-years-old."

The news hit Cameron like a sucker punch. How could he have missed that? He knew everything there was to know about

Willie and Donda Hicks. Why wasn't a child mentioned anywhere in his research? Why didn't their undercover detective or informant mention a kid?

"Deacon, do you know if the child lives here? Could she just be visiting?"

"She lives here. Found her in a back bedroom in a crib. We found a stash of weapons under it." The deputy pulled his air mask over his mouth and nose and then re-entered the house.

Cameron flushed with anger and wanted to hit something or someone. He should have found out about the little girl. They could have removed her from the house months ago. This was a major clusterfuck.

It wasn't that they hadn't found kids during meth busts in the past. They had. Cameron remembered each time as if it had happened yesterday—in distinct detail. Kids were his weak spot. A child in trouble could easily slice his heart into ribbons in seconds. There was no getting around it.

The little girl was only two-years-old? Just a baby. He tried to prepare himself. Kids found living in meth houses were commonly malnourished, improperly clothed, and neglected. Many of them tested positive for having methamphetamine in their bodies, thanks to their access to the drug. Or perhaps by exposure to second-hand smoke, resulting from their parents, a cook, or other users smoking meth in close proximity to the child. Parents were supposed to be a child's fiercest protectors, yet they were the ones putting their children in danger of serious health issues for the rest of their lives.

Pulling out his cell phone, he called Child Protective Services to report they'd found a child in a home where a meth lab was operating. He talked briefly to a CPS supervisor who promised to assign a case manager. He gave her one of his deputies' cell number and disconnected the call.

Glancing back at the emergency response vehicle, Cameron shouted to first EMT he saw. "Galloway, they're bringing out a two-year-old. Get ready. She needs to be decontaminated." Sandy Galloway, a seasoned EMT, had work meth scenes with him before. If anyone would know how to treat a small child who may have been exposed to meth, she would.

Cameron raced to his car, pulled out a clean white T-shirt, and headed back to the house. He arrived just in time to see Deacon coming out. The small child in his arms was hysterical. She wailed, flailing skinny arms and legs in a blur as she hit and kicked at him.

The officer was visibly upset. "I can't get her to calm down. I can't understand it. I have nieces and nephews who adore me."

Slipping on a pair of latex gloves, Cameron peeled back the blanket she was wrapped in and took a good look at her. Her little face was crimson and all scrunched up as she bellowed. This kid was not a happy camper. "I think she's afraid of you because of the mask. Let me have her."

Relief brightening his expression, Deacon handed the child to Cameron. She immediately stopped crying, sucked her thumb, and stared at him with the bluest eyes Cameron had ever seen. "You're okay, sweetheart. Everything is going to be fine."

Hugging her securely to his chest, he walked to the emergency response vehicle where Sandy Galloway had stacked white towels, along with a bar of soap and a wash cloth. She stood in front of the shower, adjusting the privacy curtain.

He glanced down at the child who stared right back—still sucking her thumb. After a moment, she raised her little hand to touch his face. "My name is Cameron, but my friends call me Cam. What's your name?"

She hesitated, making him wonder if she could talk. But then she pulled her thumb out of her mouth and said, "Becca."

"Becca is a pretty name." Gazing at her sweet face, he wondered how anyone could put her at such risk. Deputy Gail Sawyer joined Sandy Galloway, who was now testing the temperature of the water spraying from the side of the vehicle. It was time to decontaminate the child in his arms with a warm shower. "Becca, do you like to play in water?"

Much to Cameron's relief, she nodded and smiled.

Cameron nodded toward the running shower. "Gail, is the water warm?"

"Yes, sir. Are you sure you don't want to wait until we get her to the hospital to bathe her?"

"Have you taken a good look at her? Her clothes are filthy and so is she. Take off her clothes and put them in evidence bags to be tested at the lab. Get the camera. Take the photos that Child Protective Services needs to document any abuse, and let's get them done ASAP. I'm not taking any chances with her health. This child is getting decontaminated. If there is any chemical residue on her, it's getting washed off now."

The deputy pulled a small camera out of her pocket. "When I heard there was a child, I thought we'd need photos."

Cameron smiled approvingly. As a rookie, Gail's performance had been far-from-stellar, including the time she shot herself in the foot at the gun range during a law enforcement shooting competition. But she'd worked hard to improve his perception of her, and it was working.

"I'm ready, sir."

Cameron lowered Becca to the ground where she wrapped herself around his leg like a vine. "Becca, this is Gail. She's a deputy and she protects little girls like you."

Gail inched toward her. "I heard your name is Becca. Is that right?"

The toddler nodded and tightened her hold on Cameron's leg.

"How old are you?"

Becca held up two fingers.

Gail smiled and bent down. "Two years old? I have a niece who's two. My name is Gail. Is it okay if I take some pictures of you, Becca?"

When Becca looked up at Cameron, he bent down to her level. "Don't be afraid, sweetie. I'll be right here. As soon as Gail takes your pictures, you can play in the water. Would you like that?"

When she nodded, Cameron placed her on the ground and pulled off the blanket that was wrapped around her. Becca wore a pink nightshirt that was too small, clinging to her little body like a second skin. The garment was long overdue for washing. Cameron gritted his teeth as a surge of anger rushed through him. Obviously, her parents cared more about their damn drugs than caring for their little girl.

Through his earpiece, he heard that the deputies transporting Willie and Donda Hicks to the county jail were preparing to leave. Into his mic, he ordered the deputies to stay put. He wanted a word with both suspects.

Turning to Becca, he said, "I need to talk to your mommy and daddy for a minute. Gail will take good care of you. I promise I'll be right back, and then you can play in the water. Okay?"

Becca eyed him as if she was trying to determine if she could trust that he would return. She peered up at Gail and then back at Cameron. "Okay." Her little voice tugged at his heart. He patted her affectionately on the head and headed toward the patrol cars parked near the road.

She hadn't asked for her parents once. Not even when he mentioned talking to her mommy and daddy. That was odd. Most kids in this situation would be screaming for their parents. That Becca didn't ask for either one sent an alarm through his brain. Something was off here. Why wasn't she asking for them?

"Where's Willie?" Cameron demanded once he reached the patrol cars.

"He's here." Larry Rice, one of the Sheriff's rookie deputies, opened the back door of his cruiser.

Cameron looked inside. "Willie, we have your little girl and we've called Child Protective Services."

"Good for you. What do you want? A medal? How about a medal shaped like a doughnut?"

Ignoring the remark, Cameron knelt next to the car so he could get a better look at his suspect. Resting his head back, Willie struggled with his handcuffs and nervously scratched at open sores on his arms.

"I just thought you'd like to know what was happening with your daughter."

"Are you talking about Becca?"

"Who else would I be talking about?"

"She ain't my kid."

"You're not Becca's father?"

"No. Are you hard of hearing? I just said that. Donda and I went through a rough patch several years ago and she ran off. When she returned, she was knocked up. So Becca's *not* my kid. I could give a shit what Child Protective Services does with that brat. So get out of my face."

Slamming the vehicle door closed, Cameron glanced at Deputy Rice. "We're done talking. Take him in and book him."

Deputy Mary Hesselgesser-Wright waited for him outside the second patrol car. As he approached, she opened the back door to reveal the second suspect sitting inside.

With a smirk and a wave of her arm, Mary said, "In the back seat of police cruiser number two we have Donda Hicks, *no one's* candidate for Mother of the Year." All their earpieces were on the same frequency, and she'd obviously overheard his conversation with Willie. Apparently the deputy had made the same parental assessment of Donda as Cam had for the husband. A hint of a grin threatened Cameron's serious expression before he bent down to talk to Donda.

"Mrs. Hicks, I'm Sergeant Chase with the Sheriff's Office. I'd like to talk to you about your daughter, Becca."

"What about her?" Donda's response was more of a demand than a question. Emaciated, her dirty blond hair tied back in a ponytail, she was in constant movement in the car, twitching, scratching at her arms, and shaking. She was in bad need of a fix.

"Thought you might want to know we've called Child Protective Services."

"There's not a hell of a lot I can do about that, handcuffed in back of a police car. Now is there?" Donda scratched at her neck and glared at him.

"Do you have family in the area? Somewhere Becca can stay?"

"You're kidding, right? My so-called family wants nothing to do with me or the kid."

"How do you know they wouldn't take Becca in?"

"Because I tried to give her away, and none of them wanted her. To be honest, I don't want her, either. Christ, I'm nineteen. I never wanted to be a mother. I'm too young to be tied down by a snotty brat. She's better off with someone else."

Cameron closed the door and pushed away from the vehicle. Clenching his jaw, he cursed and tried to get a handle on his anger. He'd known stray cats who were better mothers than Donda Hicks. He made a mental note to add child endangerment and neglect to her growing list of charges.

Profile of Fear

With no relatives to take her in, the girl would go into the child protective system. There was a good chance Becca could get lost in the foster home system and get bounced from place to place, never find a loving parent and a permanent home. Was that a worse fate than living with an addicted mother who didn't care about her? Probably not, but he couldn't bear to think of the child in either situation.

If his older brother, Brody, were here, he'd say, "You can't save them all, Cam. No matter how much you want to. You can't save all of them." Yeah, but maybe if he was lucky, he'd be given a chance to help Becca.

In his earpiece, he heard Gail say, "Sergeant, just heard from CPS. The case manager will meet us at the hospital. Just finished the photos."

"I'll be right there."

When he reached the emergency response vehicle, he saw that Becca was stripped down to her birthday suit and her clothes were in evidence bags. Gail was holding the wiggling little girl, who stretched out her arms to Cameron as soon as she noticed him. He took her from Gail.

Gail looked frustrated. "I tried to get her in the shower but she wouldn't have anything to do with it. She keeps saying 'poo.'"

"What does that mean?"

As soon as the question left his mouth, Becca began chanting, "Poo. Poo. Poo."

Cameron looked at Gail. "Does she have to go to the bathroom?"

"I already asked her that, and she said no."

"Well, she has to be decontaminated. I was hoping she'd want to play in the shower water." Walking Becca to the shower, Cam said. "Want to play in the water, Becca?"

She gleefully clapped her hands and giggled. "Poo. Poo. Poo." But when she saw the shower, she shook her head and said, "No. I want poo."

Wearily, Cam asked, "Poo? Do you want shampoo—for your hair?" Cam raised his arms and moved them like he was washing his hair.

Becca giggled again, shaking her head, "No sha-poo. I wants my poo!"

"Wait a minute. I think I know what she's saying!" Gail took off running to the back of the house. Moments later she returned holding a bright pink plastic kiddie pool. "I saw this earlier when I was doing a perimeter check. Let's see what happens if I put this directly under the shower spray."

Becca jumped up and down, pointing excitedly. "My poo!"

"No, Gail. You know protocol. These idiots might have used the pool for something other than a toy."

Sandy Galloway approached them and bent down to talk to Becca. "Sweetie, if you will let me wash you in the shower, you can have this." From behind her back, she withdrew a small teddy bear wearing a white hoodie. The Shawnee County Sheriff logo was imprinted on the front of the shirt.

Becca's eyes widened with delight and in no time, the child was splashing in the water, soaking Sandy, who was determined to scrub her down with soap.

Holding her digital camera at her side, Gail leaned closer to Cameron. "Listen, there's something I need to tell you."

The shower curtain flew open and Becca ran out, exposing a series of purple bruises dotting her rib cage. Sandy quickly captured the toddler and placed her back in the shower. Inhaling deeply in an effort to subdue his anger at her abusers, Cameron turned to Gail. "What did you find besides the bruising on her ribs?"

"There's discoloration around one of her wrists. She cried out when I touched it."

"Damn it."

"The doc may find broken bones and more injuries when they examine her at the hospital. The baby has not had a good time of it."

Fists clenched at his sides, anger hummed through Cameron's body. "I want to know which one of them did this to her. Someone is going to pay."

"Sir, do you recall the training you sent me to last month? I'm now trained and certified to work with possible child abuse victims. I have a rapport with her now, and I'd really like to be the one who works with Becca."

Glancing at Gail, he nodded. In her politically correct way, she was letting him know he was biased in this case, and she was right. For reasons he had yet to understand, this child was already special to him, and his protective emotions surged through him as if a dam had broken. At this moment, he'd get great satisfaction out of throttling Becca's worthless parents.

"I agree. You do the interview with her. I'm also putting you in charge of any evidence we collect regarding her abuse. Make sure it's prepared and marked to maintain the chain of custody. We don't want some judge to throw out the case based on a glitch we could have avoided."

A soaked Sandy emerged from behind the shower curtain holding Becca, who was now wrapped in a white towel.

While Sandy went inside the vehicle to change her shirt, Cameron pulled his clean T-shirt from the back of his waistband and handed it to Gail, who quickly dressed Becca. On the toddler, his shirt hung to the ground and threatened to slide off her little shoulders. She held her arms up to him and he swept her little body into a protective embrace, as Gail handed her the teddy bear.

Sandy reappeared. "It's time we get this little one to the hospital."

Cameron looked at Becca's little face for only a second before saying, "I'm going with her." With Sandy's help, he loaded the toddler into the emergency vehicle, then climbed in himself.

Gail called after him. "I'll meet you there."

Chapter 10

Diego Santiago had been watching the house when he saw the SWAT team arrive. Damn his luck anyway. He'd waited too long to grab the kid and Donda. He'd royally fucked up this time, and just might pay for his blunder with his life.

Leaping to his feet, he hunched over and worked his way to his car, which he'd parked on the dirt road at the end of the corn field. Covered with mosquito bites, he scratched at his skin as he ran. Using a search light, the cops did a sweep of the field. Luckily, he'd run beyond the scope of the light and could see his car in the distance. Jumping inside, he fished his keys out of his dirty jeans and pulled out a small flashlight so he could see the ignition. Once he got the car started, he slowly drove ahead without headlights until he was far enough from the house and the swarm of cops to be noticed. Pulling onto a county highway, he flicked on his headlights and headed for town, hauling ass until he spotted the first convenience store. He pulled in, parked at the back of the lot, and got out his throwaway cell. His heart beating painfully against his chest, he punched in a number and waited to hear the voice of his boss.

"Yeah!" Juan barked.

"Boss, this is Diego."

"You better have a damn good reason for calling at this time in the morning." His voice rough from sleep carried the threat loud and clear. Diego's stomach clenched and prepared to deliver the bad news.

"I was watching Donda's house like you told me. The police came and surrounded the house."

"What!? Why?"

"Not sure. But I know the guy she's living with was dealing meth. Maybe he got caught."

"Where's my kid?"

"Don't know. I was in the field across from the house and got out of there when the SWAT team arrived."

"You fucking loser. You promised me that you'd get my kid!"

"There were people going in and out of the house all day. Then the cops came. No opportunity."

"No excuses!" he roared. "Just get your ass back there and locate my kid. Don't call me until you find her. Do you understand? You fail me and you die—slowly and painfully."

Diego turned the car around and headed back to the house. He'd choose what the cops would do to him any day over the wrath of Juan Ortiz. One didn't cross the boss and live to tell about it. Nor did one fail to deliver what he requested.

He arrived just as an ambulance whizzed past his car. Doing a U-turn, he headed toward the hospital.

Chapter 11

Social Worker Melanie Barrett pushed through the front doors of the only hospital in Morel, Indiana. She was not in her best mood as she entered the long hallway that led to the Emergency Department. Not that she had a best mood anymore. Bone-tired, she couldn't remember the last time she *didn't* feel exhausted.

Only twenty-seven-years-old, she felt more like seventy. When had work devoured her life? In her twenties, she was still young. She should be having fun, dating and going out with friends. Instead, she spent her life stalking child abusers and doing what she could to protect the innocent.

But everything worked against her. The overload of cases cheated her from spending quality time with any of them. The daily pressure to perform in crisis situations left her fearful, stressed, and drained. Exposure to violent family members and actual physical assault had her terrified that the next removal of an abused child could be her last.

Her workload had grown from the recommended seventeen she'd had when she trained to fifty-one cases. Lack of support from her agency and the judicial system left her gritting her teeth with frustration. Melanie had been employed by Child Protective Services for six years. Lately, she thought it was six years too long. Thinking about the horrific abuse to children she'd witnessed during that time made her want to vomit. Anger was her constant companion, and at times, even she didn't know at whom or why she was so pissed off. The constant fear of making a mistake that could result in the death of a child haunted her every minute of the day and night. How could she *not* work twenty-four hours a day, seven days a week? How could this work *not* become her life?

Melanie hated her low-paying, punishing job, along with the life she couldn't have. She was beginning to hate herself. Turns out maybe she was the pathetic loser her mother always said she was.

The previous day she hadn't left work until midnight, because she was trying to place a disgruntled teenaged boy who ran away from his second group home in a month. She'd spent hours searching all over the county for a foster family who would take him. Unfortunately, there were fewer foster parents than there were kids who needed them, and she ended up placing him with a group home that already had five teens. His running away from this one wasn't just likely, it was inevitable. She had no idea where she'd place him the next time. Melanie was out of options, which meant so was he.

She'd only gotten a couple of hours sleep when she'd had been awakened at five in the morning with the report that a two-year-old female had been discovered at the site of methamphetamine bust. Seriously? How many times had she harped at the sheriff to tell his undercover officers to look for children in the home so they could be removed at the earliest possible time—certainly before the SWAT team swept in with loaded weapons. Damn it. Now a toddler exposed to meth for God-knows-how-long was in the emergency room.

Fury sizzled her brain, so she found a coffee pot and dumped the rest of the sludge the hospital called coffee into a cup at a nurses' station. Then she plopped down in a chair in the hospital chapel to calm down before she talked to the law enforcement officer in charge and met with the toddler. Lifting the hot coffee to her mouth, she winced when the brew crossed her lips, which were still healing from the punch in the mouth she received from a drunken mother the week before. Melanie considered herself lucky it wasn't worse. The woman had grabbed a steak knife from a drawer and was heading toward her when a deputy intervened and escorted the mother to the back of his squad car.

The woman had insisted that Melanie was not going to take her kids out of their home, which was one of the filthiest the social worker had ever seen. The stench was so bad she'd plastered her hand against her nose and mouth. The young deputy who accompanied her vomited in the yard.

Used beer bottles and cat feces littered areas of the residence where the children were found playing. Because there were no beds for the kids, they slept with blankets on the soiled and stained carpet in the front room. The bathroom had a backed-up toilet, leaving no place for the children to go to the bathroom, so they went where they could. Neighbors had reported seeing the kids defecating in the back yard. Yes, Melanie had saved the three children from the squalor of their home and from an alcoholic mother who beat them on a regular basis. But did she really help them? There were no relatives who would take them, so she ended up separating the kids and putting each in an overcrowded foster home until she could put all three in the same home. But when would that be? If ever?

This particular mother had her children returned six months earlier, thanks to a child protection system whose goal was uniting families. Every time a soft judge returned an abused child to the supposedly reformed parent, she seethed. Would it be a matter of time until the child died at the hands of the people who should protect him or her with their very lives? In six years, ten of her charges were buried in the Morel cemetery. All ten had been murdered by their parents.

Things had gotten worse for children since many of the area farmers had discovered that their failed farming ventures could be turned around with an outbuilding or two and few neighbors. Meth labs were popping up like mushrooms, and God help the children who got in the way.

When it came to meth labs and their impact on children, Melanie thought she'd seen it all: toxic poisoning, chemical burns, fires, and explosions. And that was just the beginning of the drugs' impact on kids.

Meth-dependent parents and caregivers are the very *last* people who should be caring for children, because they lose the capacity to nurture. The meth makes them careless, irritable, and violent. The need to protect their children's safety becomes a foreign concept too difficult for them to understand.

So who protected their children's safety and provided essential food, dental, and medical care (including immunizations, proper hygiene, and grooming), and appropriate sleeping conditions? In too many cases, no one. If there were older siblings in these homes, they often assumed the parental role, taking care of the brothers and sisters, as well as the parents, as well as themselves.

Addicted parents typically fall into a deep sleep for days and cannot be awakened, further increasing the likelihood that their children will be exposed to toxic chemicals in their environment, and to abusive acts committed by other drug-using individuals in the home.

Older children living at meth lab sites experience the added trauma of witnessing violence, being forced to participate in violence, caring for an incapacitated or injured parent or sibling, or watching police arrest and remove a parent.

Choking down the rest of her coffee, Melanie reached into the canvas tote bag she used for a briefcase for a slip of paper, and began reading. Becca Hicks was the name of the two-year-old she would see in the ER. The child would need to be placed in a foster or group home immediately, since the mother was now incarcerated and claimed to have no relatives to care for Becca.

The toddler was the daughter of Donda Hicks, with the father listed as unknown. The address was a rural route number and there was no indication of how long mother or child had lived there. Nor was there any information on how long the residence had served as a house where meth was cooked and sold. Melanie shrugged her shoulders and sighed. There was no telling how much damage had been done to the child. She'd seen toddlers who had inhaled or swallowed the toxic substances and suffered permanent damage to their tiny bodies.

A meth house holds so many dangers for a curious toddler. Even low-level exposure to meth can cause headaches, fatigue, dizziness—symptoms she couldn't expect a toddler to describe. Melanie prayed this baby did not have high levels of exposure, which could result in eye and tissue irritation, lack of coordination, chemical burns to the skin, eyes, mouth, nose, and even death. Damage to vital organs, cancer, and brain damage were not an impossibility. Not to mention the presence of weapons, violence, physical or sexual abuse by her parent, or by outsiders visiting the home. No doubt this child's case would be added to all the other nightmares that kept her up at night.

Her stomach queasy, Melanie closed her eyes and rubbed the tense muscles in the back of her neck. Pushing her eyeglasses back to the bridge of her nose, she wished she could go home, go to bed, and pull the covers over her head. When was the last time she got a full eight hours of sleep? She just wanted to fall into a deep slumber and forget about the vicious abuse and horrific injuries she'd seen. Was that too much to ask?

Melanie didn't know how much more of her job she could take. The stress ate away at her physical and emotional health like acid. How could she continue doing a job that was killing her? How could she not?

Chapter 12

Cameron leaned against the wall in the hospital hallway. Moments earlier, a busty nurse with an attitude had pushed him out of Becca's exam room, banishing him to the waiting room until the ER doc completed her examination. He pretended to be heading that way until the nurse went back inside, and then he moved right outside the exam room so he'd know what was going on.

Becca was having none of it and was throwing a full-blown temper tantrum inside. He could hear the doctor trying to calm her down. His heart ached a little more with each ear-piercing scream. The baby was terrified, and it was all he could do to stop himself from rushing inside the exam room to comfort her.

Sighing deeply, he crossed his arms over his chest and wondered what would happen to Becca. He'd seen firsthand what happens to kids who get lost in the foster care system. Many of them moved from foster care right into juvenile delinquency, acting out their misery in a series of violent and non-violent crimes. He didn't want that for Becca.

What was it about this toddler that had wrapped around his heart and squeezed every ounce of paternal instinct he had? Was it because he'd never encountered a child who was more in need of a break? Maybe. He didn't want to think about what her reality must have been like living with a meth-addicted mother in a house where methamphetamine was cooked and sold, and a small child was just in the way. Was it two years in hell, with no one to protect her, or look out for her safety? Undoubtedly.

He'd seen the bruising on her ribs and wrists. He clenched his fists in anger as he thought about what he'd like to do to whoever put them there. Who in the hell hits a two-year-old? Did Donda do it? It wouldn't be the first time a mother lost it and took it out on her kid. Did Willie abuse Becca? Did he resent her because she belonged to another man? Was the toddler getting in the way of his drug business? Whoever hurt Becca would pay, along with the person who let it happen and turned the other way. He'd make sure of it.

His thoughts were disrupted by the appearance of a woman at the nurses' station who was asking about Becca. Aiming his laser-focus on her, he wondered who she was and why she was asking about the little girl. The woman was so thin, her thick cardigan sweater hung off her shoulders. She looked like a poster child for anorexia, with too little food or sleep. Her sharp facial features gave her a bird-like look, and she didn't wear a speck of makeup to cover the ugly bruise and cut on her lower lip.

Though the woman was talking directly to one of the nurses, she never looked her in the eye. Her eyes were always focused above the nurse's head or to the side. When Cameron heard her use the words 'social worker,' he hurried to the nurses' station.

He didn't hesitate to interrupt. "I couldn't help but overhear you asking about Becca Hicks."

Startled, the woman stepped back to put some space between them. "May I ask who you are? I was told that Becca Hicks has no relatives."

He pulled out his badge. "I'm Cameron Chase. I'm the sergeant in charge of major crimes for the Shawnee County Sheriff's Office." Cameron thrust out his hand to shake hers, but she glanced at his hand and kept her own protectively pressed against her tote bag, filled with file folders, to her chest.

Tapping the plastic work identification badge pinned to her collar with her finger, she said. "I'm Melanie Barrett. I work with CPS, Child Protective Services." Her eyes narrowed. "Your last name is Chase? Are you related to Sheriff Brody Chase?"

"Yes, ma'am. He's my brother."

A spark of temper flicked in her eyes. "Well then, you're just the person I need to speak with. Shall we have our conversation here, or in a more private place?"

Obviously eavesdropping, the nurse said, "There's no one in the conference room down the hall. I can reserve it for you."

"You do that." Melanie swung her gaze back to Cameron. "Follow me."

Chapter 13

Cameron had a good idea why he was about to get a tongue-lashing, and followed closely behind Melanie Barrett until they came to a small conference room. Trailing her inside, he paused as she pulled out a chair to sit at the head of the table, and then eased himself into a chair to her left.

"Since you're a sergeant, you can tell me who was in charge of the methamphetamine police raid of the house where two-year-old Becca Hicks was found." She lay the worn tote bag on the floor, put her elbows on the table, pushed her glasses back to the bridge of her nose, and looked at him with contempt.

Cameron cleared his throat. "That would be me. I was in charge of the raid."

"Then maybe you can tell me why Child Protective Services was not contacted to remove a two-year-old child from the home prior to the raid?"

"I'm sorry about that. Neither our informant nor our undercover detective said anything about a child living in the home. She must not have been at the house when either man made a visit. I'm not happy this happened either, and I guarantee it won't happen again."

That seemed to appease her somewhat, but clearly she wasn't finished. "It *can't* happen again. Understand? Do you realize what can happen to a child who is exposed to meth?"

Seriously? He was in law enforcement in Indiana where meth labs were popping up faster than morel mushrooms in the spring.

What kind of an idiot did she think he was? Now she wasn't the only one who was steamed. But he knew he had to tread carefully with her. She would be the one to place Becca, and he wanted to make sure she went to a good foster home. "This wasn't my first rodeo. Of course I know the chemicals used to manufacture meth pose serious dangers to children."

She shrugged her shoulders as if she didn't believe him. "I'm willing to bet that what you know about meth exposure is from seminars and articles in your cop magazines. You've never had to rush a three-year-old to the hospital because his parents made a habit of putting meth in his drinks for fun. I'd wager you never had to hold a first grader's hand while he died because he was in the wrong place at the wrong time when his father's meth lab exploded." A tear ran unchecked down her face.

Cameron squeezed her hand and watched her try to compose herself. "I'm sorry. I didn't mean to be insensitive. It sounds like you've witnessed first-hand the damage the drug can do."

"I didn't mean to go off like that. I didn't get much sleep last night."

"Yours can't be an easy job. I realize that."

She pulled a tissue out of her tote bag and blew her nose.

Cameron took the opportunity to change the subject. "Let's talk about Becca and where you'll place her."

"You mean *if* I can place her."

His brows creased as he gave her a long, searching look. "I don't understand. She *can't* stay here in the hospital."

"Shawnee County doesn't even have half the number of foster homes that the system needs. I don't know if I can find a foster family for a two-year-old."

"Then what happens to Becca?"

"If I'm lucky I'll find a group home that will take her. I have to tell you, a foster home already filled with teenagers is no place for a toddler. But I don't know what else I can do if I can't find foster parents for her."

Cameron pushed back in his chair, took a deep breath, and thought of how Becca had clung to him for safety. She was so young and had no good reason to trust anyone, but she had trusted him. He remembered how Becca had screamed his name, begging him not to leave her, when he was pushed out of her examining room. She counted on him, and by God he was going to man up and be the one who helped her, no matter what he had to do. She'd never been able to count on anyone for her safety and well-being. That was about to change.

"I want to be a foster parent to Becca. I can provide her an excellent home. Just tell me what I need to do."

Surprised, the social worker looked at him as if he'd sprouted antlers from the top of his head. "*You* want to be a foster parent?"

"Yes. You seem surprised."

"It's just that… I mean you don't look like the kind of man who would want to give up his lifestyle for all the responsibility that caring for a toddler entails."

"Exactly what kind of a lifestyle do you think I have?"

Melanie began to stutter. "I m-m-mean… You're very good-looking. I imagine you have better ways to spend your time." Her cheeks flushed pink.

Okay, now he was offended. What the hell? She was going to judge his potential as a parent solely on his looks? "You'd be making a big mistake assuming things about me based on my looks. Why don't you ask me the kind of questions you usually ask people, attractive or not, who volunteer to foster a child?"

Nervously pushing her glasses back up to the bridge of her nose, her face now blushed crimson. "I apologize. You're right. Why do you want to be a foster parent to Becca Hicks?"

Cameron considered the question thoughtfully. Hell, until minutes ago, he'd never considered being a parent to anyone. "I grew up in a good home brought up by a single mother who was an amazing role model. If I can be half the parent my mom was, Becca will be in very good hands."

Melanie only nodded. "Why Becca Hicks?"

It's a good thing Brody wasn't in the room because he'd give his little speech about Cam wanting to save the world. "Becca has lived with her meth-addicted, sorry excuse for a mother for the first two years of her life. She's a toddler who has had no one to protect her from harm, or take care of her physical and emotional needs. It's time the kid caught a break. If you appoint me as her foster parent, I intend to change all that. I'll give her all the love and attention a kid could want, along with the kind of home where she'll thrive."

There was a hint of a grin at the edge of the social worker's mouth. "I see. Tell me about where you live, where you could provide a home for a toddler to thrive."

"I live on 162 acres of land that my parents left to my two brothers and me. The property is like a nature preserve with woods, hills, valleys, two lakes, and miles of running trails, with absolute privacy. It's the perfect place for a kid. My dad built the main house with the idea it could be turned into a bed and breakfast or a nature lodge when he and mom retired. There are five bedroom suites within the main house. My younger brother, Gabe, his fiancée Kaitlyn, and I live in the main house, along with a chocolate Labrador retriever named Godiva. My suite is downstairs and has a bedroom, a living room, kitchenette, and two bathrooms. The main house also has a huge family area, kitchen, and dining room, with an outside living area."

"Are you able to child-proof the living areas?"

"Absolutely." Cameron made a mental note to research how to child-proof a home.

"Does Sheriff Chase also live on the property?"

"Yes. Brody and his wife, Carly, live in the house our parents named the "Honeymoon Cottage" that's located not far from the main house."

"You should be aware that I need to interview all members of your household. I'll also need a medical statement from a physician for each of them if you are to be considered as a foster parent."

"That won't be a problem." At least he hoped it wouldn't be. He needed to talk to his family about this fostering thing sooner than later. What would he do if they decided that adding a toddler to their lives was not such a good idea?

Melanie withdrew a pencil and a yellow legal pad from her tote bag. "I need to know more about the people who will be living on the property with Becca."

"She doesn't live on the property, but we have a housekeeper named Mrs. E. who is at the house four hours a day, six days a week. She's cooked and cleaned for our family for twenty years.

Mrs. E. is more of a family member than a housekeeper." Cameron paused for a second and grinned. "It's kind of funny. If Collette has asked once, she's asked a hundred times when my brothers and I were going to give her some kids to care for. Her two boys are grown, but aren't old enough to give her some grandchildren. If Becca joins our family, Mrs. E. will be ecstatic."

This time the social worker smiled openly before she jotted down some notes.

Chapter 14

Cameron said something about needing caffeine and left the conference room for the hospital cafeteria. When he returned, he had a large Styrofoam cup filled with hot coffee in each hand. He passed a cup to her, and settled back down in the chair next to her.

Melanie Barrett gazed at Cameron Chase and thought he was the most attractive man she'd ever seen. Not in high school, college, and certainly not on her job in Shawnee County had she ever met a man whose charisma seemed to be leaking from his very pores. With dark hair tapering neatly to his collar, he was devastatingly handsome, like the heroes in the romance books she liked to read. She wondered what it would be like to have him make love to her, and a distinct warmth flowed through her entire body.

What would it be like to have a man like Cameron Chase in her life? Actually, what would it be like to have *any* man in her life? High school was a distant memory when she dated Eddie Reynolds. She'd adored Eddie. But her mother made sure Eddie didn't come around too often, and then, not at all.

"All men are the same and after one thing," her mother often spouted, and Melanie got the message loud and clear. "Besides," her mother said disgustedly, "He just wants to get into your panties. It's not like he's attracted to your good looks and smarts. And a pregnant daughter is the last thing I want hanging around my house."

Was Cameron Chase interested in her? Not likely. That was the stuff of make-believe. Who would want someone like her? And what kind of professional lets her mind wander to such things when considering someone for the responsibility of caring for a child?

He set his coffee on the table and looked at her curiously. Her mind snapped to attention.

"Tell me about the rest of your family, Sgt. Chase."

Chapter 15

Cameron gulped down the rest of his coffee, and answered another one of Melanie's questions—this one about his oldest brother.

"You know my brother, Brody. He's the best man I know. I'd say that even if he weren't my brother. He sacrificed a lot to raise Gabe and me after our mother died. He'll make a good dad himself someday."

"Isn't your younger brother, Gabe, a private investigator?"

"Yes, Gabe's a P.I. who owns his own company, and he also does computer forensic consulting for the Sheriff's Office."

"How does he interact with children?"

"Brody's wife, Carly, has a brother, Blake Stone, who lives in Ash Grove in Sycamore County. Blake and his wife have a little boy named Shawn who's in elementary school and a baby girl named Mylee. Whenever they visit, Shawn uses Gabe as a human jungle gym and Mylee cries for Brody to hold her. In my opinion, Uncle Gabe and Uncle Brody are a hit with the kids."

"Now tell me about the women who would interact with Becca. What are they like?"

"Brody's wife, Carly, is a former FBI agent and now works out of their home consulting as a criminal profiler. She's crazy about Shawn and Mylee and often has them for sleepovers. They usually order pizza and watch a movie that the kids choose."

"So Sgt. Chase, when can I interview your family members and visit where Becca will live?"

A smile spreading across his face, Cameron said, "How about within the next hour or two?"

Chapter 16

Cameron whispered a prayer and then stepped into a small conference room equipped with an oval table with the six chairs they'd need. A coffee pot sat on a small table in the back of the room, next to a tower of Styrofoam cups the height of Mt. Everest and a plate of sweet rolls.

Brody and Carly arrived first. Carly looked relieved. "Thank God. We thought you'd been hurt on the job when you said to come to the hospital."

Cam spread his arms and she walked into his hug. "I'm okay. Don't worry."

His brother grasped his shoulder. "So why are we here, Cam? What's going on?"

Cameron started to reply, but Gabe and Kaitlyn walked in, wearing the same worried expression Brody and Carly had.

Brody poured a cup of coffee for Carly and then poured cups for Gabe, Kaitlyn, and himself. Cameron had a coffee that he was nursing at the end of the table.

Cameron waved to the chairs. "Please sit down. And know how much I appreciate your meeting me here with such late notice, and no explanation whatsoever."

Gabe squirmed in his chair and leaned forward. "The suspense is killing me. What's going on?"

"I want you to meet someone." Cameron pulled out his cell phone and retrieved the photo that he'd taken of Becca sitting on the examining table. Wearing his T-shirt, the child stared at the cell phone camera, her eyes filled with fear.

He gave the phone to Gabe who glanced at the photo, and passed it around to the others.

Brody gave the phone to Carly, then settled his gaze on Cameron. "Cute kid. Who is she?"

"Her name is Becca, and she's one of the sweetest two-year-olds you'll ever meet. We found her at the house where we had the meth bust this morning."

"At Willie Hicks' place? He had a kid?"

"Not his. Long story."

Impatiently, Gabe handed back Cameron's cell. "Just tell us what this is all about."

"There are no foster parents available to take Becca in. The group homes are filled with teenagers. That's no place for a two-year-old." Inhaling deeply, he folded his hands on the table. "I want to be Becca's foster parent, and I'm asking you to welcome her into our family."

Brody was the first to respond. "Sweet Jesus, Cam, you're a police sergeant. When are you going to have time to be a parent?"

"I'll make time. It means that much to me. But I am going to need your help to create the best home possible for this little girl. She's been through a lot. Won't know until the doc sees her, but I think she's been physically abused."

Abruptly, Kaitlyn raised her hand as if she were sitting in a classroom. "I'm in."

Surprised, Gabe turned to her. "Are you sure…"

"I'm not in the teaching profession because I *don't* want to help kids." Looking at Cameron, she said, "I'm on summer break so I'm available 24/7 until September, just tell me what Becca needs."

Gabe snaked his arm around Kaitlyn's shoulder. "The thought of a toddler in the house sounds like fun. I'm in."

With a mixture of interest and compassion filling her dark eyes, Carly turned to Brody. "We're always talking about having babies someday. Here's our chance to get some practice and to find out if we're any good at this parenting thing."

Brody cracked a smile and said, "Looks like it's unanimous. When do we get to meet our kid in person?"

Chapter 17

Dusting off the shoulder of his suit jacket, Cameron straightened his tie and wished the meeting was over so he could pick up Becca from the hospital and take her home. He'd gotten the social worker's sign-off, but he needed information from the hospital pediatrician about the child's physical condition and needs.

Dr. Phoebe Weitzel's small office had a simple, dark-wood desk with a laptop and a stack of files. It was very tidy compared to Cam's office desk, which looked like the victim of a paper avalanche. On her credenza was a wedding photo of the doctor with her new husband, and a clock that sat on top of a small replica of the Eiffel Tower. On the wall were two framed college diplomas, along with her medical license. Another wall was covered with photographs of smiling children, presumably her patients.

The door opened, and a small woman wearing a white lab coat entered the room and extended her hand to Cameron.

"Hello, Mr. Chase."

"Please, call me Cam."

"Hello, Cam. I'm Dr. Weitzel. Melanie Barrett tells me that you are stepping in as an emergency foster parent for the little girl I examined last night, Becca Hicks."

"That's correct."

"Then there are some things you need to know. Please sit down. Becca has been thoroughly examined and I want to talk to you about the results of her x-rays, toxicology screen, and blood testing."

"Is she okay?"

"Becca shows signs of physical abuse. X-ray results revealed broken rib cage bones in various stages of healing. There is also a line of purple bruising dotting her rib cage where she has been struck with a blunt object."

Cameron blew out a breath and leaned back in his chair. "I saw the bruises last night."

"There's discoloration and swelling around her left wrist." Standing up, she turned on a small light illuminating an x-ray on the wall. She explained, "See the gap between these bones in Becca's wrist? That's a broken scaphoid."

"So her wrist is broken?"

"Yes."

"Is she in pain?"

"Yes, it's undoubtedly uncomfortable for her if that area of her arm is touched."

"How long will something like that take to heal?"

"Scaphoid fractures that are this close to the thumb usually heal in a matter of weeks with proper protection. This part of the scaphoid bone has a good supply of blood, which is necessary for healing. I've placed Becca's arm and hand in a cast below her elbow. Try not to get the cast wet. Before her bath, put a plastic bag over the cast to keep it dry."

Cameron nodded. "I'll make sure."

"I'm afraid there is another health issue concerning Becca. There are trace amounts of methamphetamine in Becca's toxicology results."

Cameron sighed heavily. "One of my deputies found a half-filled glass of iced tea in the living room on a coffee table last night. We think her mother, Donda, was drinking it. It tested positive for meth. The glass was certainly reachable by a two-year-old. It's not a far stretch of the imagination that Becca drank some of the tea."

"Like I said, it was just a trace. I expect her to fully recover."

"Thank God. Did you find anything else?"

"Yes, Becca is underweight. She is thirty-three inches tall and weighs only twenty pounds. The average weight for a two-year-old girl with that height is twenty-six pounds."

"My family employs a wonderful cook and housekeeper. In addition, we take turns cooking healthy dinners. Getting Becca the nutrition she needs will not be a problem."

"That's good, Mr. Chase, because Becca tested positive for anemia. The anemia may explain why her skin is so pale. In addition, her breathing is a little rapid.

"How much of a concern is this?"

"Anemia is one of the more common blood disorders. It occurs when the level of healthy red blood cells (RBCs) in the body becomes too low. This can lead to health problems, because RBCs contain hemoglobin, which carries oxygen to the body's tissues. I suspect Becca's anemia is caused by the lack of vitamin and iron-rich food. A healthy diet is critical for Becca."

"Not a problem."

Folding her hands onto her desk, she looked at him with concern. "It's a lot of responsibility to foster a child like Becca. Right now, her emotional and physical needs are critical. Are you sure you want to take this on?"

"I've never been more sure of anything in my life. If we're finished, there is a little girl who's waiting for me at the hospital."

Chapter 18

Just back from the hospital cafeteria, Diego carried a hot cinnamon roll and a large coffee as he headed toward the visitor's room on the floor where he'd seen Juan's kid. The room was empty when he entered. He took a seat near the door so he could see down the hall, where he noticed a couple of nurses chatting outside the kid's room. He'd wait until they moved on, and then he'd have a look-see of the kid so he could report back to his boss.

Juan Ortiz was the most volatile boss he'd ever had or feared. The man had the disposition of a rattlesnake and was just as dangerous. There was no predicting what would set off his vicious temper, and when he got angry, he got violent. Lessons learned: One did not steal from Juan Ortiz and get away with it unscathed. One did not bungle a mission or disappoint. Your life depended on it.

Julio Garcia was one of Juan's drug dealers who got greedy and started shaving proceeds off the top for himself. Unfortunately, Juan found out about it, but was unable to find Julio, who had disappeared. So Juan broke into Julio's sister's house in the middle of the night, slit her throat, and wrote a message to Julio with her blood on the walls of her bedroom.

Juan Ortiz was the ultimate bully, and Diego knew a thing or two about bullies. When Diego entered junior high school, he was barely five feet tall and had a raging case of acne. That made him a target for the Disciples gang of teenaged hoodlums. When not indulging in petty crimes, they looked for kids like him to harass and use for a punching bag. One day five members of the gang followed him after school into an alley. Knocking him to the ground, they kicked and pummeled him and left him for dead. A store owner found Diego and got him to the nearest hospital, where he nearly died. His father pledged that he'd make sure this never happened again. Not to his kid. It was the only promise the man ever kept before he deserted his family.

It took Diego six weeks to heal from his injuries that included a concussion, broken facial bones and ribs, and a bruised spleen. He'd never been in so much pain. During that time his mother, Rosalita, helped him keep up with his homework; his father, Benito, taught him how to fight dirty. Knives were his dad's favorite weapon. He'd learned how to use a knife to his advantage in the Army, same place he learned to fight dirty.

Benito took Diego to a pawn shop to look for the ideal knife that was sized for the boy's hand. The pawn dealer measured his grip from his index finger to the second knuckle of his pinkie. They settled on a five-inch blade, then looked for a switchblade that Diego could conceal in the pocket of his jeans. While they were in the store, the owner took out some oil and taught Diego how to clean and maintain his new knife. A folding knife needs to be oiled regularly to keep the action as smooth as possible. He explained, "A dull knife is a dangerous one. It is important you keep your knife oiled and sharpened. It may someday save your life. A dull knife may not."

Now it was time for the training to begin. His father and his Army buddy, Rex, joined Diego on the patio. Rex went first. "It's important for you to control your environment and stay calm when your first instinct is fight or flight. The one who keeps his cool usually isn't the one who gets stuck."

Benito issued a warning. "Only pull out your knife to avoid a fight, and then use it to defend yourself if necessary. Avoid fights, if you can. But if someone comes up to you in a threatening manner, look at their hands and at their pockets. If you see a weapon, draw your knife."

Rex pulled out a hunting knife and said, "Keep your body behind your knife. Use it to protect your face, neck, and torso against your attacker. Make your body as small as possible by bringing in your shoulders and ducking your head. Secure your knife by wrapping your thumb around the grip with the blade facing down. Extend your knife-holding arm in front of you, like this." He demonstrated, then asked Diego to do the same. Benito adjusted Diego's striking arm until it was flexed at a 45-degree angle. Satisfied, he patted his son on the back and nodded his approval.

"Take off your shirt. Let's practice." As his son ripped off his shirt, Benito removed his own. Nervous sweat sliced Diego's body as his stomach tightened with fear. He was relieved and curious when he saw his father reach into his pocket and pull out a black marker, yank off the cap, and then handed it to his son. "Pretend the marker is your blade and try to mark me as many times as possible while I try to stop you."

His father bounced on his toes like a dancer, stepping backward, weaving to the left, then to the right. After several misses, Diego jabbed him with the marker to his ribs. "That's one."

Moving constantly, Benito remained facing his son at all times. He circled right and Diego poked him in the stomach. But most of the jabs did not meet their targets. He understood now how difficult it is to stab a moving target. Lesson learned.

The training continued for weeks, even after Diego returned to school. It went on until his father was convinced he'd learned the balance and precision to win the fight.

It wasn't long until six members of the Disciples gang fell in line behind him as he walked home from school, pelting him with a barrage of insults. Especially vocal was a kid nicknamed 'Bull.' Nearly six-feet-tall, Bull worked out and had the muscles to prove it. He put his strength to good use robbing classmates for their lunches.

"Hey, midget. I saw your mama shopping in the boy's department for your jeans."

They reached the same alley where they'd nearly killed him. Diego spun around to face them.

Bull stepped forward, waving the rest of the gang back. They circled around the two boys. Bull clenched his fists. "How about I kick your tiny ass?"

Profile of Fear

A voice sounded in Diego's head. *Keep calm and control your environment.*

A flash of silver. Gasps from the boys. Diego whipped his switchblade out of his pocket, clicked the button and it sprang to life. "See this knife. I sharpen it every night. Trust me. You don't want to mess with me."

"Think I'm afraid of a dwarf?" Bull goaded him in a loud voice so the others could hear his bravado. He dived toward Diego and smacked onto the cement when Diego dodged. As he pulled himself to his feet, Diego took a step backward, flexed his body, angled his striking arm and waited for Bull's next move.

He didn't have long to wait. Bull's fist whizzed by his jaw but slammed painfully into his shoulder. Diego staggered back and got into position. Bull bulldozed toward him and Diego sliced his left arm. It was a superficial wound, but Bull howled in pain as a dark stream of scarlet spilled down his arm.

Furious, Bull rushed him as Diego danced to the right and stuck the knife into his side. Bull went down this time, curled himself in a fetal position, and wailed.

One-by-one, the other boys ran down the alley, trying to get as far away from Diego as they could.

Diego eased up beside Bull and peered down at him. "Are you done, tough guy?"

"Yes. Don't cut me again. Please."

"I'll let you live this time, but the next time you insult me or mess with me, you die. Got that? Same goes for the rest of the Disciples. Make sure you warn them. I'll take no prisoners. Your blood will stain the street."

His father celebrated by taking his family out for dinner. He left his family the next day, never heard from again. Thanks to his father's self-defense lessons, the Disciples never bothered Diego again.

Diego noticed the hallway outside the visitors' area was empty, so he eased out of his chair and headed toward the kid's room. Passing the nurse's station, he noticed a group of them huddled together as if they were in a meeting. Good timing.

A man and a woman who were probably parents visiting their sick child got in front of him, so he moved closer to blend in. He stopped when he got to the kid's room and slipped in. What he saw made his heart stop. The kid was gone. The bed was made and ready for the next patient. Blood draining from his face, the hair lifted on his nape and arms. What happened to Juan's little girl? True, he'd spent a couple of hours in the cafeteria. Could the kid have died? Did they move her to another room in the hospital? Had she been discharged?

His heart was beating so fast, he thought it might explode from his chest. There was no doubt. Juan Ortiz would kill him. He'd fucked up and would pay for it with his life. No doubt. Not to mention he'd now put his mother, Rosalita, in grave danger. His mother was wheel-chair bound with M.S. Her life was already a living hell. What would she do without him to care for her? Worst case scenario, he didn't want her final moments to be a hellish nightmare at the hands of Juan Ortiz.

It was then that he saw the mousy little case worker from Child Services he'd seen outside the kid's room. Was the little girl alive? Her mother was still in jail, so there's no way she could have the kid. Had she been placed in some kind of home by the case worker? The answer to that question just might save his life.

Moving to a corner of the room, Diego withdrew his cell phone and called Juan.

"What?"

"Diego here. I have news."

"If this is about Becca, it better be good news."

"I think I know where she is."

"What the hell are you talking about? I thought she was in the hospital and you were keeping an eye on her."

Omitting the part of the story where he spent two hours in the cafeteria, Diego continued. "Child Services put her in a foster home."

"Damn it all to hell. We'll never find her."

"I have an idea on how we can do just that."

"It better be good, because right now your life expectancy is looking short."

"I saw the Child Services case worker. Noticed her name on her badge. Melanie Barrett."

Chapter 19

The Chase family celebrated Becca's first month in her new home by having a huge breakfast with cereal, scrambled eggs, bacon, blueberry muffins, cheese grits, orange juice, coffee, and Becca's favorite: cherry yogurt.

Carly and Kaitlyn had strung colorful balloons across the room and purchased a matching tablecloth. Gabe and Brody dug around in the attic until they found their childhood oak highchair and polished it until it gleamed before they set it at the table.

Cam sat at the head of the table, next to Becca, watching her slip a Cheerio into her mouth and filling her sippy cup with orange juice. A grin spread across his face when she pushed a Cheerio off the highchair tray onto the floor where Godiva snatched it up. Becca giggled and offered a piece of cereal to Cam.

Gabe peered under the table. "Notice how Godiva has strategically placed herself beneath the highchair. She's no dummy. She can identify food opportunities."

Kaitlyn touched his arm. "Actually, it's no surprise because *wherever* you see Becca, you'll find Godiva. They've become close buddies."

"So I noticed," said Cam, as he urged Becca to take a bite of yogurt.

"It's Girls' Day Out," Carly announced after a sip of her coffee. "Kaitlyn, Becca and I are going out for lunch at Mollie's Café after our pediatrician visit to get Becca's cast removed, and then we're shopping for toddler clothes, toys, and books."

"Yay! Shopping!" Kaitlyn clapped her hands and before long Becca was doing the same.

"If you have time, stop by the office, I want to show off my new niece," said Brody. He kissed Becca on top of her little head and then filled his travel mug with hot coffee. He hugged Carly and rushed out the door.

It occurred to Cameron how much had changed with the two-year-old in just one month's time. She'd gained six pounds and was now at a normal weight for her age. There were no signs of anemia in Becca's recent blood tests, and x-rays revealed her fractured rib bones were healing well. The doctor said she was showing no indications of damage from the trace amount of meth initially found in her bloodstream, and the broken bones in her wrist had healed.

Color had returned to her rosy little cheeks, and her naturally curly, flaxen hair tumbled down her back like ribbons of silk. Her eyes, the color of cornflower, were filled with curiosity and mischief.

He'd changed, too. Becca had changed him. Before Becca, he threw himself into his work 24/7, forgoing any time off. It was like he was obsessed with his work. Little else mattered. The job had sucked him in like so many of the law enforcement officers he worked with. How do you spend day after day with death and suffering, and not have it affect you? It's not like you can scrub it off in a hot shower when you get home.

That was pre-Becca. Now that she was in his life, he strived to be extra careful at work. Not that he was ever careless. But now safety was more important. What would happen to her if he got hurt? That was a question never far from the forefront of his thinking.

Cameron felt a warmth that only love can inspire, and it choked him up. There was so much of that in the room, it made his heart swell. He remembered the first time he laid eyes on Becca. Her arms flailing, crying hysterically, Becca was handed to him by one of his deputies. It wasn't long before he knew he wanted to be her father and to give her the kind of loving home she deserved. He'd worried needlessly that his family would approve his decision to become her foster dad. She'd become an important member of their family, loved and protected by each of them. Despite the hell her former home had offered the little girl, she seemed happy and loving now.

More than ever, he was determined to adopt Becca to make things permanent. He couldn't imagine not having her in his life—could not envision not being her father.

Chapter 20

Diego turned to Juan, who was sitting in the passenger seat of his car. "That's her. Melanie Barrett."

"The mousy one?"

"Yeah, I told you, she's no knock-out."

"Where does she get her clothes, Goodwill?"

"Like I said, hot is not a word I'd use to describe her."

"Prey is more like it," Juan said with a chill in his voice. "She better be the talkative type. I need to find my kid. Melanie Barrett will help me find her, or regret it."

Diego had followed Melanie Barrett for weeks, memorizing her schedule and keeping track of where she went in her free time. It was Friday, and on this day she always had a glass of wine with appetizers at the Vineyard Wine Bar on Main Street after work.

"What is this place?"

"New wine bar. They advertise themselves as a funky, modern hangout with wine tasting machines, craft beer, appetizer and gourmet sandwich menu, and live entertainment, standing room only on the weekends."

"So you're doing commercials for them now? I'm paying you to follow the bitch, not scope out new wine bars."

"I got you covered, Boss." Diego reached across him to get into the glove box and handed him a display ad for the wine bar from a newspaper. "I figured you'd want to know a little about the place if you were going to use it to meet Melanie."

"Does she meet anyone here?"

"Not that I've seen. Comes here alone."

Juan swiftly changed the subject. "What else have you learned about her?"

"She's predictable. She works in Child Protective Services. Leaves work anywhere from five to six o'clock, and sometimes leaves her house in the middle of the night."

The truth was Diego had respect for Melanie Barrett. The woman spent her days and many of her nights helping kids. Just last week, she'd left her house at two in the morning and drove to a house on Jefferson. When she arrived, the cops were already there and were dragging the husband out of the house. When the guy saw Melanie, he struggled to get free to get to her, and ended up spitting in her face before the cops hauled him away. The wife came out of the house on a stretcher, bleeding about her face, chest and arms. Later, after the woman left in an ambulance, Melanie Barrett emerged from the house holding a baby, bundled in blankets to keep it warm.

Diego respected people who helped children. He liked kids and wanted some of his own someday. He'd get married and have a couple of them. Of course, he'd need to find another job. Working for a killer and selling drugs weren't exactly the ingredients for a good father. He wanted to provide a better life for his kids. But for now, working for Juan paid well, and he needed the money to pay for his mother's medical care. Rosalita had taken good care of Diego his entire life, and now was his turn to tend to her needs.

He wondered why it was so important for Juan Ortiz to get his kid. The man didn't have a paternal gene in his body. Hell, he sold women as a part of his business, so why add his little girl to the mix? She'd be better off with anyone but Juan.

This thing with Melanie Barrett was grinding on Diego's nerves. Juan was a sick sonofabitch who would gut his own mother. How far would he go to get his kid's whereabouts from the social worker? Diego tried to avoid thinking about that. He'd done a lot of things for Juan that he wasn't proud of, but none of them included harming a woman or a child. Beating and threatening a lazy dealer who wasn't paying his dues was one thing. Hurting a woman like Melanie was another.

If it came down to that, he didn't know how he would handle it if he was asked to 'persuade' Melanie to give up the kid's whereabouts. Refusing what Juan wanted was a death sentence. Harming Melanie Barrett was a prison sentence if he were implicated.

Juan snapped his fingers in front of Diego's face. "Hey. Did you hear me? I asked you what else she did with her time."

"She visits a lot of houses. Probably foster homes."

"Have you seen Becca?"

"No. Haven't seen any of the kids. She goes inside and comes out about an hour later."

Juan looked at him as if to decipher whether or not he was telling the truth, making Diego squirm in his seat a little. To someone like Juan, everyone was a liar.

"There's a used book store on Jefferson. I followed her inside one day. She's friends with the owner and they talk about romance books. Melanie comes out with a stack of them every week or so."

"Interesting. So she's into romance?" Juan nodded, seemingly satisfied. Pulling down the visor, he primped in the mirror like a teenaged boy. And then he straightened his clothing, got out of the car, and headed toward the wine bar.

It was like watching a coyote get into the ring with a lamb. Diego sighed, leaned back in his seat, and hoped Melanie Barrett was not as helpless as she appeared.

Chapter 21

The Vineyard was a hangout for Shawnee County white collar professionals, standing-room only on Fridays. If there was any chance at all that Melanie Barrett could meet the man of her dreams, this was the place.

Melanie had gotten there early so she could get her favorite table. Her waitress, Edie, had become a friend and put a reserved card on it each Friday until she got there.

"Things are hopping tonight," Edie announced with a flip of her long hair. "Check out the hot men in here. There is more testosterone in this room than at a Pacer's game. Got to love it."

Melanie scanned the room. At least eighty percent of the drinkers were men. Her kind of crowd. The odds were in her favor. She ordered her usual cheap glass of wine, which was all she could afford on her meager salary.

Melanie tucked her over-stuffed tote under the table, grabbed her small handbag, and went to the ladies room to freshen up. Angling up to the mirror, she pulled out a small makeup bag, withdrew her new lipstick, and applied a new coat of rose cream. Next came a layer of rosy blush and a dab of concealer under her eyes to hide dark circles from lack of sleep. Brushing her hair, she stepped back for a better look. No one would say she was beautiful, but she had potential. And the right man would see that. Just like in the novels she read. All she needed was to find Mr. Right. Unfortunately, she'd dressed in a hurry for work and looked disheveled in a faded pink top, black blazer, and long outdated print skirt. It might do for work, but went a long way to repel the interest of a man. Why the hell didn't she pack another outfit in her tote bag?

Back at her table, it wasn't long before Edie returned with a chilled glass of wine that she set before Melanie. "A guy at the bar sends this glass of Cabernet Sauvignon. Turn around, he's looking this way."

A handsome man at the bar smiled and waved at her, and her heart skipped a beat. With a diamond stud in his left ear, he had a few days growth on his lean jaw. His facial features were sharp and angled, his eyes so dark, they almost appeared black. He was one of those men whose shaved head made him look dark, dangerous, and sexy as hell.

A hot blush crept over her neck and face, and the temperature in the room went up a couple of degrees.

She turned to Edie. "I haven't seen him in here before. Do you know him?"

"Can't say I do. He's Mr. Hotness, isn't he? No cheapskate either. This glass of wine is from the Ravenna Family Vineyard. 2009. A good year."

"Really?"

"I say you go for it, Melanie. What have you got to lose?" Patting Melanie affectionately on the arm, Edie returned to the bar.

Sipping her wine, Melanie looked back and noted that Mr. Hotness was moving toward her. He was tall, over six feet with a slender build, dressed in dark designer jeans with a body-hugging, gunmetal-gray silk T-shirt, topped by a lightweight navy Armani blazer. She might not have money, but she knew her fashion. He moved toward her with a slow, seductive walk. Clutched in one hand was his glass of wine; in the other, a bottle.

"May I join you?"

"Y-Yes," she stuttered, her heart in her throat.

When he sat down, she nervously lifted her glass. "Thank you for the wine. It's delicious."

He held out his hand as if to shake hers. But when she extended her own, he lifted it to his lips and kissed it, looking intently into her eyes. She nearly swooned. He was just like one of the heroes in her romance novels. "I'm Paul Richmond. I'm new in town and you're the prettiest thing I've seen since my arrival."

The line was probably older than she was, but she blushed. It had been an eternity since she dared to be this close to a man. Especially a man who gave her a second look. Not since Eddie Reynolds in high school.

"I'm Melanie Barrett."

"Melanie is a beautiful name for a beautiful woman."

He was laying it on thick, but she lapped it up like a kitten with a saucer of milk. It was hard for Melanie to hope when her hopes had been dashed so ruthlessly in the past. Clinging to the possibility he was a good man, she prayed he was genuinely attracted to her. That maybe she could have a happily ever after.

"That's nice of you to say. What brings you to Shawnee County?"

Juan sipped his wine and said, "I own eight Mexican restaurants in the Midwest, Last Stop Cantina. Three are in Indiana, in Indianapolis, Lafayette, and Bloomington. I want to build one near Morel."

She nearly choked on her sip of wine. He was not only devastatingly handsome, but successful, too. "That must keep you busy."

"I travel a lot, but I'm not complaining. It comes with the territory." He reached across the table and stroked her hand with his index finger. "Enough about me. Tell me about yourself, Melanie Barrett."

He was a man who could have any woman in the room, but he'd chosen her. He actually wanted to get to know her. Melanie was beyond flattered.

"I've lived in Morel for about six years. Moved here from Lafayette. Graduated from Purdue."

"Job?"

Melanie hesitated. Didn't see that one coming. What could she say about her job that wouldn't turn him off? Her job was stressful and punishing, putting her on the lower rung of the pay scale. Nothing glamorous about what she did for a living. What man would want to hear about endless days and nights witnessing horrific child abuse, able only to Band-Aid situations that could have a very bad ending?

"Not much to tell."

"What do you do?"

She wasn't going to lie to him. "I'm a social worker with Child Protective Services."

"Seriously?" Paul asked, leaning forward. "That's what I wanted to do. But my mother had other ideas. She made me change my major from social work to business."

"You wanted to work in Child Protective Services?"

"Damn right. Anyone who works in CPS is a hero to me. Protecting kids. It doesn't get any more important than that. That said, I bet you see a lot of things you'd rather not."

"That's an understatement." She couldn't believe her ears. Who would have guessed this desirable man would be interested in her work? "But I'm sure you don't want to hear about that."

"Actually, I do. Now that my businesses are up and running, I could go back to college and become a social worker, like you."

"You'd do that?"

"I'd seriously consider it. Now tell me about your job." Paul refilled her glass.

Melanie took a sip of her wine. "For the most part, I make home visits to investigate allegations of abuse or neglect. And usually, the allegations are warranted."

"Tell me about a home visit you've made recently."

The conversation was moving into a danger zone for Melanie. She'd be fired if anyone found out she was violating the privacy of her clients. But he was looking at her expectantly, waiting for an answer. Not wanting to disappoint him, she reasoned it would be okay as long as she talked in general terms and mentioned no names. "Not long ago, I made a home visit as a result of an anonymous tip from the Child Abuse Hotline. When I got to the house, I found three children there living in filth, the smell alone was vile. Their toilet was broken so they had nowhere but the backyard to go to the bathroom. Their mother was an alcoholic who beat them on a regular basis. They had the bruises to prove it."

"What a bitch."

Profile of Fear

"My thought exactly. And get this. The mother had her children returned to her by a soft judge who believes kids need to be with their mother, no matter what."

"Sick."

"It happens more times than you would think."

"What happened with the kids?"

"There were no relatives to take them, so I had to split them up and put them in three separate foster homes. It broke my heart, but what else could I do?"

"The mother? What happened with her?"

"She was arrested for assault and a long list of other charges, including child neglect. She punched me in the mouth and went at me with a kitchen knife. She's still in lock-up because she can't make her bail."

"Maybe the kids will find better parents and have a better life."

Melanie just nodded. She did not tell him that thanks to their mother the kids were not adoptable and would probably be bounced from foster home to foster home until they reached eighteen.

Paul urged her to tell more stories about her work, but she refused. She was off work and she certainly wasn't in the mood to tell war stories with a handsome stranger.

"Let's change the subject and talk about something more pleasant."

He finished his wine, and smiled. "You're right. Let's talk about what you like to do in your spare time."

"What do you have in mind?"

"Do you like to go on picnics?"

"I haven't been on a picnic since I was a teenager." What a romantic idea. She liked this guy. Everything about him.

"Join me for a picnic on Sunday. I'll pick you up."

Melanie wrote her home address on the back of one of her business cards and pushed it across the table. "Sounds lovely. What should I bring?"

"Let me worry about the food and wine. It would be my pleasure."

Chapter 22

Several hours had passed and Diego was getting tired of waiting in the car. He was tempted to go inside the wine bar to see what Juan was doing, but that would be asking for trouble. It would piss Juan off in 2.5 seconds and who knows what the maniac would do?

Just then Juan appeared, hopping into the car.

"Let's go. Hurry. I don't want her to see us together. She'll be coming out of the bar anytime."

Diego shoved the gear into drive and sped down the street; he saw Melanie Barrett coming out of the bar onto the sidewalk in his rearview mirror.

Juan buckled his seatbelt and appeared very pleased with himself.

"What happened?" asked Diego. "Did she tell you where your kid is?"

"Not yet. I see her again on Sunday. She will tell me then. You can bet on it."

"Do you need me to drive?"

"Now what kind of a romantic picnic would it be if I dragged you along? No, I don't need you. I want to handle this myself."

Diego sighed with relief for himself, but at the same time felt the chill of fear for Melanie Barrett.

Chapter 23

Thanks to a summer rain the day before, the air had cooled down to the sunny seventies. Perfect day for a picnic. It seemed like they'd driven U.S. Route 136 forever when Paul finally pulled off the road and parked near a thicket of woods. Leaning toward Melanie, he kissed her cheek softly, gazing into her eyes.

Wearing a brand-new blue sundress and matching sandals, Melanie worried. "I didn't know we'd be hiking or I would have worn something more suitable."

Paul smiled at her as he stroked her hair. "I love what you're wearing. No need to be concerned. There is a stream not far from here, surrounded by a grassy area. It's perfect for our picnic. The walk is worth it. You'll see. Besides, I came out here yesterday and cleared a path for us."

Melanie squeezed his hand. "That was so thoughtful of you." She may have found her perfect man. He was considerate, intelligent, interesting, wealthy, and drop-dead sexy. What more could she want? She'd spent the previous day shopping, with a quick stop at a hairdresser to shape her lifeless locks. Paul Richmond had never been far from her thoughts. In fact, he was all she could think about.

She watched him as he circled back to the trunk of the car. Wearing faded snug jeans and a pale blue Ralph Lauren shirt rolled up to the elbows, he looked handsome and dashing and she wanted him. A distinct warmth flooded the area between her legs. Was it too soon to let him make love to her?

He lay a picnic basket and a blanket on the ground, and then rushed to her side of the car to open her door. Gallantly extending his hand, he helped her out of the vehicle. "You steal my breath away, Melanie. You're beautiful." Pulling her into his strong arms, he chastely kissed her cheek again. Throwing the blanket over his shoulder, he held the picnic basket in one hand and her hand in the other. He led her up the road until they came to a freshly cut path in the tall grasses at a curve in the road. When they came to a drainage ditch, he asked her to wait. He leaped over the ditch and planted the blanket and basket on the ground, and then returned to her. Lifting her in his arms, she giggled as he carried her over the waterway. "I don't want my princess to soil her clothing."

Melanie had never met a man so romantic. Visions of having wild sex with him had her head spinning. Where had he been all her life? He was almost too good to be true.

They walked until Paul stopped and pointed to a huge oak tree. "I wanted that to be our picnic spot—in the cool shade of the tree."

"It's great."

"I changed my mind when I saw there was a wasp nest in the tree."

Melanie searched the tree until her eyes landed on a honeycombed, papery bag hanging on a branch. "Good decision."

It wasn't long until they reached a grassy clearing near a brook of cascading water, where Paul lay the blanket and picnic basket down. With the sweet smell of honeysuckle and a cool breeze embracing her bare shoulders, she admired a patch of yellow wood sorrel with its pretty flowers and clover-like leaves. Paul was right. This was the perfect place for a picnic.

She sat on the blanket, removed her sandals, and watched Paul unpack the basket.

He pulled out a bottle of wine and two glasses. "I brought a nice Zinfandel for you to try, some stout craft beer for myself. I remembered you said you didn't like the taste of beer." Filling a glass, he handed it to her and talked as he brought out their lunch. "Prosciutto-wrapped chicken with asparagus, an antipasto pasta salad, a wedge of Brie cheese with Red Delicious apple slices, and for dessert—strawberries dipped in milk chocolate. Sound good?"

"Better than good." She nearly purred when he put a sliver of Brie onto an apple slice and fed it to her. The Brie and wine were delicious. This man was a keeper.

Sampling a bite of the chicken, she moaned with pleasure and then held her plate as he filled it with Prosciutto-wrapped chicken, asparagus, antipasto pasta salad, brie cheese and apple slices. Famished, they ate in silence, and he refilled her wine glass. When they finished, he wrapped the soiled plates in plastic, put them back into the basket, and then lifted the bottle to refresh her glass of wine.

Relaxing on the blanket, Paul gazed at her thoughtfully. "I thought a lot about what you told me about your work on Friday night. I'd like to hear more. It will help me decide if I want to go back to school. Be a social worker."

"What would you like to know?"

"Tell me about the kids you've helped recently. What did you do for them?"

Melanie was flattered by his interest in her job and impressed he would consider such a life change for himself. Helping others. More proof he was a good guy, that he might be the one.

"I had a teenaged boy who'd run away from his second group home in a month. Had a hard time placing him, but finally a couple who owns a farm not far from town took him in. Last I checked, he was okay and seemed to be adjusting to his new surroundings. Maybe it will work out for him. I hope so."

"Do you mainly work with teenagers? Any younger children?"

"He's still in the hospital, but when he's released I will be placing a nine-month-old baby in another home. His mother's new boyfriend said he rolled off a changing table onto the floor, but there were too many injuries and bruising to his body for that to be true. The police arrested both the mother and the boyfriend, and the judge ordered the baby to foster care."

"Must be tough working a case like that."

"All I can do is hope for a happy ending."

She noticed Paul tensed and ran an agitated hand through his hair. Why the change in behavior? A wave of dizziness overcame her. She leaned back and took a deep breath. Was it the alcohol?" Moving her glass aside she said, "No more wine for me."

"Melanie, I read in the paper about a meth bust where a two-year-old girl was removed from the house. What happened to the little girl? Was she one of your cases?"

It wasn't the question itself, but the intensity in his eyes that made Melanie uncomfortable. Why was he asking her about that specific case?

"Let's talk about something more pleasant than my job. I'd rather hear more about you. Where did you grow up? Do you have brothers and sisters?" The light-headedness returned. Was she intoxicated? How could she be drunk if she'd only consumed two glasses of wine?

"Melanie?" Paul asked. "Are you okay?"

She opened her mouth to answer him, and that was when her world went dark.

When Melanie regained consciousness, the muscles in her arms and legs ached, her fingers numb, and something covered her mouth. To her horror, she couldn't move. She opened her eyes and pain exploded at the base of her skull. What was happening to her?

A stinging slap across her face made her wince. "Wake up, Melanie. I didn't give you that much."

Moaning, she turned her head away from the voice, blinking the frightened tears from her eyes.

"Don't bother to scream, your mouth is duct-taped. Anyway, who would hear you out here in the middle of nowhere?"

Paul stood before her, his expression ruthless and angry, the look of ice-cold fury on his face. "That wine had quite a kick, didn't it, Melanie? You were too easy. Sucked it right down, roofie and all." Bending, he tightened the rope around her ankles, painfully pressing her skin into the rough bark of the tree. Straightening, he looked at her thoughtfully. "I need to remove the duct tape. I must warn you that if you scream, I'll make sure you regret it. Don't even think about it."

With a vicious yank, he ripped the tape from her mouth, and she cried out.

"I'm warning you."

She slowly shook her head. "I won't scream. Please don't hurt me. Why are you doing this, Paul?" Her heart was racing, nearly exploding from her chest. "Who are you?"

"I'm Juan Ortiz. Does that name sound familiar?"

"No."

"You've really got to get out more, Melanie. Get your nose out of your miserable little do-gooder life. Hell, my photo is probably hanging in your post office right now. I became something of a celebrity when I hit the FBI's Most Wanted List." He pulled a serrated hunting knife from the picnic basket. Melanie gulped down several breaths to stay quiet.

"Oh, God. Don't hurt me." She pleaded. "Please put the knife away."

"Tell me what I need to know and I won't have to use it."

"I don't understand." How could she have been so stupid, so wrong about a man? She thought he was her happily ever after, yet he'd probably end her life without blinking. Things were moving too quickly to process. Why was this happening to her? She struggled with the ropes that bound her hands at the back of the tree.

"The little girl that was rescued from the meth bust at Donda Hicks' house is my kid and I want her. She's my property. You tell me where she is and you walk out of here."

"The two-year-old is your *property*?"

"You're not as dumb as I thought. Where is she?"

Becca. Melanie thought of the baby she'd visited in the hospital, her beautiful little face miserable as she cried for Cameron Chase. How she'd clung to him when he entered the room. Why did this monster, who was wanted by law enforcement, want her? His property? What would he do to her if he found her?

"I don't know what happened to her. Not my case."

His face reddened, his eyes slits of rage. She saw the flash of the knife before she felt it slice her right forearm. The wound wasn't deep but it hurt so much she could barely breathe as a trickle of blood streamed down her arm.

"Wrong answer." He gritted between his teeth. "Let's try this again. Her name is Becca. She's around two-years-old, and her worthless mother ran away. Didn't know about her until recently. No one keeps my property from me. No one."

He wrapped one of his hands around her throat and she felt the pressure squeezing her windpipe.

"Where is Becca?"

"Please don't hurt me. I'm telling you that I don't know where she is."

"You're lying." He roared, making her ears ring.

Removing his hand from neck, he jabbed the knife into the flesh of her left side. Excruciating pain took her breath away; the blood soaked her new dress and ran down her hips and thighs. A primal scream unexpressed nearly choked her as gasped for air, while the throbbing in her side escalated. She began shaking uncontrollably.

"It hurts, doesn't it Melanie? She's just one little kid that you don't even know. Not even an acquaintance. Is she worth the pain? Is she worth your life?"

Melanie had spent the last six years of her life protecting children like Becca. Removing them from deplorable conditions gave many of them a chance for a better life. She protected the weak and innocent. Wasn't that the real reason she endured a low-paying, punishing job? She was the only thing standing between Becca and a life of miserable pain from a monster who was a stranger to her. She was only two-years-old, with her whole life ahead of her. A life that would be filled with family and love, if Cameron Chase had anything to do with it.

"I don't know where she is." The dizziness returned, black spots appearing before her eyes. But her blurred vision didn't prevent her from seeing him raise the knife.

Chapter 24

Cameron gazed through the one-way glass at Donda Hicks, who sat slumped in a chair in the interview room with her head on the table. He'd gotten a message from Henry Stephens at the jail that she claimed it was urgent that she talk to him. Imagining anything the drugged-out shell of a human being had to say could interest him was a stretch. He held her directly responsible for the abuse Becca had suffered, and planned to make sure child abuse and neglect were added to her list of offenses.

Jerking open the interview room door, he purposely dropped a thick file folder that slapped noisily onto the floor. Shrieking, Donda jerked and nearly fell out of her chair, which was his intention.

"Oh, I'm sorry. Sure hope I didn't wake you up. Not resting well in your cell?" Sarcasm laced his tone as he glared at her.

Sitting down across from her, he studied her face. Dark smudges lay under her eyes, and skin stretched thin across her facial bones, making her look even more emaciated than the first time he saw her at the meth bust. Her left eye twitched as if it had a mind of its own.

"What's up, Donda? What's this urgent thing you have to discuss with me?"

Sniffing, she wiped her nose with her arm. "Look, I don't care what happens to me, but whatever you do, *don't* tell me where social services put Becca."

"I have no intention of telling you a damn thing about Becca.

You're a kid's worth nightmare for a mother. If it were up to me, I'd make sure you never came within a city block of a child for the rest of your miserable life." His words were sudden, raw, and very angry.

She visibly flinched. Her face turned red and blotched with anger and resentment. "Who the hell are you to judge me? You got no idea what I've been through."

"It's all about you. Isn't it, Donda?" He pushed back in his chair. "No room in your narcissistic, drugged-up world for a kid. Right?"

"Do you really think I'd ask to talk to an asshole like you if I didn't have to? You can go straight to hell."

"Why *are* we here? What's so important that you had to talk to me?"

Squeezing her eyes shut for a moment, Donda clenched her hands in her lap so hard her knuckles whitened. She looked up at him, and he could swear he saw a tear threatening the corner of her eye. "I just got to know something. Did social services place Becca in a good home? Will the foster parents be good to her? Is she safe?"

Cameron thought of the evening before. Kaitlyn had bathed Becca and dressed her in what the little girl called her 'doggie' pajamas. All breeds of dogs sprinkled across the soft pink material. With her tiny finger, Becca had pointed out to him the dog in the fabric who looked most like her new friend, Godiva. Gabe and Kaitlin's chocolate Lab had stuck to the child like superglue as she ran to Cameron's arms.

Kaitlyn handed a colorful book to him. "It's your turn for story time." She settled down on the sofa next to Gabe and waited for him to begin. Reading to Becca was a ritual they'd started during her first week with them. It was a time when Cameron, Gabe, and Kaitlyn could relax and leave behind the stresses of their days.

The child settled in his lap so she could see the book's pictures, and the large dog curled at his feet watching the two of them. The story was about a Siamese kitten who'd lost his mother and asked any animal he encountered, "Do you know where my mother is?" As he read, Cameron wondered whether Becca missed her mother. She had not asked for her since she'd moved into their home.

Becca listened intently and periodically touched the pages as if she were stroking the animals in the pictures. Finishing, he closed the book and looked down at her. She was fast asleep, smelling sweetly like baby shampoo, and looking angelic in his arms. Kissing her softly on her forehead, he glanced up at his brother, who smiled at him from across the room. Carrying the child up the stairs to her room, Cameron had realized how much he and his family had grown to love Becca. She was a part of them now, and he didn't know what he'd do if her birth mother tried to take her away from them.

Donda's snapped her fingers to gain his attention. "Hey. Are you listening? It's dangerous for me to know where Becca is, but I got to know that she's safe."

Lifting an eyebrow, Cameron glared at the woman across the table. A stray cat was a better mother. If she was using reverse psychology to obtain Becca's location, she wouldn't get it from him. Social services might give it to her, but he'd die before he would. The woman was poison to Becca. "Yes. She's safe. Becca's with a family who loves her and will protect her. Is that what you want to know? Is that why you wanted to meet with me? I could have told you that in a phone call."

Taking a deep breath, Donda exhaled, facing him but not really looking at him. "I need your help."

Cameron's eyes narrowed with disgust. "Seriously? What kind of help? A better question is why should I help you?"

"I have information."

"What kind of information do you have that would remotely interest me?"

Her hands balled into fists, temper flaring in her eyes, Donda leaned across the table. "Maybe you're the wrong person to talk to. I should have called the feds first."

"You think your information would interest the FBI?"

"Yes."

Leaning back in his chair, he studied her. What kind of information could a meth-head from a small county in Indiana have to offer the feds? Her husband was manufacturing meth in

Shawnee County locally, so she might have information on meth dealers and a supply network. Intel like that would definitely interest him. But the feds? Not likely.

"I'd need to hear your info before I contact the FBI. That's protocol," he lied. It wasn't protocol. She was free to contact federal agents on her own, but in the unlikely event she had information important enough for the feds, he wanted to hear it first.

"Juan Ortiz."

Incredulous, Cameron ran his fingers through his hair. "Juan Ortiz? Isn't that a fictional character created for a coffee commercial?"

"You're an idiot. Don't you ever read the FBI's Most Wanted list? I'm not saying another word until you get me someone in here that knows who Juan Ortiz is."

"If you're so smart, tell me about this guy named Ortiz."

Crossing her arms across her chest, she stiffened. "I mean it. I'm not saying a word."

Cameron left the interview room, slamming the door behind him. At his office computer, he pulled up the FBI Most Wanted list and scanned the who's who of dangerous criminals until he found Juan Ortiz.

Chapter 25

Cursing her computer, Carly Stone slapped it on the side and rebooted it. The computer techs who had been working on it for a week assured her that all was well. Apparently not.

Once her PC came to life, she opened the Internet and accessed the FBI's Next Generation Identification (NGI) database, where she re-sent a query regarding the tattoo found on the hips of murder victims Brandy Murphy and Shirley Metz. What appeared on the screen next made her heart stop and her jaw drop. Juan Ortiz. Of course, why hadn't she figured that out when she noted the initials inside the circular tattoo were 'J' and 'O'? But how could Juan Ortiz be involved with killings in Indiana, when he was hiding from the FBI in Mexico? She'd received no intelligence that he'd been found, or that he'd left Mexico.

Chapter 26

Carly hurried into Cameron's office, fighting to even her breathing. She had to tell Cameron about the tattoo. "I have something to tell you about—"

Glued to his computer screen, he interrupted. "Have you ever heard of Juan Ortiz? Just found him on the Most Wanted List."

Cameron glanced up at Carly, who had noticeably paled. He'd known his brother's wife to be unshakable, no-nonsense, and in charge, yet she now appeared tense at the mention of a criminal's name. Why? His eyebrows lifted as he drew back to study her face.

Hesitating for a moment, Carly then moved beside him to peer at Juan Ortiz's information on Cameron's computer screen. "I've heard of him. He's wanted by the FBI for human trafficking, kidnapping, and murder. That's just a few of his offenses. Why are you interested in him?"

Cameron swiveled his chair so he could see her face, but found her expression difficult to read. "I've got Donda Hicks, one of my meth bust arrests, in the interview room. She's trying to trade information on Mr. Ortiz for some kind of a favor."

Carly eased around to a visitor chair and sat down. "It's doubtful she has any information. He's been in hiding for years, conducting his business from Mexico. What did she say about him?"

Cameron shifted in his chair, picked up a pen and tapped it a couple of times. He'd screwed up. If he'd been a bit more persuasive and a lot less sarcastic, Donda might have already given him the information on Ortiz and he wouldn't feel like such a jerk. "I pissed her off and now she's demanding to talk to a Fed. She says she has important information about Ortiz."

"Do you believe her? I mean you've got her for possession and dealing meth. How credible could she be? Are you sure she's not working you for a get-out-of-jail card?"

Nodding, he chewed on that possibility. "She might be messing with me. But what if she's not? The guy's on the FBI's Most Wanted List."

Carly leaned forward in her chair. "*I'll* talk to her."

"What?"

"You said she's demanding a Fed. I'm a Fed. At least a former Fed. What would it hurt if I interviewed her?"

Cameron looked her straight in the eye. "Is there something you want to tell me about Juan Ortiz, Carly? You had a strange reaction when I mentioned his name before."

"Not much to tell. I was an agent based in the FBI's Orlando office when I first heard of Ortiz. He ran a prostitution ring there, capitalizing on the influx of tourists. We set up an undercover operation to capture him, but he got away. End of story."

There was no way this was the end of the story. Carly knew more about Ortiz than she wanted to share. She'd never held back information from him before. And that she was doing it now made him determined to find out why. Cameron shot her a cut-the-bullshit look that would have had most people spilling their guts. But not Carly. She seemed completed unfazed.

He eased back in his chair. "No reason why you can't talk to her. Like you said, she wants to talk to a Fed."

"Give me some background on her."

Cameron slid Donda Hick's file across his desk to her. "She's Becca's mother."

"She's the meth-head birth-mother that abused Becca?"

"Yeah, does that impact your impartiality?"

"I'm a little more professional than that, Cam. Did it impact yours?"

Cameron flinched. "Can't say I'm not angry with her for the way she treated Becca. So if it comes to you asking me to give her a deal for information on Ortiz, the child abuse charges stay on the table. Not budging on that."

"Seriously, Cam? You should know the chances of me asking for leniency for the woman that hurt Becca are extremely unlikely. I may not have had the time to spend with her that Kaitlyn has, but I love Becca just as much."

"I'm sorry, Carly. I shouldn't have said that. This woman unnerves me. I think she might be fishing for Becca's location. She can't know that social services placed her little girl with us. I don't trust what she might do if she finds out."

"Mrs. Hicks won't get the information from me. Have you thought about asking her to hand over her parental rights so you can adopt Becca? I mean, that little girl is as much a part of the family now as I am."

"I can't ask her now, not when she's looking for some leverage."

"Sorry, Cam."

"Let's get back to Donda's background. As you will see in her file, she's been arrested for petty thefts as well as prostitution, but that was several years ago in Indianapolis. Nothing since she moved here, married Hicks, and gave birth to Becca."

"I'm not seeing an obvious connection to Ortiz. Like I said, he's been hiding in Mexico for years."

Cameron sat quietly for a moment, chewing on his lower lip as he thought. He remembered talking to Donda's husband when he was in the back of the police cruiser. The man had told him Becca wasn't his—that Donda had run off a couple of years ago and came back pregnant. He scrubbed wearily at his face. He had a bad feeling in his gut. The girl could be telling the truth. Cameron wanted to see if Carly found out this same information.

"This all might be a ploy to get out of jail, but I appreciate you talking to her."

Chapter 27

Carly paused before the one-way glass window to get her first view of Donda Hicks. The woman inside the interview room was gaunt and wore the worried expression of someone who had made too many mistakes in life to count. She wore an orange jumpsuit with a worn gray sweater too large for her small frame. Pulling the cuffs over her hands, she was worrying the frays of yarn with her fingers. As if she sensed she was being watched, she crossed her arms and stared at the one-way glass.

Cameron moved beside her. "What do you think of our informant?"

"She looks angry, but she also looks scared."

"I get the angry part, but what are you seeing that suggests she's afraid? Not seeing it."

"Look at her, Cam. She's just a scared kid. See her arms folded under her breasts? It's a typical gesture of defense. There is something she thinks she must defend herself against. Something or someone she fears. I'd be willing to bet she'll ask for some type of protection."

"I doubt if Donda Hicks has the kind of information to warrant *any* kind of protection."

Carly shouldered past him to enter the small interview room. Once inside, she sat across from Donda without saying a word, putting her briefcase on the floor. She pulled out the information Cameron had printed about Ortiz and placed the pages on the table, right where Donda could see them.

Donda shot her a suspicious look. "Who are you?"

"You asked for a federal agent. "I'm Special Agent Carly Stone."

Donda eyed Carly suspiciously. "Yeah, and a long-lost Kardashian. Notice the family resemblance?"

Reaching into her briefcase, Carly pulled out her identification card and slid it across the table. "Is this proof enough for you, Ms. Hicks? Now start talking. I'm too busy to play games with you. If you have information on Juan Ortiz, spill it."

"I need some promises from you first."

"No deal. You get consideration if the information is useful. Period."

Donda blew out a breath, and then crossed and uncrossed her arms. It seemed to Carly as if she were wavering between talking or not. "How do you know Juan Ortiz?"

"I fell for one of his modeling schemes."

"What does that mean?"

"Ortiz puts these ad things on Craigslist and Backpage for models. The ads said I could be famous and make a lot of money, so I emailed my photo. Why not? I was living with my mom and my grabby, pervert stepfather at that point, so what did I have to lose, anyway? At least that's what I thought. I get a response almost immediately. The email had a flyer attached that gave a time and place for model tryouts."

"Where?"

"A fake office he'd set up in Indianapolis. There are two other girls waiting when I get there. They were dressed up with makeup and shit like a pro on Saturday night. A sour-faced beeach sitting at a desk tells us we have to wait fifteen more minutes for two more girls to arrive. One of the girls who was here before me gets up and says, "I'm not waiting. I'm done with this gig," and she leaves.

The rest of us waited, and when they don't show up, the boss, this Ortiz guy, has another place for the modeling tryouts, and that there is a van in the back waiting to take us there."

Carly wrote notes on a yellow notepad. "Was Ortiz in the office?"

"No. There were two badass dudes, who alternated between

speaking Spanish and English, and the hostile secretary who said as little as possible. She mainly glared at us."

"So what happened at the tryouts?"

"That's a joke. There is no modeling tryout. Once we are, like, herded in this van, this one girl, she starts freaking out. She leans forward and demands to know where they're taking us. The dude in the front seat turns around and slaps the shit out of her. That's the first sign that tells me we are in deep trouble, so I just keep my dumb-ass mouth shut. The second sign is when we are blindfolded."

"Where did they take you?"

"Lady, haven't you heard a word I said? I was blindfolded. How in the hell would I know where we were going?"

Tapping her pen on the table, Carly gazed at Donda. Not expecting to believe anything the woman said, Carly was beginning to think she was telling the truth—at least this part of her story. It was like the tales she'd heard from the few women who were willing to talk about Ortiz's operation. "Go on, Donda. What happened next?"

"When the van finally stops, the men lead us through a house and didn't remove the blindfolds until we were shoved into a small room together. The house stank like cigarettes, booze, and sex."

"Even though your eyes were covered, do you remember anything about the house that would help us find it?"

"No. We were kept in a small room on the second level and the windows were covered from the inside with plywood. We broke our damn fingernails trying to pry off that plywood."

"So the house has more than one floor?"

"Yes, but the only room I seen downstairs was the kitchen when we ate our chow. Afterward, we were marched back up the stairs."

"You couldn't see into the other rooms?"

"The house had few lights and the staircase led right into the kitchen. The only other rooms I saw upstairs were the three rooms where we had sex with customers."

"You claim you know Juan Ortiz. Before you tell me how you met him, give me a good description of what he looks like."

"The girls call Juan 'the man of many faces.' He's always

changing his look and identity. When I knew him, he had a deep tan and had black, curly hair over his forehead, to just below his ears. If you could overlook his cruel streak, he'd be hot."

Carly glanced at her skeptically. "You could have gotten that information from the Internet. I need more to believe you actually know him."

Donda pulled the waist of her skirt down and stood up to reveal a tattoo on her hip—a small circle with the initials J.O. inside. It looked like a brand cowboys use on cattle. "I'm telling the truth. He called me his special bitch. This tattoo means I'm Juan's property. All his girls have them. But no one knew him like I did. I'm the one he chose for sex, not the other girls."

"Tell me more."

"When it came to doing it, he liked it rough—meaning he had to slap me around, hard enough to leave bruises, before he could get it up. I think he was more turned on by hurting me than by the prospect of hot sex. He was touchy about questions, too. One time I asked him how he got the thick, white scars on his back. He said to drop it or he'd slit my throat. Then he backhanded me so hard, it knocked one of my front teeth loose." Donda opened her mouth to reveal a space in her front row of teeth.

"Anything else you can remember about him physically?"

"Yes, he has this weird scar on his right shoulder, looks like it was an open wound that should have had stitches but didn't."

Carly's eyes narrowed. "It's a gunshot wound."

"How do you know that?"

"Because I gave it to him."

"Oh, shit. You're the one who shot him?"

Carly became uncomfortable and shifted in her seat realizing her mistake. Why had she blurted out a secret, only she and a few undercover cops knew? A secret she'd guarded for years. And now a woman desperate for her freedom knew her name and location. Now Donda now had a bargaining chip with one of the FBI's most dangerous criminals. A man who would stop at nothing to take Carly's life, as well as the lives of those she loved.

"No one can do something like that to Juan Ortiz and live," Donda warned.

Carly swiftly changed the subject. If she could get to Ortiz first, it wouldn't matter if he found out her name and location. "So far you've given me enough info to make me believe you knew Ortiz in the past, but that was years ago. But we need information about where he is and what he is doing *now*."

"I saw him weeks ago, shortly before I got busted."

"In Indiana?"

"No, the North Pole. Of course I saw him in Indiana. I knew it was a matter of time for him to find me. No one gets away from him. He warned me that I was his property and that if I ever escaped, he'd use his many associates to find me. He's got meth cooks, dealers, and distributers all over the Midwest. But once I found out I was pregnant with his kid, I knew I had to escape."

Carly's eyes widened, her heart lodged in her throat. "Wait a minute? Are you suggesting that Becca belongs to Juan Ortiz?"

"I'm not suggesting, I know she does. I always used protection with the johns. But Juan wouldn't hear of it. He didn't like sex with a rubber and refused to wear one. Finding out I was pregnant with Becca was the most terrifying day of my life. If he found out, he'd either kill me or take my baby and sell her, or both. That's why I ran."

"How did you escape?"

"Back then a thug named Mateo worked for Juan and ran the house. He's the one who offered me as a gift to Juan in the first place. Mateo ran the ads on Craigslist and Backstreet, and delivered us for sex in hotels close by. One day, he'd hooked a big spender but there was no one to send to the hotel. It was the weekend of a big Colts game, and all the other girls were working parties. I begged him to send me. He agreed as long as I didn't tell his boss. Juan didn't want me leaving the house, but greed got the best of Mateo and he let me go. Once I got inside the hotel room, I started crying hysterically. I told the john I was pregnant and was being beaten and held captive. He felt sorry for me. Paid me $500 for staying with him that night. In the morning, he took me to the bus station."

Growing impatient, Carly sighed and ran her fingers through her long hair. She fished an elastic band out of her briefcase and then tied her hair back. "Let's skip to the part where you saw Juan Ortiz weeks ago."

"Gee, pardon me if I'm boring your ass."

She met Donda's glare head-on. "Go on."

"There's this farmer's market set up in a field on Route 41 on Saturday mornings."

"I've been there."

"On this particular Saturday, I had Becca with me in her stroller. Wanted to see if I could find some used toddler clothes and get some fresh veggies. You know, for the kid. As soon as I got out of the truck, I sensed something was wrong. Made me jittery and looking over my shoulder. Once we got going, I decided it would be a quick trip, look for the clothes, buy the veggies, and get the hell out of there."

"You saw Ortiz at this farmer's market out in the country. How would he even know it was there? I don't think I could find it by myself, not without someone local driving."

"How should I know how he got there? I just know it was Juan I saw."

"Keep going."

"Like I said. Things felt creepy. I felt someone was watching me, but every time I turned to look, no one was. After a while, I decided I was just being paranoid, so I relaxed a little. I was filling a bag with sweet corn when I heard Becca let out the most terrifying scream I'd ever heard. I ran to her stroller, and saw Becca crying hysterically with her index finger pointing to a man in the next booth. It was Juan. He wore a ball cap that covered most of his face, but I knew it was him, the same slender build, the same dark eyes filled with hate. Becca had caused a commotion that must have freaked him out, because he got out of there in a hurry, disappearing in the crowd. I unbuckled Becca from the stroller. I was so scared I left the stroller there. I held my kid to my chest and ran like my feet were on fire to the truck and got the hell out of there."

Carly felt the blood rush to her face. She didn't want to believe that Ortiz was in the state, let alone the small county where she lived. "And you're certain the man you saw was Juan Ortiz?"

"Seriously? Are you asking if I could recognize the bastard I had to screw for years? He wore a ball cap, there's no way he could disguise those eyes. They're dark as death."

When Carly didn't answer, Donda leaned across the table. "I'm begging you to promise me that my kid will be protected. Juan may not know exactly where she is now, but he'd be an idiot not to think she's living somewhere in this county. And he may be a monster, but he's not stupid. If Becca isn't in a safe place and protected, he *will* get to her. It's only a matter of time. And when he does, he'll sell her to the highest bidder, or even worse, keep her himself. Her life won't be worth living."

Cameron was waiting for Carly when she left the interview room. She brushed past him and sprinted down the hall like she was in a relay race. Shouting her name, he rushed after her. By the time he caught up with her, Carly was in her car, gunning it through the parking lot.

He pulled his cell phone out of his pocket and called the jail. "Inmate Donda Hicks is on her way back. Put her in solitary. No phone calls. No visitors and no communication with other inmates."

Chapter 28

Carly broke the speed limit getting out of Morel, ran a stop light, and nearly got T-boned by a grain truck whose driver angrily pumped his horn. Alarm closing like a fist around her heart, she reached the edge of town, and burned rubber as she made a turn and headed toward home. Fishing her cell phone out of her purse, she called Kaitlyn, but got her voice mail and disconnected the call. Where was Kaitlyn? She had Becca with her today, and had no clue that she and the child were in danger. Carly glanced at the rearview mirror to make sure she wasn't being followed. Clear.

Carly forced the gas pedal down until she reached 80 mph, which was an insane rate of speed for the curvy two-lane highway. She didn't give a damn. The sooner she could see for herself that Kaitlyn and Becca were safe the better. Glancing in the rearview mirror, she saw a hopped-up red pickup with a gun rack in the back window bearing down on her, matching her speed and then some. Pulling her small handgun out of her ankle holster, she placed it on her lap, prepared for confrontation. In her mirror, she could see the truck had closed the distance between their vehicles and he was riding her bumper. A car passed from the other direction, and the truck whipped around her and zipped ahead. It was just a kid. The teenaged driver laughed and waved at her as he passed. Carly cursed, focusing her fear and anger on the driver, and then pumped the brake as she neared a curve in the road.

She thought of Brody and what a mistake it had been to keep

Profile of Fear

what had happened with Juan Ortiz from him. Sharing good memories with Brody came naturally, but how did she marry a man she couldn't trust with the ugliest details of her life, as well as the good? God knew how much she loved him, but she couldn't seem to open the door in her psyche and let him in. Why did she guard this one memory so closely in the vault of her mind? Clearly, she should have seen the psychiatrists that upper management demanded she see, if she wanted to return to active duty as a federal agent. Instead, she had resigned and fled to Shawnee County, where she took the consultant job with Sheriff Brody Chase. Her flight wasn't far enough away, nor would it ever be. The memory was alive and well, and resided in her nightmares, from which she'd never be free.

Cameron would tell Brody what he learned from her interview with Donda. He'd show his brother the recording. She was sure of it. Carly would have done the same if her brother, Blake, had married a woman with secrets.

But what did Cameron really have to tell? That she was involved in a botched FBI op to capture Ortiz in Florida. So what? He knew she'd been a federal agent. She'd participated in many setups to catch criminals. The clincher was that Cameron had to have overheard her telling Donda that she was the one who'd given Ortiz the gunshot wound scar. Blurting that kind of personal knowledge to a suspect was idiotic, and she'd never done it before. No personal knowledge. That was the rule. Most of the agents she knew didn't wear their wedding bands so that suspects wouldn't know they had a family. You could never be too careful. So what does she do? She gives Donda Hicks knowledge about her identity and location that Ortiz would give his right arm to know. Information that could get her and everyone she loves killed.

Carly chewed on her lower lip and ran her fingers through her thick hair as she slowed to turn into the long drive that ran past the main house to the Honeymoon Cottage. Seriously? Was she actually considering *not* telling Brody the truth? That train had left the station. There was no way she couldn't tell him—not when their very lives could be at stake.

Glancing one more time in the rearview mirror to make sure

she hadn't been followed, she turned into the driveway. Kaitlyn's car was parked in one of the four-car garage spaces. Becca must be inside with her. She'd talk to Kaitlyn as soon as she made contact with the federal agents currently assigned to Juan Ortiz. If they had new intelligence on him, it was critical that she get it.

She'd unlocked the door and was heading inside the cottage, when Carly heard the crunch of gravel and saw a white SUV with tinted windows pull in and park next to her car. Oh God! What if Ortiz already knew where she was? What if she had brought death to her home? Her heart beat erratically.

Easing her handgun out of her ankle holster, she slid inside and leaned against the doorframe, waiting to see who the driver was.

A man with short-cropped blond hair unfolded his long legs, got out of the SUV, and leaned lazily against the side. He wore a gray pin-striped suit and looked like he could do a modeling stint for *Esquire* magazine. "Good to see you, Agent Stone. If that's a gun in your hand, you might consider the penalties of aiming at your supervisory special agent for the FBI."

She slipped the gun back into her waistband. "Since it's you I'm aiming at, the bureau may actually give me a medal. *And,* Sam Isley, you are not my supervisor or anything else to me."

"I'm sensing hostility. Come on, Carly, what happened between us was a long time ago."

"Not so long that I can't see in vivid detail you screwing my trainee on your desk as I stood in the doorway, holding a bottle of champagne to celebrate my return to you. You remember, I'd been on assignment for a month. Thought you'd be glad to see me and all that."

"I wanted to marry you, Carly."

"Thus making the humping even worse. You. Cheated. On. Me." Gritting her teeth, she glared at him for a long moment, descending the steps to the driveway. "I think I've made it perfectly clear that I do not want to see you. I've moved on. I'm happily married. So why are you here?"

He gestured with his head to the cottage. "It's not a social call. May I come inside to talk?"

"No."

Nodding, he unbuttoned his suit jacket, thrust his hands in his pockets, and leaned lazily against his vehicle again. Carly's fingers dug into her palms to keep herself from slapping the smirk off his face. If there was one person she was not in the mood to deal with today, it was Sam Isley. Not that it was likely that she'd ever have a yearning to spend time with her former supervisor/lover. "Say what you have to say, Sam."

"Last night someone broke into your place in Orlando. Because you're still tagged as a federal agent, the city cops called the Orlando field office, who called me." He opened the car door to retrieve a photo in a clear plastic evidence bag from his passenger seat. "This was found on your bedroom wall, painted in red paint, before they dumped the rest on your bed."

Carly looked at the photo. Oozing red paint covered her bed, splashes of it on every wall except the one above her headboard. On that wall, someone had carefully painted a red circle with the letters 'JO' inside it. It was the same return-to-owner symbol tattooed on Donda Hicks' hip. The symbol Juan Ortiz had branded on each of his girls, his property. If Ortiz didn't know her identity, how did he find her house in Orlando?

"How did he...?"

"How did he find you? That was my question until I saw this." Isley handed another evidence bag to her. "This was found in your living room."

Carly withdrew from it a folded newspaper article about a charity event she'd headed for the Orlando FBI field office. Along with the text was a photograph of her, holding the Lucite award the mayor had given her. "I guess I don't need to ask how Ortiz found me."

Wrapping an arm around her shoulders, Isley said, "I'm sorry, Carly. This kind of thing isn't supposed to happen to agents."

Jerking out of his embrace, she backed up a couple of steps. "Do you have anything else on Ortiz to tell me?"

"Yes. Two months ago, we received information that Ortiz is in the Midwest and heads a group of men who are trafficking young girls they've abducted or duped into working for them. They recruit their victims through online modeling ads where they are promised high-paying glamorous jobs."

Carly nodded, taking it all in.

"I shouldn't be telling you this."

"Don't you dare stop," she warned.

"The Indy field office has a long list of missing women they believed were abducted as a result of answering these ads. Some of the girls are sold as nannies or maids. The others are trafficked for exotic dancing, prostitution, and janitors, restaurant waitresses or dishwashers.

"Restaurant workers? He owns restaurants? How is he getting away with that?"

"Under a variety of names, Ortiz owns a dozen *Last Stop Cantina* restaurants throughout the Midwest. In Indiana, he has one in Indianapolis, Lafayette, and Bloomington."

"All three towns have universities. Is he focusing on coeds?"

"Not necessarily. Several of the missing girls are teenagers."

"Why is he here in the Midwest? Why would he risk capture when he can conduct his business safely from Mexico? It doesn't make sense."

"We've had no sightings of Ortiz. We don't know that he's actually here."

"He's here. I just interviewed a confidential informant who saw him a few weeks ago."

Isley's jaw dropped open in surprise, and anger flickered in his eyes. "Damn it, Carly. You cannot withhold that kind of information from me. You know better."

"Seriously? Should I have contacted you as quickly as you did me when you first learned of Ortiz's operations in the Midwest?"

"Okay, that's fair. I didn't contact you right away because you shouldn't be involved in anything that involves Ortiz."

"Since when do you get to make that kind of judgment call?"

"I let you down—"

"When I needed you most. And this time, you put me in harm's way."

"How many times do I have to say I'm sorry?"

"Forget it. I have."

"That's a lie, Carly. You *haven't* forgotten it. I wished you'd seen the shrinks like I asked you to."

Swiftly, she changed the subject. "I want in on your op to catch Ortiz."

"No chance. No personal agendas. Robynn Burton with the Indiana State Police will be in charge of creating the task force to focus on finding Juan Ortiz. Right now she's focused on a series of murders. The bureau is stepping back to let the state police handle it. We're in on a consultant basis only."

"I want to be on the task force when it forms."

"Not a good idea."

"Why not?"

"So you can go vigilante? Not on my watch."

"What's that supposed to mean?" Carly snapped back, a little too intensely.

"Come on, Carly. Give me a little credit."

They heard Brody's SUV before they saw it, thundering down the driveway toward them, the big tires spitting gravel onto the lawn. Pulling in behind Carly's car, he got out of his vehicle, anger radiating off him in waves.

"Agent Isley. What are you doing here? I'll give you exactly two seconds to get off my property."

Isley got into his car and powered down his window. "Carly can fill you in. Good to see you, Sheriff." Backing his car up, he turned around and headed toward the highway.

Brody focused on Carly. "Do you want to tell me what that was all about?"

She headed for the house. "Not now. I'm going to get dinner started."

Chapter 29

Robynn Burton was waiting for Cameron when he returned to his office.

Standing to face him, hands on her hips, she was clearly annoyed. "Where have you been? I've been waiting for you for thirty minutes."

"Nice to see you, too, Sergeant."

"Didn't you get my email? I wrote you that I'd be here today by eleven."

"I haven't had time to have coffee, let alone check my email. Sorry. What's going on?"

Cameron eased into his chair and took a moment to check her out. Robynn was still trying to hide her lush curves beneath a nothing-but-business black pant-suit, with a white blouse buttoned all the way up to her slender neck. She reminded him of Melanie Griffith's character in the movie *Working Girl*. Robynn had a head for business, and a body made for sin. The latter being the subject of many a fantasy involving him pinning her to his bed, with Robynn moaning with pleasure beneath him. His eyes moved to her face, their gazes locked, and there was a moment of sizzling awareness that ended when Robynn blinked and then cleared her throat.

"Three women were murdered Tuesday in Indy. Same M.O. as the Brandy Murphy and Shirley Metz killings. One of them was from Shawnee County."

"What's her name?"

Profile of Fear

"Carol Sue Henley. The coroner identified her by her dental records."

Cameron scrubbed his hands over his face. Could his morning get worse? "Damn it. I was hoping we'd find her alive. She's been missing for nearly a year."

"The other two victims had been reported as missing, too."

"Carol Ann disappeared from a shopping mall. The mall surveillance tape showed her getting into a white Dodge utility van with a man and a woman, who were savvy enough to keep their backs turned away from the cameras."

"So no identification of the couple?"

"No, and God knows I tried. No license plate either." She pulled out a thumb drive and pushed it across his desk. "Here's a copy of the tape if you want to view it yourself."

"Thanks."

"Did you know the girl?"

"Yes, I've known the family for years. Her parents, Bob and Sue, own a farm near our property. After our mom died, Bob and Sue checked on my brothers and me every week, always bringing a casserole or a pie. They had us over for holiday dinners. Good people. Carol Ann was just a baby then, but I watched her grow up. I saw her just before she disappeared. She was with her parents at Mollie's Café. She'd just gotten her learner's permit to drive and they were celebrating. This is going to devastate them."

"I'm sorry. They were notified earlier this morning."

"Tell me what happened. Start from the beginning."

"I got a call from dispatch reporting bodies found at a house fire. By the time I got there, the whole place was engulfed in flames, and there were so many neighbors in the streets gawking, it looked like a street party. We had to send for backup to clear the area before someone got hurt."

"Arson?"

"Yes, but the fire isn't what killed the girls. The response team was able to carry the bodies out, at least what was left of them, before the house burst into flames."

"What do you mean?"

"All three of them were in the upstairs bedroom where they were found with their throats slit."

115

"Just like Brandy Murphy and Shirley Metz. Did they have the tattoos?"

"All three."

"It's our perp. That makes five victims that we know of." He shook his head with disgust. "What kind of an animal does something like that?"

"The same kind of animal that gets himself a starring role on the FBI's most wanted list."

Cameron felt the blood drain from his face. "Who?"

"Juan Ortiz. He's wanted for—"

"I know who he is and why he's wanted. How can you be sure it's him?" It was as if he were entering his own private nightmare, and he feared he'd never get out.

"We've got an eyewitness. We had intel suggesting Ortiz was in Indiana last month, so we put out a BOLO on him. I had a photo of him along with some of his crime buds that I showed to the neighbor. She picked Ortiz out of a photo lineup and insisted that was the guy, along with two other men, she saw entering the house that night before the fire. Said she was looking out her window because she couldn't sleep, and saw a black SUV pull up in front of the house next door. She'd become curious and concerned about its occupants because there were men visiting the house at all hours of the night. Once or twice she'd seen an older woman leave the house and come back with shopping bags. Although she was away the day they moved in, the woman across the street told her a mother and her daughters lived in the house."

"Did she ever see the girls?"

"No. She was just going on what she heard about them. I interviewed the woman who lived across the street to get confirmation."

"Any DNA or fingerprints?"

"Not at the house, but we got lucky. A patrolman found a black 2013 Cadillac Escalade with Illinois license plates abandoned behind an empty, foreclosed house. He ran the plates and discovered the SUV was stolen. CSI techs dusted it for prints, and guess whose prints they lifted from the seat adjustment lever? Mr. Juan Ortiz."

Cameron paled and swallowed to push bile back down his

throat. As much as he wanted to believe that Donda had hatched those stories she told Carly about seeing Ortiz in Shawnee County, he now had to face the facts. Ortiz *was* in Indiana, and the threat to Becca and his family was very real. The only safety net was the fact that no one but Social Services and his family knew where Becca was living. At least not yet. If Donda had a chance to exchange Becca's location to save herself, he was sure she would. He pulled out his cell and texted the county jail to make sure Donda had been placed in solitary. When he did not get an immediate response, he decided to check it out for himself. Something was wrong. Alarm tightened his gut.

"What's wrong?"

Cameron shook his head and grabbed his keys. "Robynn, let's take a ride. We have an inmate who says she has information about Juan Ortiz."

Chapter 30

The first thing Cameron and Robynn noticed when they pulled up to the Shawnee County Jail was one of the Coroner's white vans parked outside.

"That's odd," Cameron said, as he opened the driver side door. "Wonder what happened?"

He and Robynn entered the jail and spoke to the jail administrator, Paul White. "We're here to see inmate Donda Hicks."

Paul's face drained of color. "Sgt. Chase, I was about to call you."

"What's up?"

"We just discovered Donda Hicks hung herself in her cell."

Cameron exploded. "What the hell are you talking about? I just saw her an hour ago."

"Yes, sir. When they brought her back to the jail, the other inmates were on their break in the yard. She said she didn't feel well and wanted to go straight to her cell. So that's where they took her."

"My order was that she be put in solitary with no visitors."

Paul nodded nervously. "They were going to do that after the yard break was over and they'd done roll call. During roll call, by the time they got to her cell, she was hanging from the top bunk by bed sheets. She died before they could get to her."

"I'd like to see her cell." Robynn said.

"So would I." Cameron agreed, thinking they might find

something in Donda's cell that would tell them why she killed herself.

Cameron and Robynn checked in their weapons and a guard led them to Donda's cell. The inmates in the cells surrounding Donda's were visibly upset and stared at them as they passed by.

Donda's cell was sparse, with two metal structures jutting from the wall across from the bunk bed, anchored to the floor. One structure served as a table, the other as a chair, while a stainless steel toilet was attached to the far wall. Donda's body had already been taken to Bryan's facility for autopsy.

On the metal table were four paperback books. Cameron flipped through each one then set it aside. As he was flipping through the pages of the fourth book, a slip of white paper fell out.

"There's writing on the paper. What does it say?" Robynn leaned toward him.

Cameron held out the note so they both could read it.

The kid is dead or you are. You choose.

Just then a guard came to the door. "Sgt. Chase, you have a phone call. Said it was an emergency."

Cameron took the guard's cell phone and lifted it to his ear. "Sgt. Chase."

"This is Brody. Another body's been found near Hillsboro by a family of campers."

"On my way."

Chapter 31

Following Brody's directions, they got onto U.S. Highway 136 heading toward Hillsboro. Once he reached the crime scene, he noticed one of Bryan Pittman's Shawnee County Coroner vans was already parked at the side of the road, just before the curve.

"You've got to be kidding me. This is where Shirley Metz's body was found." Robynn exclaimed.

"Unbelievable. I don't need Carly to tell me if this is the same killer, he's shoving it into our faces."

Once they'd walked to the curve in the road, they turned right and crossed the drainage ditch. That's when Cameron noticed a freshly cut path leading deeper into the woods.

"This path wasn't cleared last time we were here. Remember how we had to plow through the brush? Did the killer actually take the time to come out here to make a path to the body? That's pretty damn brazen."

Robynn considered that. "Maybe. But there could be other reasons for creating a trail. Maybe his victim was alive when he brought her here, and the cleared path was part of his con to get her here in the first place."

The pathway led them by the huge oak tree where Shirley Metz's body had been found. The papery wasp nest still hung on a branch. They moved farther until they came to a grassy clearing near a brook. They saw Bryan Pittman standing next to a bloodied young woman tied upright to an elm tree.

Cameron approached him, while Robynn moved closer for a better look. "Bryan, what do we have?"

"Looks to be a woman in her late twenties or early thirties. Just a guess, but it looks like she's been dead twenty-four hours or so. I'll know more during the autopsy."

"Cause of death?"

"Deep cut to her throat."

"Like Brandy Murphy and Shirley Metz?"

"Yes, her throat was cut like theirs. But there's a couple of differences here."

"What's that?"

"No tattoo, and she has smaller cuts and jabs all over her body. I counted twenty. Looks like she was tortured before her death."

"That's new. Why would he torture this victim and not the others? What did he want from her?"

Cameron stepped around Bryan to get a better look at the victim. Long brown hair covered her face, her legs and arms had horizontal cuts, and blood soaked the blue sundress she was wearing.

"Any identification?" Cameron asked Bryan.

"No purse or anything."

One of the crime scene technicians appeared with a camera, another tech was at his side. While one pushed the victim's hair away from her face, the other took photos. When Cameron was able to see her face, his heart stopped.

He turned to Bryan. "I know her. That's Melanie Barrett. She's a social worker."

"Why would anyone want to torture a social worker? What could she have that the killer wanted?"

Cameron pulled out his cell phone to call home. "She was *Becca's* social worker."

Chapter 32

Robynn jumped into the car, slamming the door behind her. "What's wrong? You look like you've seen a ghost."

Not answering, Cameron speed-dialed Kaitlyn's cell number and got her voice mail. "Kaitlyn, call me as soon as you get this message. It's important."

He then called dispatch and ordered a deputy to do a wellness check at the main house. Tossing his cell on the console, he revved the engine and did a U-turn onto the highway.

"Talk to me, Cam. What's going on?"

"It's a long, *personal* story. You don't want personal from me, remember?"

"If it has to do with this case, and I have a feeling that it does, I need to know. From the beginning."

He shot her a quick glance, worry lining his mouth, deep and drawn. "Yes, it probably has something to do with this case."

"Talk to me."

"Not long ago, at a meth bust, I met Becca, a two-year-old who had been physically abused and exposed to meth. Both parents were jailed with a laundry list of charges and faced lengthy prison terms. I made a request to be her foster dad and was approved."

"You're fostering a little girl?"

"Don't sound so surprised." He snapped.

"I didn't mean it like that. It's just that I had no idea you'd do something like that."

"That's on you, Robynn. You've kept your distance and I've respected that. If you had wanted to know more about me, I figure you would have asked."

"I deserve that. But what does this little girl have to do with our case?"

"According to her meth-head mother, Donda Hicks, Juan Ortiz is Becca's biological father. I believe her. She thought Ortiz tracked her to Shawnee County because he wants his kid."

"What does any of this have to do with the victim at the crime scene?"

"The victim's name is Melanie Barrett and she's Becca's social worker. Besides my family, she was the only one who knew where Becca lives."

"Cam, we have no evidence that Juan Ortiz killed this woman."

"He has plenty of motive. She stood between him and the kid he's searching for."

"Others might have motive, too. Social workers put their lives in danger every time they remove a child from his or her home. The parents get angry, as do the grandparents, and the rest of the family. How do we know that someone from her work didn't kill her?"

"You may be right. But what if you're wrong? I have a two-year-old who depends on me to protect her. And right now, I have no clue where Kaitlyn and Becca are."

He flicked on the light bar atop his SUV and stomped on the accelerator. "I've got to get home. I don't know what I'll do if anything happens to Becca. Christ, that maniac could abduct her and take her to Mexico and I might never find her. He's a trafficker who would sell his own mother, if he thought he would profit."

"We'll get there in time, Cam. We'll protect Becca."

"We?" Surprised, he glanced at her.

"We. I'm involved now, and I'm in it for the long haul."

They reached the house and Cam turned into the driveway. Kaitlyn's car was parked in one of the four-car garage spaces. Slamming the gear to park, he jumped from the car and ran into the house, Robynn not far behind. With guns drawn, they searched the house, clearing each room. No one was there. They met downstairs in the kitchen and Cam searched for some kind of note from Kaitlyn that might let them know where she and Becca were. There was no note to be found.

Robynn peered outside the kitchen window. "Cam, come here. There is something you need to see."

Cameron moved next to her. In the garden, Becca stood over some tomato plants, watering them with a sprinkling can with Godiva at her side. Kaitlyn was nearby, pulling weeds.

Relief washed over Cameron. She was safe.

Robynn nudged him. "What are you waiting for? Aren't you going to introduce me to your little girl?"

Chapter 33

Carly Stone didn't need to look at her clock to know it was two in the morning. Although the nightmares had slowed down, they still grabbed her by the throat and squeezed at least twice a week at precisely two in the morning, the same time of day she was nearly raped and murdered. Drawing a blanket over Brody's shoulders, she slipped out of bed and went to the kitchen to make a cup of chamomile tea.

Soon Brody joined her and sat at the end of the table, rubbing sleep from his eyes. Gazing at his wife, he asked himself why she hadn't confided that she knew Juan Ortiz…who might be the star of the perpetual nightmares she experienced.

He'd awaken to the sound of Carly's rasping breaths and whimpering cries. Each time he'd wanted to reach for her, pull her body tightly against his to make the bad dreams go away, to make her feel safe. But he dared not do that. He'd made that mistake once, and had been pummeled by a flurry of blows from Carly, who was still fighting demons in her sleep. Brody had learned to lie still until the nightmare ended. Sometimes she rolled into the safety of his arms and he'd hold her until the first light of morning.

"Want to talk about it?"

"Look, I know Cam must have told you about my interview with Donda Hicks and our conversation about Juan Ortiz. It's nothing, Brody. History. Over. The end." Pulling out her tea bag, she opened the lower cabinet door and threw it away, then sat down at the table with her husband.

"I'm having a hard time believing this piece of your history is 'nothing.'" Brody understood that working as a federal agent, Carly had lived her own scary movie, including her partner's beheading by a sex trafficker in Florida. It was one of her off-limit topics, ones she refused to discuss. He knew of that incident from her brother, Blake.

And then there were the most recent bloody crimes scenes, created by serial killers, Jim Ryder, and the 'Gamers,' teenagers Evan and Devan Lucas. If those weren't the stuff of nightmares, he didn't know what was. Carly had trained herself well, excelled in compartmentalizing, and had not shed a tear at gruesome crime scenes. Nor had she joined his deputies, puking their guts out on the sidelines. Her sense of control was admirable for a law enforcement officer, but he wondered where she packed away all that horror in her mind.

"It's just the job, Brody. I'm sure I'm not the only one in police work who has bad dreams. We see a lot of bad stuff. I just don't like to talk about it."

"You can't keep all that inside and not have it affect your life, Carly—*our* lives, together." What bothered him most was that she wouldn't confide in him about her demons. He'd finally stopped asking because it pissed him off so much.

Carly was the woman he wanted to bear his children, to spend the rest of his life with. He loved her fiercely and shared his darkest secrets with her. If she loved him just as much, why wouldn't she talk to him? What could be so terrible that she wouldn't tell him about it?

"It's not about us."

"Bullshit. It's about you not trusting me. What kind of a marriage can we have without trust? Stop shutting me out. There's nothing you can tell me that will change my love for you. Nothing."

He was her husband. Whether he had a right to know everything in her personal history was up for grabs. But it was obvious what had happened was disrupting her sleep and intruded upon their relationship.

Profile of Fear

Carly started a pot of coffee, took out two mugs from the cabinet, and then returned to the table.

She thought back to the days that led up to her personal nightmare. "I was working as special agent in the Criminal Investigation Division of the FBI office in Tampa. Sam Isley was the Special Agent in Charge, and my boss. Juan Ortiz was in Florida, heading a major sex trafficking operation. Sam discovered through an informant that Ortiz was actively looking for a specific type of woman to sell to a customer in Orlando—an American girl with Italian features. It was decided that I fit the bill, and they prepared me for an undercover assignment that could bring down Juan Ortiz's entire operation. It was my first time undercover in two years, and I'd begged for the opportunity."

When she paused, Brody urged her to go on.

"They knew Juan Ortiz was a middle man who could lead them to the man who orchestrated the sale of young women throughout the state. My mission was to identify the leader and help my team bring him down, along with his nasty group of pimps and murderers. And in the process, free the young women they held captive, forced into prostitution.

"The first time I saw Juan Ortiz, he was leaning against a wall in a downtown Orlando bar called Chillers, looking very much like a lead in the old *Miami Vice* television series. Hispanic with angular facial features, dark eyes and skin. He worked a white blazer, pastel-blue silk T-shirt, and new jeans almost as well as actor Don Johnson.

"I headed for the ladies room, checked to make sure it was empty, and then counted out loud to test the microphone taped between my breasts. I also made sure my Colt Defender semi-automatic was securely holstered on the inside of my thigh.

"Within seconds, I heard the voice of Agent Dan Levitt through my earpiece; he told me he could hear me perfectly."

Carly became so lost in the story, it was if she were reliving what had happened.

Chapter 34

Dan lowered his voice to a whisper. "Thought you might like to know that Special Agent in Charge Sam Isley is heading toward the van. Did you know he'd be here tonight?"

"No, I didn't. Thanks for the heads up." Carly frowned as she checked her look in the mirror. Why was Sam here?

He was getting protective again. And Carly hated it. Just because she slept with him did not mean she needed him to go guard dog on her. Didn't he think she'd learned how to protect herself in all that training in Quantico? What would her team think about his presence? Sam was giving the impression he didn't think she couldn't handle herself on this assignment, and it pissed her off royally.

Pulling a small brush out of her purse, she pulled it through her long ebony mane, making sure her hair covered the wireless earpiece in her right ear. Glancing in the mirror, she barely recognized herself. Camille, the only other female on the team, had applied the foundation, blush, and mascara so thick that she looked like she just stepped out of a department store makeover. Good lord, she was supposed to look like a call girl, not *America's Top Model*.

Carly applied some scarlet lip gloss to her lips and straightened her dress. She'd brought three dresses to the team meeting for a vote, and all three were vetoed. Then Camille pulled out a shopping bag from beneath her chair and handed it to Carly. Inside was a beaded, red wrap-dress with a full mini-skirt, the neckline cut into a deep V in front.

When she'd balked about wearing it, Camille had said, "Carly, you're supposed to be a high-class call girl. How many call girls do you know who dress in starched, button-down shirts and blazers, like you usually wear?"

"What about the three dresses I brought from home?"

"Yeah, you could wear those to church, or maybe if you ever have to chaperone a junior high school dance," Camille had said, as the rest of the team howled with laughter. Carly's face burned. They were right. She was not the type to dress provocatively. Could she pull this off?

Carly checked out the dress in the mirror and realized she disliked it as much as her team enjoyed her having to wear it. It was so tight she could barely breathe, and the beading scratched her legs when she walked. Thanks to the four-inch red pumps, she wouldn't be walking that much if she could help it. It was more like teetering on stilts and heading for a fall.

Tugging the top of the dress, she thought she'd be lucky if her breasts didn't pop out to say hello. She wished she'd taken Camille up on her offer to tape her into the dress. Too late now. It was time to meet Juan Ortiz.

Back in the bar, a band had started playing and the lead singer was doing a really bad impression of Robin Thicke. Juan Ortiz was now sitting at the bar, talking with a blond-haired woman. Carly knew the second Juan noticed her; his eyes widened and an almost feral expression lit his face. She gave him her best come-hither look, and sat down at nearby table. A waitress asked her for a drink order, and just as she was about to order a Coke, Juan Ortiz appeared at her table holding two frozen strawberry daiquiris, and said, "I have the lady's drink."

As the waitress returned to the bar, Carly asked, "Are we celebrating something? If so, I should know your name."

Juan pulled Carly's hand to his mouth and kissed it, then said, "My name is Juan Ortiz, and this might be the luckiest night of your life."

"Hello, Juan. I'm Charlotte," Carly began. "And why is this the luckiest night of my life?"

"You are very beautiful," he said as he fingered a lock of her hair and brushed it away from her face. She nearly flinched. If he uncovered the earpiece, she'd be made.

Backing slightly from his touch, she asked, "And why would meeting you be lucky for me?"

"That is for you to discover before the night ends," Juan responded. "Do you model?"

"Does that line usually work for you?" Carly asked with a flirtatious smile.

Looking like a spider weaving his web around his next victim, Juan said, "I work for a very powerful man who owns a modeling agency. He is looking for someone like you to model in the show he has planned in Paris next month. Are you interested?"

Carly feigned surprise and delight, and shot him her best smile. "Very. I've always wanted to model."

"If you will give me a moment to make a call, I may be able to introduce you to him tonight."

"Awesome!" Carly said. She watched Juan Ortiz pull his cell phone out of his pocket and walk toward the bar. Soon he was speaking to someone and emphatically nodding his head.

"Did you hear that?" Carly said to Dan.

"Yes." His voice sounded through her earpiece. "This is working so much better than we imagined. We thought it'd be weeks before Ortiz took you to meet the big boss. Good job."

"Are you ready to follow us?"

"Yes. We're using the GPS inside your cell phone to keep you in our range. Ortiz drives a new Jag and our van is parked right behind him. Don't worry. We won't let you out of our sight."

"Not worried."

Juan Ortiz returned to the table and said, "My friend can see us. He doesn't live far from here. Let's take my car. It's out front."

Ortiz led her to a gleaming, black Jaguar and helped her into the sports car. Soon they were shooting through the streets of Orlando like a bullet. Juan Ortiz drove as if he were a competitor for the Daytona 500, squealing the tires as he took turns.

They'd only gone a few miles when he pulled into a shopping plaza parking lot and stopped.

"Why did you stop?" Carly asked.

Profile of Fear

"Give me your purse," he demanded. When she didn't move, he grabbed it from her.

"Hey, what are you doing?" She cried out.

Juan Ortiz ripped her cell phone out of her purse and threw it out the window.

"I'll buy you a new one," he said, as he shoved the car in gear and blasted onto the street like a rocket.

Carly fought back the panic that rioted inside her. Glancing at the side rearview mirror, she saw her backup in the white van, two cars behind them. They were still there. When would they realize they could no longer track her by the GPS in her cell?

Racing through the streets, Juan Ortiz took the turns so fast that the car glided on two wheels. He made a sharp right into an alley; at the end he made a left turn onto a busy highway, then onto the westbound ramp of I-4.

"What's the hurry?" Carly asked, as she glanced in the mirror again. The white surveillance van was nowhere in sight. Her stomach clenched tight. What if they'd lost Juan's car?

"The boss is eager to meet you," he said, as his eyes openly appraised her body.

Soon they were near the attractions, Disney World and Epcot, the traffic thick on I-4 with tourists. Without a warning or signal, Juan Ortiz veered the car onto a ramp, and turned left onto a busy boulevard. Carly saw a sign announcing Kissimmee city limits. Juan pulled into an upscale subdivision, then entered the driveway of one of the most beautiful and largest homes she'd ever seen. The house was painted white, with plenty of large windows facing a lake. A dark Mercedes sedan was parked in front. Apparently sex traffickers made a good living off the pain and suffering of others.

Entering the home, he led her into the living room that held two white leather sofas in front of a white-brick fireplace. The room was huge, with most of the walls made of glass. It looked more like a designer show house than someone's home.

"Where is your boss?"

The feral look was back in his eyes. "I'm so sorry, but something came up and he can't make it. He asked me to interview you and send him my thoughts on whether he should hire you."

Alarm bells sounded in her head and a chill rushed down her spine. She was alone with a maniac, and backup was nowhere in sight.

It was then she heard a pounding sound that seemed to be coming from the floor beneath them. "What's that noise?"

Ortiz visibly squirmed and said, "That's my dog. He wants out. He'll just have to wait until after we take care of business."

She hadn't identified the noise, but it was not coming from a dog. A dog would have scratched at the door and barked. Her team was certain that Ortiz held the women in an out-of-the-way warehouse, but they may be wrong. Was Ortiz holding women hostage in the floor below?

Ignoring the sound, Ortiz moved toward a bar and lifted a bottle of wine. "Pinot Noir?"

"Yes, thank you." Carly said, although she would not be drinking it. Ortiz was known for lacing drinks with roofies to disable the women he abducted.

More sounds from below. Muffled cries. Frantic hammering against the door.

"You might check on your dog. He sounds upset."

Ortiz placed his beer on the bar. "Excuse me. I'll be right back."

The second she heard his steps on the stairs, Carly began exploring the house. There was a living and dining area on her level, along with a kitchen. A short hallway led to a small guest room and an office. Taking a thumb drive out of her purse, she copied the contents of his hard drive, nervously checking the hallway and listening for sounds of him returning.

Soon she heard muffled crying and Ortiz's hostile voice as he entered the living room. Carly peered around a wall. He was not alone. With his arm around her neck, he pinned a young woman—no more than a girl, maybe thirteen or fourteen— against his body. The girl had duct tape sealed across her mouth and binding her wrists.

Carly withdrew her gun and entered the room. "I'm a federal agent. If you are as smart as you think you are, Ortiz, you will let the girl go."

Profile of Fear

Ignoring her, Ortiz withdrew something silver from his pocket, clicked a button, and a switchblade sprang to life. The girl's terrified, muffled screams filled the room as she began to struggle against him. He squeezed her neck in a choke-hold until she was barely conscious, and then pressed the knife against her throat. The girl's eyes bulged in terror.

"Put down the gun, bitch."

"Not happening." Carly tightened her grip on the gun, and struggled to get a good shot, but he kept the girl positioned as a human shield.

"This does not have a good ending. You're both going to die and I am going to move on, build my businesses, and live the good life."

"Don't bet on it." Carly yearned to hear sirens. Where the hell was her backup?

"It's too bad about you, Charlotte. A customer in Orlando was going to pay top dollar for you. This should have been easy. You drink your wine, get drunk, and lose consciousness. It's my three-step plan for success. I deliver you to my customer, and he makes sure you have plenty of the drug of his choice so he can control his new sex slave."

"You're a sick bastard. How many women have you done this to?"

A slow, evil smile spread over his face. He was enjoying this talk. She'd use it to stall until help could arrive. "What about this girl? What's her story?"

"Got a client who wants to play 'Daddy,' and this stupid girl fit the bill. Found her at a bus station. Runaway from Chicago. She's looking for a new life, and I was going to give her one."

"You call that a life. Selling her to a pedophile?"

Carly's heart was beating so hard; she wouldn't have been surprised if Ortiz could hear it across the room. This was her first big case and if backup didn't arrive soon, she was probably going to die.

She tried to swallow, but her throat was dry. Think, Carly, think. You can do this. Got to stall. Carly's thoughts were all over the place, like a group of first graders let out for recess.

"He was also willing to pay top dollar, so what do I care?"

133

She heard the faint sound of a siren in the distance. "Hear that siren? That's my backup."

His expression twisted with indecision before he lifted the knife and slashed the girl's throat. Carly could hardly believe her eyes as blood flooded down the girl's neck.

As she slumped to the ground, Ortiz dived for Carly, slamming into her before she had the chance to get off a shot. The gun, knocked from her hand, spun crazily as she dropped it onto the floor, and so did his knife.

Carly rammed her forearm up and into his throat and his airway. Ortiz choked and struggled to breathe. She then pushed him off her and managed to break away. Where was the gun? Realizing Ortiz was pushing to his feet, she spun around and stomped down on his fingers, making him howl with pain.

Diving under a table, she retrieved the gun, and stood to aim it at Ortiz. But he was gone! There was a dead girl on the floor. Who knows how many other victims… And she let the bastard get away.

The sirens grew louder as she searched the house. Clearing each room on the upper level, there was no sign of Ortiz. She was about to search downstairs when Dan Levitt and Sam Isley knocked down the front door.

"He may have gone downstairs."

The basement was massive, with many small rooms. Three women were in the first room they searched; duct tape covered their mouths, and shackles fastened their legs to the floor. The next four rooms were empty.

Carly heard the twisting of metal of a door unlocking and ran toward the sound. Ortiz was standing at the top of a short staircase, before the door that led to the garage.

"You haven't seen the last of me, bitch. I am your worst nightmare. I will find you if it's the last thing I do. I will slice your throat and kill those close to you. That's a promise."

As he turned to go through the door, Carly got off a shot and a crimson stain covered the shoulder of his white shirt. Running toward him, she tripped on the second step of the staircase and fell. By the time, she regained her balance, Ortiz was in a Hummer parked in the garage. He slammed through the garage door, making his escape. Carly let him get away—again. She blinked back the tears that threatened to spill, and choked back the hot bile rising up her throat.

Chapter 35

Carly felt Brody's hand grasping her own. He had moved next to her, and with a finger wiped tears from her cheeks.

"I failed."

"How can you say that? You rescued three women, who owe their lives to you."

"But not the girl. She bled out before the ambulance arrived. I should have done something different to get him to release her." She looked into Brody's compassionate eyes. "It was *my* responsibility. I should have saved her."

"That wasn't going to happen, Carly. No matter what you did, the result would have been the same. She was his shield from you. When he heard the sirens, he must have freaked out and killed her so he could get to you. Thank God you were able to fight him and get your gun back. You could have died, Carly. I have no doubt he would have killed you, too. You did what you had to do. End of story."

"I wish it *was* the end. But it isn't, Brody. Ortiz has not forgotten his promise. He has people looking for me.

"Sam Isley was here to tell me they think Ortiz or some of his men broke into my Orlando house. They poured red paint all over the bed, splashed it on the walls. Plus they painted a red circle with the letters 'JO' inside. That's Juan Ortiz's brand; he puts it on all the women he traffics." Her words tumbled out, fast and clipped, as fear gripped her.

"How could he have found the house in Orlando when he didn't know your true identity? You told him your name was Charlotte."

"He found a photo of me in the *Orlando Sentinel* from several years ago, where I was accepting a charity award. Once he had my real name, it wasn't hard to find my address. I hoped he'd think I still live in Florida. But now that we know he is in Shawnee County…"

"You think he tracked you here?"

"I'm not sure. Cam's informant, Donda Hicks, thinks he is after Becca. It seems the monster is Becca's father."

She stopped, started, and stopped again, trying to find the words. "That evil bastard is Becca's father. I'm so sorry, Brody. I've put all of us in danger! I've led him right to our door."

Chapter 36

Hailey Adams sat at a table at her mother's café, filling salt and pepper shakers and lamenting about how boring her young life had become. She'd practically grown up in Mollie's Café, owned and operated by her mom, Mollie Adams. The place was filled with timeworn red Formica tables in the dining area, with red vinyl booths lining the perimeter, and framed record albums adorning the walls. Everything was fifties style, from the gingham curtains, to the uniforms the waitresses wore. If her mother had her way, the waitresses would be serving food wearing felt poodle skirts and roller skates. That idea was quickly squashed the first week when Belinda Ross fell—while carrying a platter of tenderloin sandwiches, fries, and sodas—and broke her arm. Thus inspiring her rich daddy to threaten a lawsuit.

An old jukebox, a gift from a customer, still blasted out songs by Elvis, the Everly Brothers, and Nat King Cole, among others. The fact that Hailey knew all the fifties songs and the people who sang them was a testament to how much time she'd spent at the diner. Too darn much. She wasn't one of the popular kids, nor would she ever be, thanks to working at her mom's café while the rest of her class was out having fun.

She heard her mother's voice in the kitchen and the rich aroma of freshly baked cinnamon rolls filled the air. Cinnabon had nothing on her mom, who soon appeared at her table, gripping steamy cups of hot cocoa and coffee in one hand, and four hot cinnamon rolls on a plate in the other. She set the items on the table and sat down.

"Let's take a break, sweetie."

Hailey eyed her mother with distrust. "This isn't another one of your mother-daughter talks where you do all the talking, is it?"

"Suspicious much?" As Hailey rolled her eyes, Mollie nibbled at a cinnamon roll and then sipped her hot coffee. "Would it be so bad if it was?"

"I'm sixteen-years-old, so it's a little late for the sex talk."

"*Barely* sixteen. You just had your birthday, and we've already had the sex talk."

Hailey's mouth watered as she eyed a cinnamon roll, before plucking it from the plate and biting into it. That diet she and her best friend, Niki, had discussed just flew out of the window on wings of savory cinnamon and rich butter.

"What's on your mind, Mom? Let's get this over with."

"I was thinking that maybe you'd like to have a slumber party and invite some friends over."

"What friends?"

"I don't have names, but I just thought maybe you'd like to get to know some of the other girls in school. You spend a lot of time with Niki."

"I get it. This is about Niki. She's my best friend, Mom. Get over it."

"With her black eye-shadow Goth-look, purple-streaked hair, and bad attitude, she's a lot for a mother to get used to."

Niki was Hailey's BFF, the only one at school who got her. There was no way she'd let go of their friendship. No way. But getting mad at her mother usually got her grounded, so she took a slow, calming breath to dial down her anger from an all-out temper tantrum, to just plain annoyance. "Yeah, well, let me tell you, Mom, getting used to Dr. Hot Stuff hanging around hasn't exactly been a party for *me*."

"That's different, Hailey, and stop calling Bryan that. It's disrespectful."

"How is it different? I'm not throwing confetti over your new man, and you don't like my best friend. Sounds like we're even."

"Why is it so hard for you to give him a chance?"

"He's not Uncle Cam. Not even close."

"Hailey, Cameron Chase and I haven't been together for a long time."

"Uncle Cam always helped me with my homework and taught me to play basketball. He even went to my soccer games. You can't say that about Dr. Hot Stuff, can you?"

Mollie fidgeted with her napkin. "He's interested in getting to know you, but you don't help things by leaving the room every time he starts a conversation with you. Please give him a chance, Hailey."

"No, he's interested in you, not me. Didn't he stay over again last night?'"

Her mother's face flushed crimson and she averted her eyes.

"Yeah, that's what I thought."

Hailey's cell phone alarm sounded, and she got to her feet to pull off her apron. "Saved by the bell. Got to go. Don't want to be late for school."

"We can talk about this later."

Hailey shot her a smirk, raced toward the door, and said over her shoulder. "Can't wait."

After school, Hailey pushed Niki in a swing at the park playground. Niki was barely five-foot-one inches tall and ninety pounds, compared to Hailey at five-foot-five and one-hundred-and-ten pounds. The girls were as different physically as they were close emotionally.

They moved to a picnic table and Hailey sipped a coke, while Niki played with the ash on the end of her cigarette. A car filled with teenaged boys drove slowly past. "Hey, Niki. Let's hook up Saturday night."

"Bite me." Rolling her eyes at Hailey, she brushed back a lock of purple hair. "Stupid boys. So sick of them."

"I'm sick of this boring, hick town."

"Did you have another fight with your mom?"

"She keeps trying to push her new boyfriend down my throat. So why is it so important that I like him? She does. That's for sure. He's started to sleep more at our house than he does his own."

Profile of Fear

"So why don't you like him? Dr. Pittman is hot. Seems nice, too."

"Just don't."

"It's because of that detective your mom used to date, isn't it?"

"Uncle Cam's a sergeant now, not that it matters. I miss him, and I just don't see why Mom can't get him back."

"Maybe it's a lost cause like my mom and dad."

"That's different."

"I guess so. It would be a pretty miraculous, tabloid-worthy moment if my mom got my dad back, since he took off when I was born and hasn't been seen since."

Hailey sighed. "I want to do something exciting and fun for a change."

"Now that you have your license, we could go to the mall Friday night."

"That's a great idea. But my mom will have a hissy fit."

"I've got some ideas on how we can get around your mom. Keeping moms clueless is one of my super-powers.

Chapter 37

Carly, Cameron, and Robynn gathered in the Shawnee County Sheriff conference room with Brody.

Brody glanced at Cameron. "Before we get started, what's the latest on keeping Becca safe from Ortiz?"

"Everyone in the house is aware of the situation and certainly more aware of security, including using the security system. No more forgetting to set it or leaving doors unlocked."

Carly interjected. "When Kaitlyn and I are watching Becca, we will be armed or will have a weapon nearby. Don't worry. We won't let anyone get near her."

"He'd have to be pretty stupid to try to abduct Becca from a family of law enforcement officers," Cameron added.

A frown slipped across Brody's face. "No one said that criminals are smart. But we don't know who's working for him, so we need to look out for more people than Juan Ortiz. He's known to hire others to do his dirty work."

Brody turned to Robynn. "Can you give me an update on information the state police have about Ortiz?"

"Yes. State police have launched an undercover investigation into sex trafficking operations within Indiana. We've discovered that Juan Ortiz is the leader of a group of men running prostitutes throughout the state."

"How is he supplying the women? I know there are different methods, different cons, or outright abduction." Carly wanted to know.

Profile of Fear

"Although many girls are runaways picked up at bus stations, most of their female victims are recruited through online modeling ads, where they are promised high-paying, glamorous jobs. Our criminal investigation field office in Indy has a long list of missing women they believe were abducted as a result of answering these ads."

"How does this connect to Juan Ortiz?"

"We've received intelligence that indicates Ortiz is in the Midwest and is trafficking girls for exotic dancing, prostitution, and forced domestic labor as nannies, maids, janitors, and restaurant dishwashers. He is also known to sell girls to the highest bidder so they can be personal sex slaves. Under a variety of names, Ortiz owns eight Last Stop Cantina restaurants throughout the Midwest. Three are in Indiana: Indianapolis, Lafayette, and Bloomington. There are rumors that a Last Stop Cantina will be built somewhere in Shawnee County. The girls who are illegal immigrants are forced to work in these restaurants for little or no pay."

Brody interrupted. "The three places you mentioned are college towns. Does that mean Ortiz is targeting coeds?"

"It's possible. His depravity also extends to targeting females as young as twelve or thirteen. Once the girls are in his custody, they are advertised in prostitution chat rooms and transported throughout the Midwest, and are housed in rented or leased homes in middle-class neighborhoods. Most, if not all of the victims, are threatened, beaten, and raped. All of the women are told their families or children will be harmed or murdered if they try to escape, or tell anyone about their situation. Two of his victims last month *did* escape one of these homes. We have them in safe houses in return for their testimony once Ortiz is captured."

With his elbows on the table, Cameron leaned toward her. "The modeling con. Is that the only scheme he is using to recruit?"

Robynn opened a file folder and withdrew some papers. "One of our informants says that Ortiz and his minions actively recruit female prisoners from the Rockville Correctional Facility for Women, promising them high-paying jobs when they get out. Upon their release, Ortiz's thugs transport the women to one of his homes, where the windows are barred and they are repeatedly beaten and provided drugs like meth, heroin, and cocaine to keep them in line. They are not allowed to leave the house unless accompanied by one of Ortiz's men."

Brody pushed back in his chair. "I'm still not understanding why Ortiz would want to set up operations in Shawnee County. We're a rural community, for God's sake."

Carly glanced briefly at Robynn and then said, "Brody, you've got to change your 'not in my backyard' attitude because it's just what traffickers are counting on."

"Carly's right. Traffickers are moving their businesses to unsuspecting rural communities. They don't necessarily want to work in big cities. They're drawn to small towns because they think they won't get caught," Robynn added.

"If their focus is Shawnee County, they better rethink their damn plan," Brody growled.

Robynn continued, "Traffickers like rural areas because when homes are spread apart, it's harder for victims to escape. It may be miles until they reach safety or the closest residence. Even with a head start, the traffickers have a good chance of finding them."

"Is that the only reason?"

"No. Lack of job opportunities may make women more vulnerable to traffickers because they don't have the means to support themselves."

"And then there are truck stops," added Carly. "Rural areas are loaded with truck stops, which aren't so prevalent in the city. Truck stops are lucrative for traffickers to sell sex to travelers or lonely truckers, with minimal concerns about detection. A truck stop can be an easy place for a trafficker to sell victims night-after-night to a new group of customers."

"So the general thinking is that Ortiz is here to set up another trafficking operation?" Brody asked the group.

Cameron took just a second to respond. "I think he's already here, and his people are working his cons this very second. I also think he is very motivated to find Becca. But I don't know why. He's a monster, not a parent. But there is some reason he is desperate to find her. Becca's safety is my top concern, and I won't rest until I find him and learn what that reason is."

Chapter 38

The woman sitting in a visitor chair across from Gabe's desk looked like she'd rather be getting a root canal than telling a stranger her personal business. Annoyance lined her face, but distress flickered in her eyes. Camilla Essick looked bone-tired, the kind of fatigue that comes from stress overload and too many sleepless nights.

Gabe poured some hot coffee into a mug and handed it to her. "Let's start by telling me why you want to hire a private investigator."

"It doesn't seem like I have much choice. The police aren't doing a damn thing. All they're good for is telling me that sometimes kids run away. Well, my Lea didn't run away. I would know. The problem is they don't believe me."

"Are you telling me your daughter, Lea, is missing?"

"Yes. I reported her missing to the police two weeks ago."

Gabe made a mental note to talk to Cameron about this girl's disappearance. "How old is Lea?"

"She's seventeen."

"Has she run away from home in the past?"

Camilla shifted in her chair. "Twice. But that was a long time ago." She paused while he jotted down the information. When he looked up, she'd leaned toward him, her dark eyes imploring him. "You've got to believe me. She did *not* run away this time."

Gabe gave her a brief nod and poured them both another cup of coffee. He'd learned long ago that parents rarely thought their kids ran away from home, but sometimes they did. For whatever the reason, the son or daughter came to believe that taking flight was a whole lot better than staying in what they perceived to be a bad situation. "When was the last time you saw Lea?"

"Two weeks ago on a Saturday night. I was sitting on her bed and talking to her while she got ready for work. She'd gotten her first part-time job working at the Sycamore Mall in one of those cell phone kiosks. She didn't want to be late, so she rushed out the door and I followed her to her car. We had plans to go out for pizza after the mall closed." The woman teared up. "We had plans."

"I see. Do you have a photo of Lea?"

Camilla pulled a leather wallet from her purse, found a photo and slid it across the desk to him. "This is her senior picture. It was taken a couple of months ago."

Gabe scanned the photograph. Lea Essick looked older than seventeen, with dark waves framing her full square face. Her cheekbones were high, her mouth wide and well-shaped. She wasn't a knockout, but close enough to have her male classmates burning up her cell phone. He held the photo up between two fingers. "May I keep this?" When Camilla nodded, he continued. "I need to know more about your daughter. Does she drink, smoke, or do drugs? Who is she dating? Who are her best friends? Are there any co-workers that she's mentioned?"

Camilla pursed her lips as if offended and shot Gabe a glare. "My daughter does *not* drink or smoke, nor does she do drugs of any type."

"I'm sorry, Mrs. Essick, if I seem rude. I need to ask these questions so I have a better chance of finding Lea."

"She doesn't have many friends, but she's been dating a young man named Rick Foster. I know his parents from the country club. Nice people. As for co-workers at the mall, she sometimes talks about Teri Tanner. I think Teri went to Lea's school, graduated last year."

"That helps. You said before that Lea had run away twice before. Why?"

"Why is that important? I already told you that she didn't run away this time."

Profile of Fear

"It's helpful to understand why she ran away the other times."

Temper flashed in Camilla's eyes, coloring her cheeks. "Her father died. Lea had problems at school. We argued a lot. She took off. I found her. Satisfied? My daughter has grown up a lot since then, saw a therapist, and got her act together. And for the last time, she didn't run away. Are you taking my case or not?"

Gabe pressed back in his chair, a memory sizzling in his brain. He remembered when he learned that Kaitlyn had been abducted by a pair of sociopaths who would think nothing of killing her for fun. His gut kicked at the memory, and he remembered feeling panic and fear like he'd never known. The same emotions Camilla Essick must be experiencing.

"I'll take the case. I'll look for your daughter." Opening a desk drawer, he pulled out a form that he gave to Camilla. "This form contains a series of questions that will help me find your daughter. The questions run the gamut from a full physical description to Lea's bank account and credit card numbers. You need to answer the questions as truthfully as possible if you want us to have any chance of finding her."

Chapter 39

Gabe pushed his way through the doors of the Sycamore Mall, noting a dome-shaped security camera above him as he entered. If he had his way, metal detectors, armed guards, and bag screenings would be commonplace at shopping malls. Undoubtedly, mall owners wouldn't agree. Anything that might discourage shoppers from heading to the mall was a definite no-no in their world of economic survival.

Walking into the mall brought back memories. What was it about a tragedy that cements the date and event in your mind for a lifetime? Gabe remembered exactly where he was and what he was doing on January 25, 2014, when 19-year-old Darion Marcus Aguilar entered a Zumiez store in the Columbia Town Center Mall in Maryland on the second floor. Armed with a Mossberg 500 12-gauge shotgun with a pistol grip, he fired six to nine shots, killing two employees—21-year-old Brianna Benlolo and 25-year-old Tyler Johnson—and injuring five others before committing suicide.

Aguilar wasn't the first mall shooter nor would he be the last, a fact that filled Gabe with apprehension whenever he or Kaitlyn visited a shopping mall. With several entrances, multiple parking levels and lots, plus the networks of corridors, the very design of a mall provides an attacker with endless prospects for cover. Soft targets. That's how security experts referred to retail malls. You've got groups of people coming into and leaving the building through numerous exits, making it easy for an attacker to enter and exit quickly. It also made shoppers vulnerable, at risk.

From the main entrance of the mall, Gabe made his way toward the cell phone kiosk on the second floor where Lea Essick was last seen. Stepping onto the escalator, he climbed the steps, brushing past shoppers who were taking in the bright store lights and bustling crowd below. Glancing at his watch, Gabe hurried past the food court until he saw the cell phone kiosk. He waited as a young woman with a shock of spiky, dark red hair took care of a customer. After she finished up, he moved toward her.

"Teri Tanner?"

The girl looked down at her name tag then at Gabe and smiled. "Yes, sir. What kind of a cell phone can I show you?"

"I'm Gabe Chase. I called you yesterday about Lea Essick."

"Sure, I remember." She bent over the counter to talk to a kid unloading a box of cell phones. "Ely, I need to take a break. Can you take over for a while?"

She joined Gabe, looking him over, and not in a professional way. "You're sure not what I expected. I thought all P.I.s smoked a cigar, had a pot belly, and gruff voice. Like in the movies. You're sure not what I expected. You're hot."

She flashed him her sexiest smile. In the past, he might have toyed with her attraction to him to get information from her. It was different now. He'd become a one-woman man since he'd fallen in love with Kaitlyn. Flirting with anyone but her was no longer in his repertoire. He cleared his throat. "I appreciate your taking the time to talk about Lea. Since you're on break, how about a coffee? I saw a Starbucks in the food court."

"That's perfect. I haven't had my caffeine fix today."

As they stood in the Starbucks line, Gabe listened as Teri chatted about working in the mall at the kiosk. The barista at the counter seemed to know Teri and chatted with her, while whipping up her chocolate-drizzled whipped mocha.

Gabe found a small table in a section of the food court that was probably going to be as private as it got near the busy coffee shop. As he waited for Teri to get settled, his gaze bounced from couples leaning towards each other at the chic bistro tables to the laughing groups of teenagers lining up at the restaurant booths. Sipping his hot coffee, he swept his attention back to Teri.

Gabe pulled a small notepad from his jacket, along with an ink pen. "How long have you known Lea Essick?"

"Gosh, I guess about two years. We went to the same school. Like I told that cop, I knew her well enough to say 'hi' in the hall between classes. But I got to know her better when I got this job at the kiosk."

"Did the police question you about Lea?"

"Yes, last week sometime. He really didn't act as interested as you'd think he'd be about someone who was missing. He mentioned that Lea may have run away."

"What kind of person is Lea?"

"She's great. Easy to talk to and all that."

"Was she happy? Did she share any problems she might be having?"

"Yeah, she was happy. In fact, she said this was the best school year she'd ever had. She really likes her boyfriend. She talks about him non-stop." Teri took a big slurp of her coffee and quickly licked the cream foam from her upper lip.

"So she and her boyfriend were getting along?"

"Sure. When she was working, he'd come in and spend time with her during her breaks. He seemed real nice, and not hard to look at, either."

Teri flicked a glance at her watch and rose from her chair. "Listen, I'm sorry that Lea is missing. I wish I could think of something that could help you find her. But I can't. I have to get back to work."

Gabe handed her his business card. "Thanks for talking to me. Call me if you think of something."

A slender kid with a buzz cut and an expression too serious for his years immediately moved into Teri's chair and sat down across from him, placing his coffee cup on the table. "I overheard you talking to Teri. I hope you don't mind. I'm Rick Foster, Lea's boyfriend."

Gabe considered him, remembering his name from Camilla and Teri, and outstretched his hand. "I'm Gabe…"

Rick ignored the gesture and kept his hands tucked in his pockets. "I know who you are." He interrupted. "You're the private investigator that Lea's mom hired. Teri called me last night and told me you were trying to find Lea. I want to help."

"When was the last time you saw Lea?"

"We had a date the Friday night before she disappeared. Went out for dinner at O'Charley's restaurant, then caught *Star Wars* at the mall movie theater."

"And after that?"

"I followed her home. She hopped into my car outside her house and we made out until her mom turned on the porch light. That's her signal for curfew."

"Are you and Lea close?"

Rick nodded and looked down at his coffee. "I love her enough to want to marry her someday. I'm nineteen and she's only seventeen, so we have to wait. Lea wants to go to college after high school, and I'm taking classes at Ivy Tech."

"Let's talk about Saturday, the day she disappeared. Did you see her that day?"

"No. Couldn't call her either. I bus tables at the Wrangler's Steak House outside of town. My boss made me work a double shift. Asshole. I may never see Lea again because I worked that shift. I wish I had called in sick or something."

Rick Foster drew in his shoulders, tucking his elbows into his sides—obviously filled with self-blame. If he was ever on Gabe's suspect list, he was off it now. That was the thing about a missing person or homicide victim, their loved ones inevitably blamed themselves for what happened, often for a lifetime. He didn't wish that on anyone.

"Don't be so hard on yourself. It probably wouldn't have made a difference, Rick. Is there anything that Lea may have shared with you that might be important?"

"I've racked my brain, but I'm coming up with nothing. I know one thing. There is no way she would have run away. No way."

Chapter 40

Gabe waited until the lunch crowd died down, and then showed Lea's photo to the food court workers. Later Gabe visited store owners with Lea's photo. Many had seen her working at the kiosk as well as eating in the food court, but didn't have any pertinent information about her activities on the Saturday she disappeared.

Gabe got back on the escalator to the lower level to visit the security office. After he introduced himself as a private investigator, he was referred to Rob Nelson, head of mall safety and security. A talkative man, Nelson had a husky build with salt-and-pepper hair worn in a military cut. He waved his arm as he referred to the shopping mall as if he were a land baron overseeing his acreage.

Although he was on a tight schedule, Gabe listened patiently to Nelson as he talked about his department. Eventually, he got him to talk about systems put in place to protect customers and retailers, so he could transition into some questions about Lea Essick. "Sycamore Mall was built in the seventies, so until three years ago, the security system was pretty antiquated. And that's saying it politely."

"I'd heard the mall put in more sophisticated technology."

With a derisive snort, Nelson scowled and continued. "Yeah, it's a great system, but three guards lost their jobs over it. The system turned out to cost more money than the mall owners bargained for. Losing those guards means we're down to one guard to patrol the upper and lower levels, and one to oversee the security monitors. She can't leave the monitors, so if something happens, how quick help arrives depends on where the guard is on his rounds."

"What about the parking lots?"

"We don't have the manpower to patrol the parking lots. We're dependent on the external bullet cameras."

"Not good." Gabe shook his head as he thought about what safety implications this had for unknowing customers entering and leaving the lots. It was no secret that people are often victims of crime in mall parking lots. Great setup for car thieves, purse snatchers, carjackers, and sexual predators. At least with surveillance cameras, mall security personnel can review videos and help law enforcement track down the perpetrators. Somehow, that didn't ease his mind. With no guards actually driving around the parking lots, help might not come soon enough for a crime victim who was being abducted, raped, or worse. It was certainly not a model for crime prevention at its best. He made a mental note to brief Brody and Cam about the situation, in the hope that deputies could do more patrols through the mall parking lots.

Nelson led Gabe into a room that had three large monitors mounted on the wall. Beneath them sat a female security guard tapping on a computer keyboard. She briefly acknowledged him by nodding her head, and then returned her attention to the monitors. "Misty's job is to monitor the property by watching video feeds from security cameras located at various sites both inside and outside the mall. Our closed-circuit television security system has software and cameras to track bags left behind, count shoppers entering and exiting through doors, and it detects when a person enters a restricted area."

He pointed to the first monitor. "On this monitor we get feeds from thirty-six cameras strategically mounted throughout the inside of the mall, including walkways, escalators, and the food court. Each of our one-hundred specialty and anchor stores have their own security cameras, which tie into to our system. That footage appears on the second monitor. Parking areas are on the third."

Gabe gazed at the first monitor. "Would you please pull up the cell phone kiosk on the second floor?"

"Sure." With a click of her mouse, Misty pulled up the cell phone kiosk, which was now surrounded by customers.

"Is that why you're here? Something going on at that kiosk?"

"I'm looking for a young woman who worked at the kiosk. Lea Essick. She disappeared two weeks ago."

"Yeah, so I've heard. The cops were here. Didn't seem too worried though. They think she ran away."

"From what I've heard from the people who know her, that doesn't seem likely."

Nelson glanced at him, seemingly sizing him up before he invited Gabe into his office and closed the door. "I found that girl's car parked outside Macy's at the end of the mall closest to the kiosk where she works. The county police have already had the car towed after their crime scene techs worked it over."

"Do you know whether any prints were found on her car?"

Stroking his chin, he regarded Gabe warily, then leaned across his desk, talking in a low, bitter voice. "As usual, the cops told me to get lost. Asshats. Even though I used to be a cop for the city, those guys have no respect for mall security. None. Like I said, I'd already found the girl's 2004 silver Honda CRV, so I hung around outside Macy's and watched the CSI team dust for prints. They got nothing. Only prints they found were the girl's."

"Good to know. Did they find anything else?"

"Nah. The girl didn't make it to the car that night." Abruptly Nelson stopped talking; his face reddened and his mouth froze in a grim line. It was as if the words had escaped his mouth before he'd had a chance to cage them inside.

"How do you know?"

The security officer's face darkened another shade of crimson and he shifted uncomfortably in his chair. Wordlessly, he stared at the surface of his desk.

It was then that Gabe realized exactly what he'd done. Fueled by his resentment toward the investigators, Nelson had withheld information about Lea Essick. Considering his jumpiness, it was likely an important piece of the puzzle needed to find the teen. Gabe felt his temper rise, but worked to keep it in check. How could someone who had what could be critical information needed to find a missing girl suppress it over a perceived slight by law enforcement?

The mall cop was damned lucky that it was he who sat across from him instead of Brody or Cam, who would have slapped him with a well-deserved obstruction charge and a personal tour of a county jail cell.

Swallowing his anger, he spoke calmly, as if he hadn't heard Nelson's admission.

"Any chance you've got a surveillance recording of the Saturday when Lea Essick was last seen?"

Sullenly Nelson rifled through his top drawer a moment before pulling out a USB drive and handing it to Gabe. "Here. It's a copy. Thought the cops would ask for this, but they didn't, so I didn't offer."

"I'd also like any footage you have focused on the kiosk, as well as the food court for the last thirty days."

Rob left the room. Gabe could hear him talking to Misty. Soon he returned to the office with another USB drive.

Slipping it into his pocket, Gabe stood abruptly to end the conversation. Pausing at the door, he shot a glare back to Nelson. "You've got fifteen minutes to call those investigators and tell them what you found on the surveillance recording. Spin it however you want, but give them the information, because in fifteen minutes *I* will."

Nelson sank into his chair. "Oh, shit."

Gabe tapped the face of his watch. "Fifteen. And counting."

Chapter 41

Gabe entered the Vineyard Wine Bar and waded through the after-work crowd until his found his brother, Cameron, at a table near the front window. They exchanged hellos and Gabe sat down.

Cameron smiled. "I saw that the builder has poured the foundation for your new house."

"Kaitlyn and I walked down there last night. We're getting excited."

"Will there be wedding bells soon?"

"Not sure. Kaitlyn wants to take her time. But after watching her with Becca, I think her internal baby alarm is going off. We may get married before you know it. At least I hope so."

"Really appreciate the time she's spending with Becca."

"She enjoys it. Cam, thanks for meeting with me."

"No problem. But is there a reason why you couldn't talk to me at home?"

"Aside from taking time you'd rather spend with Becca, I think this particular conversation is better left private."

Cameron nodded and held up a finger to get the waitress's attention. He ordered two Heinekens, and turned his attention back to his brother. "What's going on?"

"I've got two things I want to discuss with you. Let's start with the research you asked for about online sex trafficking. I found a lot of information, most of which makes me sick to my stomach."

Profile of Fear

"I hear you," Cameron agreed.

"What I found are a lot of places for sex advertising on the Internet, like Craigslist, Backpage, and a variety of underground chat rooms. The difficulty is distinguishing between the sex traffickers and the voluntary sex workers."

"According to federal law, all minors involved with commercial sex acts are treated as victims of trafficking."

"I know that. It's why I turned my focus to ads for underage girls. I started out by looking for photographs, but it seems the traffickers are on to those searches by law enforcement and they rarely post images on their ads. They exchange photos with the buyer after arranging a meeting."

"Tricky bastards."

"Starting with Craigslist, I went to the "Casual Encounters" and "Women for Men" sections. I noticed there were certain common phrases, key words, and codes that can help narrow the search for underage sex workers."

"What are some of them?"

"Sometimes they are brazen enough to use actual ages like: Age 17/18/19, which indicates the age without specifically advertising the girls as underage. Other key words they use are: young, new in town/back in town, dirty old man, and daddy/daughter incest. Disgusting, right? And ads like this skyrocket during big sporting events like the Super Bowl."

"So how can we use these ads to find our missing girls we think Juan Ortiz has abducted?"

"It won't be easy, Cam. You'd need someone constantly combing the ads looking for underage workers, and then you'd have to cross-reference by location. The next step would be to investigate the person who posted the ad. Sites like Craigslist require a court order, search warrant, or subpoena before they release information. But I've heard they are very cooperative once they receive the warrant. They can give the investigator the Internet protocol (IP) address of the poster, which will help identify which computer the posted ad came from, and thus identify your perp."

"Crap. I don't have that kind of manpower and time."

"I think you should consider setting up a sting of your own.

Create an ad to use on the sites I mentioned. Lure the traffickers to provide underage girls to a hotel room you've secured, and see what shakes out."

"That might be a good idea. I'll discuss it with Robynn. Good job, Gabe. Now what else did you want to discuss with me?"

Gabe opened his briefcase, withdrew a folder, and opened it on the table. On the top was a photograph that he handed to Cameron.

"This is Lea Essick. She's seventeen and a Shawnee High School senior. She's been missing a little over two weeks. Her mother hired me to find her."

"Wait a minute. Isn't my team already working this case?"

"Cam, Mrs. Essick doesn't feel like they are taking her daughter's disappearance seriously because she's run away in the past."

"Well she can get in line. All parents believe that, no matter how hard we're working the case. Listen, I assigned Dean Maxwell, one of my rookie detectives to the case. I'll ask him for an update, and see what's going on. What have *you* found out?"

"Lea disappeared from Sycamore Mall where she worked at a cell phone kiosk. She had plans with her mother after work, but she never came home. I went to the mall where she worked and talked with a co-worker, her boyfriend, and mall security."

Gabe pulled his laptop out of his briefcase and opened it on the table with the screen placed so both could see. He pulled a USB drive from his pocket and inserted it. "I got surveillance footage from mall security. This first clip is from the day before Lea disappeared." Gabe pointed to the screen. "There is Lea now at the cell phone kiosk. She's not very busy until this man and woman approach her with a stack of what looks like flyers."

"Can't see their faces."

"I'm sure that was their plan. They talk to Lea for about five minutes before they hand her a flyer that she tucks under the cash register. I returned to the mall and her co-worker found the flyer and gave it to me." He pushed a bright pink flyer across the table to Cameron. "The flyer advertises a call out for models. Perfect con for a young woman. Promises glamor and big bucks."

"So you think this flyer is connected to her disappearance?"

"Hell, yes. Especially after what you said the other night about schemes used by Juan Ortiz's men to recruit young girls. But I'm not sure Lea Essick fell for the con. You'll see why I say this when we skip ahead on the tape to the night she disappeared." Gabe fast-forwarded the tape to the time in question. "Here is Lea leaving work and going through the back exit to where her car is parked. See the white utility van parked near the exit? The side door is open and there are two young girls inside. Watch what happens as Lea tries to walk by them. One of the young girls calls out to her. She stops and immediately this guy in a black hoodie grabs her and shoves her into the van. He slams the door, jumps in the passenger seat, and they drive off."

"We can run that license plate."

"I already did. It was stolen from a car parked in the Kroger grocery store parking lot. Dead end. And the faces are so blurry, you can't make them out."

Cameron thought for a moment and said, "I bet this is what happened to Brandy Murphy."

"Who's that?"

"Murder victim who was around Lea's age and worked at the mall. Brandy left with a suspect driving an Escalade. I'd bet anything he used this exact con with her. When we found her body, she had Juan Ortiz's ownership tattoo on her hip. I think you've identified his recruiting scheme. We'll search her father's house again to make sure. And I hope we can find Lea Essick before she becomes his next murder victim."

Chapter 42

Kaitlyn did a quick 360-degree scan of the parking lot before she lifted Becca out of her car seat. Carly secured the baby in the shopping cart and they headed toward the GoodBuys store entrance. GoodBuys was a new store in town, a Target wannabe, and they were celebrating the store's grand opening with bargains in all departments. Of interest to Kaitlyn and Carly were the sales in the children's department. Becca was outgrowing her clothing and they planned to stock up for fall weather, even though it was months away. Armed with Cameron's credit card, they headed toward the area where they might save some money on clothing, toys, and children's books. Cameron had given them the green light to purchase anything Becca needed.

Deciding to divide and conquer, Carly headed toward children's clothing and Kaitlyn turned the cart into the aisle that had toys for toddlers.

Kaitlyn had made a stop to look at a *LeapFrog Shapes and Sharing Picnic Basket* when she noticed Becca pointing to a colorful book. "Bunny. Bunny," she called out. Kaitlyn made a closer look at the book and discovered that, indeed, there was a rabbit on the cover. She picked up the board book and handed it to Becca.

"Can you point to the bunny?"

Becca extended her chubby little finger to touch the baby rabbit on the cover and Kaitlyn planted a kiss on her cheek. "Very good, sweetie."

Profile of Fear

Proud of the way Becca was learning new words, Kaitlyn had worried about how the baby's consumption of meth would impair her development, but so far, so good. The pediatrician assured them she was progressing well.

Kaitlyn added a few more books and toys and then joined Carly in the toddler clothing aisle.

"Check out these little dresses I found." Carly held up a blue jumper with a pink flowered top. "Do you like this, Becca?"

The little girl quickly glanced at the outfit. She was too busy looking at the baby animals in her new book to give it her full attention.

Kaitlyn looked over the other outfits Carly held and then put them in the cart. "These are great. She's also going to need new jeans and long-sleeved shirts and sweaters. I see a clearance sale sign down there. I'll check it out."

Carly dug in an overstuffed bin of toddler pajamas and pulled out a couple in Becca's size. She turned to put them in the cart.

That's when she made a dead stop in the middle of the aisle, a chill rushing down her spine, the hair on the back of her neck standing up. Something was wrong. Her intuition had saved her more than once and there was no chance she'd ignore it this time. Doing a 360-degree turn, she checked her surroundings. Nothing out of the ordinary. Kaitlyn stood not far from her at the opposite end of the aisle, checking out a display of little girl's blue jeans. A woman with a shopping cart was thumbing through a rack of toddler shirts. Carly's eyes swept back to the end of the aisle. The shopping cart! Where was the cart? Where was Becca?

Carly called out to Kaitlyn as she rushed to the end of the aisle. "The cart's gone! Where's Becca?"

Racing down the aisle, they looked in every direction, but Becca was nowhere in sight. They reached the main corridor, finding it clogged with shoppers, and ran in opposite directions to cover more ground.

Once she'd checked every aisle in her section, Carly hurried into the women's restroom. It was empty. She then barged into the men's restroom, hitting a man coming out with the heavy door. No sign of Becca.

Carly found the small customer service area and slammed her

identification on the counter. "Listen closely. I am a federal agent and I work for the Shawnee County Sheriff. A child is missing. Lock down the store." Her eyes wide, the panicked employee behind the counter froze.

"Move it! Lock it down. No one leaves."

"Oh, God. I don't know how."

"Get your store security manager here *now!*"

"I'll get my manager." The employee with the name Sam on her nametag paged the store manager. A thin man moved next to her, pulled out a pager and called the checkout manager, and told her to alert the checkout clerks.

Carly stepped back into the shopping area. Her hands on her hips, she scanned the area again for a little girl with bouncing blond curls.

Her heart in her throat, Kaitlyn cursed herself as she frantically searched each aisle for Becca. It was all her fault. She should never have left the child alone in the cart, even for a second. There was no excuse. Now Becca might be in the hands of a child predator. The thought was unbearable and tore at her insides.

Kaitlyn was nearing the front of the store when she found their shopping cart filled with clothing and educational toys—but no Becca.

Up ahead she noticed a short man in a hurry, dressed gangsta style, with low-hung jeans exposing his underwear like a white beacon, and a gray hoodie covering most of his face. He held a small child on his hips like it was a sack of potatoes, its legs flailing. Who carries a child like that? And why was he in such a hurry?

He moved faster as he neared the front doors, so Kaitlyn picked up speed and pushed a shopper's cart out of her way, ignoring the woman's protests. Pulling her pepper spray out of her purse, she slipped it into her pocket. Breaking into a sprint, Kaitlyn dug deeper and found her stun gun at the bottom of her handbag, clutching it in her hand as she ran toward him. He was going down.

The child's small body jerked against the man with each step he took. The child kicked and screamed and cried hysterically. It was Becca!

Getting closer, Kaitlyn shouted, "Stop that man! He has my baby!"

The man heard Kaitlyn, glanced back at her, and then rammed into an elderly woman's cart. Stunned, the woman snatched up her purse and began hitting him with it as she screamed for help.

"Stop him," Kaitlyn shouted. Chaos ensued as a crowd of shoppers nearby rushed to the elderly woman, still screaming for help. A teenaged boy in an athletic jacket stuck out his foot and tripped the man, who tumbled onto the floor, releasing Becca from his grasp. The boy grabbed Becca and ran in the opposite direction. Kaitlyn turned to see Carly making her way to the boy and Becca.

The man in the gray hoodie struggled to his feet, stumbled, then sprinted toward the store's front doors with Kaitlyn close behind. He charged through the exit door and disappeared in the parking lot. She'd lost him.

Kaitlyn turned to see Becca in Carly's arms, standing near the checkout area. With tears streaming down her face, she hugged both of them tightly and repeatedly said, "My fault. All my fault. I'm so sorry."

"I share the blame, Kaitlyn. My attention should have been on the cart. It all happened so quickly. He had to have been following us."

The store manager approached them. "What happened?"

Carly stepped in and held out her I.D. "We can explain that later. Right now we need to see your surveillance tape."

Inside a glassed security office upstairs, Carly handed Becca to Kaitlyn and sat next to the security manager, who looked like he was an eighteen-year-old high schooler. She told him the area in which they were shopping and he alerted her attention to the second computer display. He backtracked the tape until they could spot Kaitlyn, Becca, and herself in the toddler clothing aisle.

"Go slow. Take it frame-by-frame."

He slowed the replay to a crawl until the man in the gray hoodie came into view. The man inched his way along their aisle, pretending to look at children's clothing, until he came within a couple of feet of their shopping cart. Still eyeing them, he waited until Kaitlyn walked to the opposite end of the aisle, and Carly bent over the clearance bin. At that point, he handed Becca a small object, perhaps a book, and smoothly moved the cart, picking up speed as he neared the end of the aisle. In the corridor, he moved at a natural pace so as not to attract attention, weaving in and out of clusters of shoppers, aiming toward the front of the store. Then he turned to see Kaitlyn chasing after him, and he accidentally slammed into the elderly woman's cart. He stops and removes Becca from the cart

"Please enlarge the picture, and take it back again, still going frame-by-frame, so we can get a better look at him."

She turned to Kaitlyn. "Does he look familiar?"

"No," Kaitlyn replied, as she patted Becca's back to calm her. "Thanks to the hoodie he's wearing, I can't really see his features on the display. But I can describe what I saw when I was chasing him. He's very short for an adult male. He's younger, maybe in his twenties or thirties. Dark hair and features. I'm guessing he might be Hispanic?"

Carly switched her attention to the display. "Let's see the surveillance camera shots from the parking lot." Soon the man in the hoodie came into view, running from the store. He got into a late model Ford truck and skidded his tires in an effort to flee the parking lot.

"I'd like a copy of the footage from both cameras."

He soon handed her a thumb drive, which Carly slipped into her pocket. Once they reached the store's first floor, she turned to Kaitlyn and winced. "Now I have to call Cam to tell him what happened. Hope he stays calm."

"Not likely. He'll probably go ballistic and not allow Becca out of the house until she's thirty."

After Carly and Kaitlyn discussed the matter further, they decided not to tell Cam until dinner. It was Gabe and Kaitlyn's turn to cook, and they made meatloaf, mashed potatoes, and steamed fresh green beans, with a German chocolate cake for dessert—Cam's favorite meal.

Carly didn't have to wait until dessert was served to broach the subject of Becca's aborted abduction attempt. Cameron got the topic rolling.

"So how did your shopping trip go today?" Cameron asked as he mounted a scoop of mash potatoes on Becca's plate.

"About that..." Carly began. "Something happened at GoodBuys that you should know about. But I want you to promise not to freak out."

"Does it have to do with Becca?"

"Yes."

"Can't promise. What happened?" The tone in Cameron's voice changed and his words were clipped.

"We were in the toddler clothing aisle when a man took off with Becca in the shopping cart."

"What the hell? One might assume a child would be safe shopping with an armed federal agent and a woman who has a self-defense arsenal in her purse."

Kaitlyn interjected. "We take full responsibility, but it happened so fast. Wait until you see the surveillance tape."

"Did you identify him?"

"No. He was wearing a hoodie that covered his facial features. He was short, maybe five feet something, with dark hair. Might be Hispanic."

Cameron clenched his jaw to keep from exploding. "Hispanic? Like Juan Ortiz?"

Carly spoke up. "We can't automatically make that connection with what we have, which is zero evidence and no identification of the perp. The guy doesn't fit Juan's physical description. Ortiz is much taller. In addition, we have no way of knowing if Melanie Barrett gave out Becca's location."

"Don't you think it's just a little too coincidental Becca's mother, Donda Hicks, was found hanged just hours later?" Cam scrubbed his face with his hands in frustration. His gut was saying this had Ortiz written all over it.

"We ran the license plate on the old truck the jerk was driving and it had been reported stolen. It was found later today in a ditch near a 7-Eleven convenience store near the town limits. Dusted the truck for fingerprints, but the entire vehicle had been wiped down."

Cameron was incredulous. "That doesn't sound like a professional to you?"

"Hell, Cam. You know yourself that anyone with a television watches CSI and would know to wipe down a stolen car to get rid of prints," said Brody.

"I know. It's just that when it comes to Becca's safety, I get a little crazy." He wiped mashed potatoes from his child's little face and hands, and then pulled her out of her high chair to sit on his lap. "I don't even want to think about anything happening to her."

"It may have been a fluke. A child predator and not Juan Ortiz. We've beefed up security at the house, and we are either armed, or have a weapon nearby when we're home alone with Becca. I can't tell you how sorry I am that this happened, but please don't make her a prisoner in her own home. We'll be more careful. I promise. She's safe living here, and she's safe with us," Carly pleaded.

Chapter 43

Diego held his cell phone as he sat in his room at home. He'd just checked on his mother and she was immersed in a Lifetime movie in the living room, so he knew he'd be safe talking business behind his locked bedroom door. His mother thought he worked a janitor job at the hospital. He wanted to keep it that way. It would kill her if she knew what he did with his time, and who he spent it with. Hurting his mother was not an option.

He thought of the events of the day: one could get him killed, the other should make Juan Ortiz a happy man. That is if anything could make Ortiz happy. The man was a monster on every level. A fact that never wandered from Diego's mind. He regretted ever getting involved with Ortiz. No matter what the man paid him, it wasn't worth the fear of disappointing him and losing his life. His mother depended on him as her caregiver, and as her sole source of income. What would happen to her if he should be killed? What would happen if Ortiz took out any disappointment on Rosalita? It was a thought he wouldn't let himself consider.

Earlier, he'd had Juan's kid in his grasp. He'd been watching the Chase house since that social worker had given up the kid's location to Ortiz. Diego had read in the paper how her body had been found tied to a tree with her throat sliced. No doubt the handiwork of Juan Ortiz. If Ortiz had been a sane man, he would have abandoned his plan to get his kid back when he learned she was living in a house filled with law enforcement officers, including the county sheriff. Not Ortiz. He loved a good challenge. He only seemed more determined, more threatening, placing sole responsibility for nabbing the kid on Diego's shoulders.

When it came to children, Diego had a soft spot. Ortiz was the last man on earth who should have a kid. Who knows why he wanted her back? The man trafficked women for sex. What would he do with a little girl? The whole thing made him want to throw up. If anything bad happened to the kid, it was on him. He'd have to live with it the rest of his life. That seemed worse than getting caught, like almost happened today.

He'd followed the two women and Juan's kid from the house to GoodBuys, and sat in the truck he'd stolen as they emerged from their car. The women seemed unusually watchful and he had to duck down when they looked in the truck's direction. Once they entered the store with the kid in the shopping cart, he lifted the hood to his jacket to cover his face and entered the store. One thing he had going in his favor was that people usually didn't notice him. Except for his height, he was nondescript. People looked past him, not at him.

Finding the women and little girl in the kid's department, he waited until the right time to grab their shopping cart with the kid inside. He'd almost made it to the entrance when the blond bitch, running like a gazelle, began closing in on him. From there, it was all downhill, and he ended up fleeing the scene without the kid, just grateful he could get away. Maybe the whole thing was a sign that he shouldn't grab the little girl. His mother believed in signs like that. Maybe he should, too.

Lifting his cell, he punched in Juan's number. He hadn't told Juan about his plan to abduct the girl in the department store, so he had no intention of telling him now. Who knows what Juan, with his quick temper, would do to him if he knew?

"Hello, boss. I've got good news."

"It better be."

"Got a job on the construction crew I told you about."

"What construction crew?"

"The crew that's building the new home on the Chase property. I start tomorrow. I'll be able to avoid their security gate

Profile of Fear

in front and enter through the construction road in the back. I'll have my eye on things at the main house where your kid is living."

"You'll do more than that. You'll figure out a way to break in and get my kid. I'm tired of waiting."

"I was thinking maybe one of your other guys, like Carlos, could do the breaking in. He's better at break-ins than I am."

"What are you saying? You won't do it?"

"No, boss. Of course not."

Juan paused for a second and then said in a low, menacing voice, "I met your mother, Rosalita, today."

Diego's heart pounded painfully hard and he could barely breathe. "You met my mother?"

"Yes, I paid her a visit when looking for you. Poor woman, trapped in that wheelchair like she is. Who knows what could happen to her, helpless like that."

"Leave my mother out of this. I'll do what you want."

"Just think of all the unfortunate things that could happen if you don't, Diego. To you, to your mother. Do you understand?"

Diego understood perfectly. He understood exactly what he had to do. Remove the threat. Kill Juan Ortiz.

Chapter 44

Hailey hopped on the escalator, stood behind Niki, and rode up to the second level, to the H&M store. The air practically buzzed with excitement as teen shoppers hustled to snap up the newest CD deals with fragrant cups of Starbucks in hand to give them a caffeine boost.

Escalators were great for people-watching, and Hailey spotted Tim Branson, super-popular high school basketball star and all-around hottie, at the cell phone kiosk below. Sending him a friendly wave, she tugged on Niki's shirt and told her Tim was in the mall.

"Of course, he is. All the popular kids are at the mall on Friday night."

"Just so we've covered our bases, I told my mom I was staying all night with you tonight. She'd have a fit if she knew I'd driven to the mall," said Hailey.

Niki nodded, pushing a strand of purple hair away from her lips. "Stop worrying. Your mom will never know we drove to the mall. Our plan is solid."

The girls leaped off the escalator onto the second floor and entered a Bath and Body Works store. Zeroing in on a fragrance sample, Hailey spritzed her forearm with 'Pretty as a Peach.' "Smell this, Niki. Isn't it awesome?"

"Makes me hungry for fruit."

"Very funny. Try this one." Lifting a spritzer of 'French Lavender and Honey,' she sprayed Niki's wrist.

Profile of Fear

"Oui, Oui. Getting that one." Grabbing the bottle, she giggled, and aimed herself toward the body lotions, where she picked up one with the same scent.

At the checkout counter, Niki declared it was her treat, and paid for all their purchases with a gift card she'd been holding onto since last December.

Exiting the store, the girls stood at the railing to look over the crowd below. Hailey spotted a handsome man in his early twenties with an armful of pink flyers and pointed him out to Niki. "That guy in the navy shirt is too hot to be hot."

Niki looked him over. "Agree. We're talking rock star hot."

"Wonder what he's selling?"

"Let's go down, get a flyer, and a closer look."

By the time they reached the lower level, rock star guy was gone, so the girls went to the food court, which was brimming with teenagers. They each got a hot pretzel, packets of mustard, and bottles of Pepsi, then sat down to eat at a small table.

The food court was a hub of commotion with teens sitting at tables talking on their cell phones or texting, while others called out to friends they'd just spotted. The aroma from the many small restaurants wafted in the air: meat grilling, buttery popcorn, cinnamon, BBQ, and more. Hailey's stomach growled.

Hailey had taken a couple of bites of her pretzel when she jabbed Niki in the ribs with her elbow. "There he is. The rock star guy."

Six-foot-three or so, he looked athletic and had a face like a movie star, and a smile that would make a young woman want to follow him anywhere. A mane of black hair curled from his forehead to just below his ears. They made eye contact and he flashed Hailey a brilliant smile as he headed toward their table.

Chapter 45

Carlos Rodriguez glanced at the caller display on his cell and groaned. Juan Ortiz. Just what he didn't need, his boss checking up on him again. He resented the constant grilling about his business decisions. Carlos's operation was running smoothly long before Juan Ortiz decided to return to the states from his hideout in Mexico to take charge and take a third of his profits. It was a bitter pill to swallow.

Carlos accepted the call. "How are you liking Indiana, Boss?"

"This isn't a social call. What's going on with your operation?"

"Things are going well. We're still recruiting runaways at bus stations and—"

Shouting, Juan interrupted. "Where are you? It's so fucking noisy I can barely hear you."

"I'm at the mall."

"What the hell are you doing out shopping? You've got a job to do."

Carlos clenched his jaw, fighting a rush of anger. "I *am* doing my job."

"At the mall?"

"Where do you think young girls go on the weekends? We're using the modeling scam to recruit, and we're getting some beauties. We'll take them back to the house to break them in. Some of them will be workers for your restaurants, or nannies for our clients. The others become escorts we advertise on Backpage. 'Dial-a-Ho' on the Internet. Easy."

"You don't have to explain the modeling con. I created it. If it's so damn easy, why are your numbers down? Mateo in Ohio is making twice the money you are with his girls."

"Mateo is a meth-head thug. He's just stupid enough to get us all locked up."

Juan ignored his remark. "Bring up your numbers or Mateo comes to Indiana to teach you how it's done." Juan disconnected the call, and Carlos shoved the cell in his pocket. He was so pissed he wanted to hit something.

Looking over the railing to the floor below, he noticed a kid swipe an accessory from the cell phone kiosk. That's what they get for not keeping a better eye on their merchandise.

Carlos never took his eye off his merchandise, and that's why he was successful. No matter what Juan Ortiz thought.

Turning, he scanned the food court, looking for teenaged girls who looked naïve enough to fall for his modeling con. Sitting at a table near the pretzel place was an auburn-haired beauty who was a dead-ringer for Britta.

Carlos remembered the last time he'd seen Britta, and how much she'd repulsed him. She was five-foot-six and weighed maybe 90 pounds soaking wet. A field of open sores covered her arms, and every time she opened her mouth she revealed rotting or missing teeth. She was not the go-to babe she'd been when he'd met her the year before. Not by a long shot.

Once upon a time, Britta had been the most requested of his team of escorts. That was before her love affair with meth began. The drug he used to control her had taken over until she was lost to him. She'd become a liability—not an asset.

If she disgusted him, what must her clients be thinking? It wasn't surprising that requests for her services had narrowed down to occasional calls. How was that impacting his bottom line? Stupid question. How in the hell did he think she was adding to his business? She wasn't. He'd have to get rid of her soon. Maybe ask his cousin, Pedro, for a ride in his single-engine Cessna and drop her ass over the Wabash River.

Carlos made eye contact with the Britta-look-alike and flashed her a brilliant, practiced smile as he angled across the crowd to reach her table. She looked young, maybe sixteen, just the age his clients wanted.

"I apologize for staring. It's just that you're so beautiful," he said to Hailey, and then grinned when she flushed with color. "Let me introduce myself. My name is Carlos, and I'm a talent agent for Vogue Modeling Agency."

"I'm Hailey, and this is my friend, Niki."

Glancing at her friend, he noted her eyes widening under a thick veil of mascara. Her hair black with streaks of purple. She was trying too hard to get attention. Carlos made a snap decision to recruit them both.

"Are you two already with an agency?"

Hailey seemed confused. "Agency?"

"Modeling agency. Are you models?"

Niki choked on her soda and Hailey stuttered, "N-n-o."

"Then it's my lucky day. My clients are looking for models, and you two fit the bill perfectly. One of my customers heads a huge retail chain and is looking for fresh new faces to headline his new lines of designer clothing."

"And you think we could model?" Niki asked.

"I wouldn't be here if I wasn't sure of it." Carlos watched as the girls exchanged smiles. They could barely contain their excitement. He'd hooked them, now all he had to do was to reel them in. "But let me tell you about Vogue Modeling before we continue.

"Our agency is the Midwest's premier resource for professional models and actors, as well as video production services. As a full-service talent agency, we provide our clients with the best professional talent for print, television, promotion, and runway, and offer on-site or remote casting, based on the company's needs. We currently have too many clients and not enough models. That's where you two come in."

He pushed a pink flyer to each of the girls. "This flyer describes our casting call. Sorry about the late notice, but our next call-out is tonight. I can give you a ride from the mall. We'll go to our facility where you'll have professionals do your hair, makeup, and nails. Our photographers will then take pictures of you so that we can have 8x10 glossies made to show our clients."

"And you think your clients would be interested in one of us?" asked Hailey.

"I know it." Carlos replied. "Let me share some information with you about salary and perks our girls have received. Many of our models make more than $100,000 a year and receive free beauty care, products, and clothing."

"We'd have to talk this over with our parents," Hailey said, as Niki kicked her under the table and gave her a don't-ruin-this look.

"That's no problem. In fact, I will meet with your parents personally to answer all their questions. But only if you participate in the casting call." Carlos pulled out a lined piece of white paper and pushed it across the table to Hailey. We already have three participants in tonight's casting, so if you're interested, sign your name on lines four and five. Be sure to list your home address, as well as your parents' names." Amusement flickering in his eyes, Carlos watched as the girls signed the papers. "My SUV will be parked outside Macy's at closing time. You can't miss it. It's a new, silver Lexus RX 350. Be on time, we have a lot to do. The sooner I can get your information to our clients, the better."

Chapter 46

Hailey pulled her car around to the Macy's parking lot at the far end of the mall. There were few cars parked in the area, and a couple of sales clerks straggled out of the building. Parking, she turned the headlights off and removed her seat belt. Niki finished her call, then put her cell phone in her purse.

"Okay, it's all set. My mom thinks we're going to stay with Cheryl Timms tonight. I told her that Cheryl and her boyfriend had a bad breakup and needed some shoulders to cry on."

"She bought that?"

"Sure. Getting me out of the house so she has more private time with her man is one of her priorities. I could have told her I was boarding a spaceship to Saturn and she would have agreed."

"This is crazy. My mom is going to kill me if we get caught. She'll ground me until I'm thirty."

"We're not getting caught. We're getting discovered. The new faces of modeling. Remember?"

A gleaming, silver Lexus RX 350 with tinted windows arrived and parked at the mall entrance.

"Oh, my God," Niki exclaimed. "Is that Carlos? That car is amazing."

Just then, a man got out of the car, zipping up his hoodie.

"That's definitely Carlos."

As they approached the Lexus, Carlos opened the back door for them and made an exaggerated bow.

"My ladies. Your chariot has arrived."

Profile of Fear

The girls slid across the sumptuous leather back seat and inhaled the intoxicating new-car smell. A glass roof opened to a million sparkling stars above. Neither girl had ever been in such a luxurious vehicle.

"Very cool car," gushed Niki.

"The agency spares no expense when it comes to taking care of our models. Just think. In a year or two, you ladies can afford to buy a car like this." Gazing at the girls in the rear view mirror, Carlos added, "There are iced bottles of water in the console. Help yourself."

Thirsty, Hailey took a bottle for herself and gave one to Niki. She thanked Carlos and lifted the opened bottle to her lips and let the cold liquid sluice down her throat. She leaned back to watch as a slice of moon scuttled behind some clouds, while he drove the car out of the parking lot.

Carlos pushed a DVD into the player, and soon Justin Bieber with a group of dancers were strutting across the two LCD screens mounted behind the front headrests. Wearily, Hailey let her head drop to the headrest as her mind drifted into a fuzzy haze.

The next thing Hailey was cognizant of was Carlos and another man helping her out of the SUV. So weak that her limbs felt like Jell-O, she found she couldn't manage to stand on her own. Looking back, she saw Niki sprawled across the backseat, so passed out she was breathing through her mouth. The men half-carried and dragged Hailey into a large house, into a kitchen with dark cabinets and granite counters. There was a man seated on a stool near the granite island. Carlos was not happy to see the man, and some harsh words were exchanged. She didn't understand. Where was she? Why did her eyelids feel so heavy she could barely keep them open? Was she dreaming?

Carlos opened a door, flicked on a light, and began the descent down wooden steps that creaked. Holding her tightly with one arm, he braced himself against the railing to balance himself. A musty, mildew odor pierced the air, reminding Hailey of her grandmother's basement. When he reached the floor, he deposited her on a rug where she closed her eyes and fell into a deep, blissful sleep.

Chapter 47

In addition to the home under construction, there were two other structures on the Chase property: an A-frame cottage, where the sheriff and his wife lived, and a massive two-story. Diego had been watching the two-story house while working on the construction site, and knew the family's comings and goings. Most activity occurred at the larger house, and he was sure that was where Juan's kid lived. He'd seen the little girl, but never alone, always with an adult, making it too risky to get to her.

It was the dead of night, and the only sound he heard was the mooing of a cow in the distance. No one was home at the sheriff's house, and one car was parked outside the main house. It belonged to the blond. She was inside, alone with the child.

All the lights in the house were out, and he prayed the woman and child were in a deep sleep. He'd seen a white crib in a window on the second floor, so he knew Juan's kid was in a room upstairs.

Earlier in the day, he'd noticed the blond-haired woman take the big dog in her car. When she returned, the dog was not with her, and Diego realized this was the chance he'd been waiting for.

Juan had given his word, whatever that was worth, that Diego and his mother's safety depended on the safe retrieval of his daughter. Once that was done, Diego would be paid $10,000, and his work with Juan Ortiz would be done. He'd never contact them again. If Juan didn't honor his promise, Diego would move to

Profile of Fear

Plan B, which was to kill Ortiz and flee the country with his mother. They'd go to Mexico, where his mother still had friends and relatives.

Slipping on a sock hat to cover his hair, and latex gloves to prevent fingerprints, he moved quietly through the tall trees that bordered the Chase property until he reached the back of the house. His plan was to use a method he'd used many times to burglarize fancy homes like this one. It was one of the rare times his small stature worked in his favor. Dropping to his hands and knees, he lowered his body and slid through the doggie door into the kitchen. Once he got his bearings, he listened carefully for any movements within the house. Hearing nothing, he stepped into a dining room and then crept through a huge living space to the stairway. Upstairs in the hallway, he headed for the room at the end. It was a nursery, softly illuminated by a child's lamp that revealed a large Peter Rabbit painted on a wall, and Juan's kid lay in the crib near the window.

Looking angelic, the child was sleeping peacefully with her little arms wrapped around a stuffed toy rabbit. Diego's heart ached. How could a monster like Juan Ortiz have created such a beautiful baby? A better question was: How could he deliver this angel to a predator who took pleasure in slicing the life out of others?

Diego backed away from the crib. He couldn't do it. He'd done some things he wasn't proud of, but he'd never hurt a woman or child. He wasn't going to start now, no matter how Juan Ortiz might threaten him.

His senses on heightened alert, he knew without looking that he was no longer alone in the room. Spinning around on the balls of his feet, he saw her near the door.

"Get away from the baby." The blond-haired woman sprung forward, viciously swinging a long, aluminum flashlight in her right hand. The blow hit its mark and stars exploded in front of his eyes. A thin trickle of blood ran down his face. He slammed into the crib, waking the baby, who let out a terrified scream. The woman swung the flashlight again, but he dodged before it slammed into his jaw.

A rush of adrenaline shooting through him, Diego pushed her

away with all his strength and rushed into the hallway, heading toward the stairs to make his escape.

"Stop!" The woman stood at the top of the stairs with a Glock aimed at his chest. "I will not hesitate to shoot, so you better stop."

Ignoring her, Diego took the steps two and three at a time until he reached the lower level. Racing through the kitchen, he dived through the doggie door.

Chapter 48

By the time Cameron and Gabe reached the house, Deputy Gail Sawyer's police cruiser, lights ablaze, was parked in front, and Kaitlyn was holding Becca tightly in her arms in the kitchen.

Gabe rushed to Kaitlyn, and Cameron pulled Becca into his arms and planted kisses on her little face. "Are you okay, sweetie?" The little girl tightened her arms around his neck and lay her head on his shoulder. A pang of guilt shot through him. He should have been here to protect her. He'd let Becca down.

Gail leaned against the kitchen counter, a small notepad in her hand. "It seems the Chase family had a visitor tonight."

Cameron glanced at Kaitlyn and Gabe, then focused on Gail. "We have a security system. How is it possible that someone got into the house without the alarm going off?"

"It's my guess he used the doggie door."

Incredulous, Cameron glanced at Gabe. "Isn't that wired too?"

Gabe shook his head with an apologetic shrug. "Sorry, Cam. We didn't think a door that small would be an issue."

"Obviously, it *wasn't* an issue for the bastard who broke in. Please call the security company tomorrow to wire the doggie door, Cameron turned to Kaitlyn. "Is anything missing?"

Kaitlyn pulled her Glock out of her robe pocket and carefully placed it in a cabinet. "No, Cam, nothing is missing. He wasn't here to steal; he was here to kidnap Becca. I found him standing over her crib."

Fear and anger playing out on his face, Cameron held Becca closer and said, "Tell me what happened."

Kaitlyn returned to the kitchen table and dropped down in the chair next to Gabe. "I was getting out of bed to come downstairs for some chamomile tea. I always check on Becca when I wake up at night. That's when I saw the man leaning over her crib. I hit him with the flashlight and he went down. But not for long. He pushed me and made it into the hallway. I followed him, but made a stop in our bedroom for my Glock. By the time I reached the top of the stairs, he was close to the bottom. I shouted for him to stop but he just ran faster. When I reached the kitchen, he was gone. He had to have used Godiva's doggie door. It's is the only escape route he had that wouldn't trigger the alarm."

Gabe sat down at the table. "Did you get a good look at him?"

"Not the best. It was dark. But I think it was the same man who tried to abduct Becca from GoodBuys. He wore a stocking hat tonight, so I couldn't get a good look at his hair, but he had dark facial features and the same short body as the man in GoodBuys. I'm convinced it was the same person."

Gail looked up from her notes. "Think it's time for Kaitlyn to meet our sketch artist, Sergeant?"

"Yes, and I want the crime scene techs here to dust for fingerprints."

Kaitlyn interrupted. "Cam, he was wearing latex gloves."

"Great. Just great."

"I'll have them dust just in case he didn't have them on the entire time he spent in the house," said Gail.

"Wait a minute," said Gabe to Cameron. "How did he know you and I wouldn't be here tonight? How did he know that Godiva wouldn't be here?"

"Obviously he's been watching the house."

"Exactly. Once we get that sketch, I'll run it by the construction foreman. Our guy may be working on his crew, and has had a bird's eye view of the main house and the Honeymoon Cottage."

Cameron, with his small child still in his arms, leaned against a wall and breathed deep. "No one is saying it out loud, but we're all thinking it."

Kaitlyn folded her restless hands on the table. "Thinking what?"

"Juan Ortiz knows Becca is here, and he's sending his men to get her."

Chapter 49

Cameron took one look at the menu at the new Java Lava coffee shop and ordered a large coffee with three shots of expresso. That's when he heard a voice behind him.

"Rough night?"

He turned to find Robynn Burton behind him in line. "That's a fair assessment. What are you doing here at seven in the morning?"

"Looking for you, Sgt. Chase."

Cameron paid for his coffee and pulled the warm cup off the counter. He stood aside and waited for Robynn to get her order. Searching the place for an empty table, he saw a couple of millennials sipping coffee behind their open laptops, and an elderly couple sitting near the window sharing a blueberry scone. The new coffee shop was brimming with early risers, like him, who needed some high octane to start their day. He waved to Bryan Pittman, who was leaning back in a cozy reading chair with his newspaper in the corner. There was no empty bistro table to be found.

Robynn paid for her coffee, blew on her steaming brew, and groaned with pleasure after taking her first sip. A creamy foam coated her lips, tempting Cameron to lick it from her mouth. Resisting the temptation, he handed her a paper napkin instead.

"Follow me." She led him out the door to an empty park bench that faced the courthouse. Sitting down, she patted the place next to her and Cameron settled in.

"So why are you here, Robynn?"

"I told you. I was looking for you." Pausing for second, she added. "I heard about your break-in."

"News travels fast."

"Like lightning speed on the cop grapevine, especially when something like that happens to one of our own."

"And of course I wasn't there when it happened." A mixture of bitterness and guilt lined the tone of his voice, whether he wanted it to or not.

"So it's your fault someone decided to burglarize your house?"

"It's my job to make sure my family is safe—especially Becca. I'm all she has."

"Wouldn't it be great if we could build a protective shield to surround the people we love? Great, but not realistic. You're only human, Cam. You can't be there to protect Becca 24/7. I learned that lesson the hard way when I almost lost my daughter, Ellie."

"What do you mean you almost lost Ellie?" Cameron stared at her, clearly surprised that Robynn's daughter had been in a life-or-death situation, and he didn't know about it. He was even more surprised she was opening up a private part of her life to him. This was the woman who claimed she wanted things to be all-business between them.

"It was last year. I had a sitter named Angela, who usually came to my house to care for Ellie. But on this day, Ellie was playing in Angela's yard with a ball. On the front porch, Angela's cell phone rang and she raced to get the call. It was a college admissions clerk who needed more information about her application. She didn't see that Ellie's ball had rolled into the street. Nor did she see the blue Camaro racing toward Ellie. The screech of the car's brakes drew Angela's attention to the street, but it was too late. Ellie lay unconscious near an easement in the road. The driver didn't stop, instead he gunned the car and sped away."

"I'm so sorry this happened. How badly was Ellie hurt?"

Robynn glanced at him with despair, her eyes darkened with pain. It was as if she were re-living the memory. He fought the impulse to pull her into his arms to soothe her.

"The car didn't hit Ellie head-on. The force of the impact

threw her little body off to the side of the road. When I arrived at the hospital, the doctor said she had suffered a broken arm and had a concussion. As I sat next to my little girl's hospital bed, all I could think about was how I'd failed her. I was her mother. I should have been there. Instead, at the same time Ellie was hit, I was involved in a high-speed chase with a hit-and-run driver who'd struck an elderly pedestrian and fled the scene. I put that man in a jail cell. The driver who hit my own child, I never found."

Cameron reached out and caught her hand in his, grateful she didn't try to pull away. Instead, she wrapped her fingers around his thumb.

"So I know how you feel about protecting Becca. That's why I came here this morning looking for you. I knew you would blame yourself for the break-in."

"Does it get better? Do you ever stop blaming yourself for not being there?"

"Yes, it does, and I have. When I moved to my house outside Morel, my foster parents, Eddie and Barb, purchased a home down the street. When I'm working, Ellie stays with them. She's very happy with the arrangement, and why wouldn't she be? She's their only grandchild and is getting all the love and attention she needs while I'm away. Eddie and Barb would give their lives for her, and they support my work. They want me to put away the bad guys to make the world we live in a little safer."

Bryan Pittman strode out of the coffee shop and leaned against an elm tree across from them. Robynn withdrew her hand from Cameron's grasp. "I heard there was a burglary at the Chase house."

Cameron glanced at Robynn, who had a grin tugging at the corner of her mouth. To Bryan, he said, "For pity sake, is the whole town abuzz with the news? How much do you know?"

"A pint-sized idiot got in through your dog door. I mean, who tries to rob a house where two officers live? Not to mention, Kaitlyn the amateur ninja lives there, her purse filled with a self-defense arsenal. Plus a former FBI agent and county sheriff live next door. Who would be stupid enough to target your house?"

"Not stupid—desperate and determined. He was there to

abduct Becca. This was his second attempt. Kaitlyn found him in her room, standing over her crib."

"How would he know Becca was there?"

"Melanie Barrett, Becca's social worker. She's only person outside my family who knew where Becca was living. Juan Ortiz tortured Melanie for the location before he murdered her. I'm sure of it."

"I agree she was tortured, but I couldn't find any trace evidence on her body. No defensive wounds or DNA under her fingernails. Have you found anything concrete to prove he was the one who killed her? Any witnesses?" Bryan asked.

"No." Robynn interjected.

"Just my gut. And it hasn't failed me yet," Cameron said with quiet emphasis.

"So you're thinking the guy who broke into your house works for Juan Ortiz?"

"Yes. Gabe and I think he's been watching the house for a while because he knew when Kaitlyn and Becca were alone."

"Is Becca okay?"

"For now. But if I'm going to keep her protected, I've got to move her into a safe house."

"You're not thinking of moving her into that safe house on Elm Street, are you? So many people know about that place, you may as well put a neon sign out front."

"What choice do I have?"

Bryan gave it some thought. "Remember that house on Shadow Lake my mother left me in her will? All the renovations are finished, and it's a good place to hide Becca. It's surrounded by woods, and no neighbors for close to a mile."

"Who knows you own that house?"

"No one but you. And it can't be tracked to me in public records because it's still in Mom's maiden name. Becca will be safe there. Promise." Bryan dug in his pocket for his key ring and peeled off a house key, which he handed to Cameron.

"I can't thank you enough, Bryan."

"Who's going to take care of Becca while she's there?"

"Gabe and Kaitlyn, along with Brody, Carly, and me. We're going to take shifts."

"Count me in for a shift," Robynn said.

Cameron shot her a curious glance, and then continued. "There will be one or more adults with her at all times."

A ding from his cell alerted Cameron to a text message. "Just got a text from Gabe. He's waiting for me in my office, and he says it's urgent he talk to me."

Chapter 50

When Cameron and Robynn reached his office, he found Gabe pacing in front of his window.

"What's so urgent?"

Gabe spun around to face his brother, worry darkening the color of his expression. He held out a USB flash drive in his hand and sat down behind Cameron's desk. "A woman who works security at Sycamore Mall sent this surveillance recording to me this morning. It's from Saturday night after the mall closed. You need to see it."

With Cameron and Robynn at the back of his chair, Gabe plugged in the USB. Soon a grainy image of the mall's parking area came into view. A light-colored SUV approached and then parked in front of the mall exit. A man got out of the driver side of the car, zipping up a dark hoodie that shadowed his face. Opening the rear door, he angled his body toward the east end of the parking area and took a bow.

"Who is this guy?" Cameron wanted to know.

Robynn pointed at the computer screen. "Can we freeze and enlarge this shot to get a better look at his face?"

Gabe adjusted the image. "Sorry, this is as good as it gets for this section. Just keep watching. There's more."

Two young women came into view and Cameron's heart sank. "That's Hailey Adams. That's her friend, Niki, with her."

He watched as the two girls slid across the back seat and the man closed the car door. With the hoodie still covering his face, he opened the driver-side door and climbed inside. Soon the SUV moved out of the camera's viewpoint.

"Gabe, do you have a shot from another camera so we can see where the car headed?"

"Yes." Gabe clicked a couple of keys and the rear of the car appeared as it raced out of the parking lot. He froze the image to get a better look at the license plate, but the image was too grainy to make out the numbers.

Cameron pounded his fist on the desk. Anger narrowed his eyes, stiffened his jaw. "That sonofabitch knew we couldn't identify him with that hoodie covering his face. Damn it. Can we not catch a break?"

"Not so fast, Cam. Here's a section of the recording from earlier that evening. There's our guy wearing a navy shirt and gray pants. He's handing out some type of flyer on the main floor." He used the mouse to move to another camera. "Here he is approaching Hailey and Niki in the food court."

"I'd like to know what's on the flyers he's showing the girls," said Robynn.

"So would I," Cameron replied. "Both girls look very interested in whatever he's talking about."

"This could be the same perp who abducted Lea Essick and Brandy Murphy at the mall."

"I agree," said Robynn. "They both disappeared from Sycamore Mall and Brandy was last seen leaving with a man wearing a hoodie in a newer model vehicle."

"Gabe, please get me the best quality image of this bastard's face, as well as a clear shot of the vehicle—make and model. I need it for a BOLO. I also want you to email it to Carly. Maybe one of her buddies in the FBI can run it through their facial recognition system. We need to find this guy and those two girls before it's too late." Cameron touched Robynn's arm and then rushed to his office door.

"Where are you going?" asked Robynn.

"You and I need to talk to Hailey's mother."

Chapter 51

Cameron and Robynn stepped onto Mollie Adams' front porch. He hesitated before knocking on her door. The last thing he thought he'd ever do was tell Mollie that her sixteen-year-old, who used to call him Uncle Cam, had most likely been abducted. He couldn't imagine why Mollie herself had not reported her daughter missing by now.

Robynn touched his arm. "How do you want to play this? You knew Hailey, so it's personal for you. Let me take care of the difficult questions."

Cameron nodded and pounded on the front door. He waited a couple of seconds. When there was no answer, he knocked on the door again. Finally, Mollie answered the door, tightening the belt of her robe, looking sleepy and disheveled. She seemed surprised to see him.

"Cameron? What's wrong? It's barely eight in the morning, you're going to wake up the whole neighborhood."

"Mollie, may we come in to talk to you?"

Mollie's glance swung to Robynn. "Who are you?" When Robynn introduced herself and held out her badge, Mollie's face froze in fear as she opened the door for them. "What's happened?"

She led them to a small living room, where Cameron and Robynn sat on a sofa, with Mollie nearby in an easy chair. There was a school photo of Hailey on the lamp table next to her. Cameron swallowed past the knot of emotion lodged in his throat. "We're here about Hailey."

Mollie paled, her hand pressed against her chest. "Has there been an accident?"

"No, Mollie, but we have reason to believe that Hailey may have been abducted from the mall Saturday night."

"That's not possible," Mollie insisted, denial ringing through her voice. "Hailey stayed the weekend with her friend, Niki Smith. You must understand, Hailey just got her driver's license. She's not allowed to drive to the mall. She's staying at Niki's house. Let me call her mother." Before she could get out of her chair, Cameron's hard hand gripped her wrist.

"Niki is missing, too. A deputy is at Niki's house right now."

"Oh, my God," Mollie cried. Realization that her daughter may be in danger sunk in. She paled and had difficulty breathing. "How do you know she's missing?"

Robynn interjected, "We have a surveillance recording from the mall. Hailey and Niki are seen getting into a light-colored SUV. We'd like to show you the tape to see if you can identify the man they're with." Robynn pulled out her cell, and pushed play on the recording. She then handed the phone to Mollie.

Eyes wide and horrified, Mollie watched the surveillance recording of the two girls joining a man and then entering an SUV. "Oh, no. Why would Hailey do something like this?"

Robynn fast-forwarded to a better shot of the man's face. "Do you know this man?"

"No, I've never seen him before. Where has he taken my daughter?" Mollie gulped hard, hot tears slipping down her cheeks.

Cameron placed his hand on Mollie's arm to comfort her. As he did, he heard the creak of a door opening in the back of the house, footfalls sounding in the hallway, and Bryan Pittman appeared in the room, barefoot, wearing sweatpants and buttoning his shirt. Hadn't he just seen him in the coffee shop?

Cameron stood up, and was momentarily speechless in his surprise to see one of his best friends half-dressed in his old flame's house. For a second, both men froze, too surprised to do more than nod.

One look at Mollie's face and Bryan rushed to her side, easing down into a squat beside her. "Mollie, what's wrong?"

"It's Hailey." Her shoulders slumped, tears blinded her eyes and choked her voice as Bryan wrapped his arms around her.

"I'll get you a glass of water, Mollie," Robynn said as she left the room searching for the kitchen.

Cameron dropped down to the sofa with his elbows propped on his knees, feeling more than a bit awkward as Bryan consoled Mollie. What he had with Mollie ended a long time ago, and it was none of his business who she dated. But he was confused as to why Bryan hadn't told him he was involved with Mollie.

Robynn returned and handed Mollie a bottle of cold water she found in the refrigerator. "Mollie, we need to move quickly to find Hailey. She's already been missing over seventy-two hours." She pointed to the framed photograph of Hailey on the end table. "Is that a recent photo of Hailey? May I borrow it?"

Mollie nodded and handed the photo to Robynn.

"Does Hailey have a cell phone? Is it here, or with Hailey?"

"I'm sure it's with my daughter. She never goes anywhere without it."

"I'll need the number so we can get a warrant. We need her call history, cell tower history, latitude and longitude of where the phone was when it was used." Robynn handed Mollie her small notepad and Mollie provided the number.

"What is the make, model, and year of the car Hailey was driving?"

"I bought her a blue, 2014 Honda Civic when she turned sixteen. I have the license plate number in my desk."

"Thanks," Robynn said. "We'll also need her date of birth and the account numbers of any credit or bank cards."

"Of course. I'll help any way I can. You have to find my girl," she pleaded. "I don't know what I'll do if anything happens to her."

Though he didn't answer, Cameron's expression spoke for him. There was nothing he wouldn't do to bring Hailey home safely. Nothing.

"There are some things that you can do, Mollie," said Robynn. "Call and email everyone you know and tell them Hailey is missing. Create missing flyers with her photo and get them posted in the windows of all the local businesses, and use social media to get help finding Hailey. Keep your cell with you at all times, in case Hailey tries to reach you."

"Thank you. I'll get started right away."

"On our end," Cameron interjected. "We're issuing a BOLO so that deputies can be on the lookout for the SUV, and for Hailey's car. We'll find out if this case meets the criteria for an Amber Alert. I believe it does."

Robynn and Cameron were heading toward their car when Bryan pulled Cameron aside.

"Are you thinking that the guy who kidnapped Hailey is the same one who abducted Lea Essick and Brandy Murphy?"

"I can't be sure of that."

"Bullshit. It's the same M.O. Both girls were abducted from Sycamore Mall. Brandy Murphy had been missing six months when her body was found, and I performed her autopsy."

"And Lea is still missing. There's a good chance she's still alive. Same goes for Hailey and Niki. It's too early to play these kinds of guessing games." Bryan looked so disconsolate that Cameron felt he had to give him some hope, even if it was just a sliver.

"Hailey may not have much time. You have to find her."

"Doing my best."

"I'm sorry I didn't tell you about Mollie and me," Bryan began.

"Not my business. Mollie and I were over a long time ago."

"I love her, Cam. I want to marry her and adopt Hailey."

"That's serious."

"I've never been more serious of anything. I want to build a life with them. Hailey has to come home, Cam. She has to."

Chapter 52

Three in the morning was Sgt. Cameron Chase's favorite time for serving a warrant or arresting a subject. Most people were asleep in bed at that hour. Great time for a surprise visit. Unpleasant surprise, but a surprise just the same. It served law enforcement well, and undoubtedly saved many lives. He was banking on the early hour to help them successfully hide his little girl from a maniac.

Standing outside, Cameron could see Kaitlyn with Becca inside the house through a window. Becca was stroking Godiva's soft fur as Kaitlyn tucked her hair into a baseball cap, and dressed her like a little boy. Kaitlyn decided that Godiva would accompany Becca and stay with her in the safe house. Any precaution, no matter how small, would be taken to ensure the safety of his child. What would he do if anything happened to Becca? It was a question he didn't even want to consider.

With high-beam flashlights, deputies searched the construction site and the dark wooded areas surrounding the house, their squad cars lining the entry roads on both sides of the property.

The Chase property was blazing with lights, the glittering rotating beacons on top of county deputy cars, and beams from the sheriff's helicopter looming overhead. Gabe piloted the copter and was using heat-seeking technology. With the thermal imager, his brother had the ability to see a suspect's body heat, which made it very difficult for a suspect to conceal his position, whether he was hiding inside a structure or outdoors. The circumstances surrounding the break-in convinced them that the perp was watching the house. If they got lucky, they'd find him before he could harm Becca. They were taking no chances.

Four cars were parked in the driveway. The plan was to load three of the cars with toddler-sized dolls, wrapped in blankets, each with an amazing resemblance to Becca. The fourth car would carry Becca to her safe place. Only immediate family members knew which car would contain a small child who had just begun referring to Cameron as 'Daddy.'

Cameron had accepted offers from both Bryan Pittman and Prosecutor Michael Brandt to use their lake houses as places to hide Becca. Michael and Anne Brandt owned a beautiful A-frame home across the lake from Bryan. With one of her armed family members, Becca would alternate living between the two homes, making her location that much more difficult to find. Gabe had called to report he'd already flown over the two lake homes twice and discovered no activity around either house, other than Bryan's van parked in his driveway. He was stocking the refrigerator with food and was waiting for them.

Cameron's cell sounded with a text from Robynn. It was time to move. He sent a text to all the deputies working the property to alert them. After a moment, Brody emerged from the house carrying one of the toddler-sized dolls. He opened the back door of his vehicle and strapped it in a baby car seat. Cameron was amazed at how well his older brother cared for the "baby". He guessed that caring for two younger brothers gave him some good experience. Brody slipped into the driver seat and drove off the property heading for Tippecanoe County, far from the safe houses. A deputy fell in line behind him.

Next Kaitlyn appeared dragging a small suitcase and holding a doll in her arms, and like Brody, strapped the doll into the back seat. Her destination was a friend's house in Lebanon where she would spend the day. A deputy would watch the home to see if she'd been followed. Smiling at Cameron, she waved as she started her descent to the highway.

Once Kaitlyn's car disappeared, Carly came out of the house holding a doll and carrying a diaper bag. Once she had the doll

Profile of Fear

situated in the back seat and had left the property, Cameron went inside the house.

What he saw first made quick tears come to his eyes. Robynn, looking gentle, serene, and beautiful, sat in the family rocking chair holding Becca, who was peacefully asleep on her shoulder. It was a vision of which he had dreamed. The woman he loved holding his child. Cameron was in love with Robynn. It was high time he admitted it to himself. He'd loved her since the first moment he looked into her hunter-green eyes. A man could get lost in those eyes. He had.

"Children absorb the stress around them," Robynn began. "I think all the activity tonight tuckered this little sweetheart out."

Cameron crossed the room to Robynn and lightly kissed her on the forehead. "I can't tell you how much I appreciate your helping with this." Kneeling down beside the chair, he softly placed his hand on her arm.

"If it were Ellie in this situation, I have no doubt you'd do the same for me. My little girl is sleeping peacefully in her room at her grandparent's home. This darling child needs to be in her safe house, tucked in her crib, fast asleep. And I want to be there to help you keep her safe. I'm ready to leave when you are." Robynn wrapped a soft blue blanket around the little girl and handed her to Cameron. Together they made their way to the car.

Chapter 53

Carlos was eating breakfast when Juan Ortiz burst through the back door and slammed a newspaper on the table, sloshing hot coffee all over him.

"What the hell?" Carlos leaped to his feet and grabbed a kitchen towel to blot the hot liquid from his shirt and chest.

Glaring at him, Juan barked, "Look at the front page. We've got trouble."

Carlos smoothed out the front page of the newspaper. A photo of the two young girls he held captive in the basement was under the headline: 'Two More Missing Girls.' He looked up at Ortiz, who hovered over him with his hands on his hips. "Okay, it's not the best thing that could happen, but I can handle it."

"You're a moron. You couldn't stick to runaways or new releases from the women's prison, you had to focus on young women who would be missed. Stupid. Stupid. Stupid. Now you've got every cop in the state looking for these two girls. Everything we've built is at risk because of you. I should slit your throat and watch you bleed out on the floor right now."

"I said I'd handle it."

"You'll handle it all right. You'll kill both of them and leave their bodies where they won't soon be found. If you draw any suspicion to our businesses, I will personally end your pitiful life. Do you understand?"

"Perfectly."

The minute Juan Ortiz left, Carlos headed for the stairs to the basement. Lying barely conscious on old mattresses with their legs handcuffed to the floor were Hailey Adams and Niki Smith. They were still sleeping off the latest dose of Rohypnol. It would be hours before they were conscious again.

He shook his head with disappointment. He'd had plans for both girls. Once she was broken in, Niki would be answering ads for escorts that he'd place on Backpage. Hailey was another matter. Carlos had thoughts of keeping Hailey for himself. He didn't know if it was her close resemblance to his ex, Britta, or her natural wholesomeness, but he'd never met anyone like her. He experienced a protectiveness, foreign to him, about the girl with the long auburn hair and beautiful face. He wanted her for himself, sharing her with no one. He wouldn't let drugs destroy her as they had Britta.

But things had changed. Ortiz wanted them dead.

Chapter 54

Robynn sat next to Cameron in the sheriff's conference room, both working on their laptops. "No activity on Hailey's credit cards after a couple of small purchases at the mall on Saturday before closing time. Same for Niki."

Cameron nodded with disappointment as if the information was what he expected. "Just got the girls' cell phone history, as well as the cell tower report. The last ping from both of their phones was to a cell tower near the Brownsburg Exit on I-74. It looks like one of them or their abductor turned off their cells at that point. They were heading toward Indianapolis."

"I'll issue a BOLO to our troopers in Marion County with our girls' photos."

Cameron's cell phone sounded, the display indicated the call was from Carly. "Hey, Carly. Are you and Brody still in Florida?"

"Yes, we're working on the damage the vandals did to my house down here. Brody and I are so sorry to hear about Hailey. But I have news on that surveillance image that Gabe emailed me."

"Good news, I hope."

"I think so. A friend at the Bureau ran it through facial recognition software and got a hit. He's a low-level criminal named Carlos Rodriguez. He's served time for meth possession and battery. He also had a prior for promoting prostitution. He was caught selling girls at a truck stop off the I-74 exit in Crawfordsville. Did six months and paid a fine."

"Nice guy."

"Oh, it gets better. He's a known associate of Juan Ortiz. My intelligence is that he runs a con to recruit young girls for Juan's escort services."

Cameron shook his head with genuine concern. "That's what he was doing at the mall. I'd bet anything that the pink flyer he was showing the girls was part of his con to abduct them."

"I think you're right, which makes it even more important that we move fast to find them. Get Mr. Rodriguez's photo to the media. When we find him, we find Hailey and Niki."

Chapter 55

Hailey had been awake for at least an hour, but the room spun each time she moved her head. Her mind was fuzzy, and her attempts to move were met with an overpowering weakness in her limbs. Something metallic rubbed against her ankle and trapped her left leg in place. Panic seized her brain like a vise. Where was she?

The only light in the room flickered through a small dirty window from a street light outside. The clammy chill of the air made her shiver. A moldy mustiness in the air turned her stomach. The odor was familiar. The last time she'd smelled it was when she'd helped her mom clean her grandmother's basement. But this was not her grandmother's basement.

Pinching her eyelids shut, she struggled to remember how she got to this dark place. She and Niki were at the mall. They were talking with a man who promised them modeling jobs. So exciting. The girls were giggling. They could earn enough money to buy splashy cars, gorgeous clothes, and new houses. They'd fly to exciting new places, far away from their boring hometown. All they had to do…

Her mind flashed ahead. She and Niki were entering the back seat of a new SUV. The man named Carlos, who promised them modeling jobs, was in the driver's seat, and offered them cold bottles of water. They were both so thirsty. As if hitting a wall, the memories stopped. Where was she?

Profile of Fear

Hailey heard faint breathing next to her. She turned her head, waited for the room to stop spinning, and then focused on the person beside her. Niki! Hailey tried to call her name, but the words came out slurred. Willing her arm to move, she touched Niki's hand and tried to speak to her again. But Niki didn't budge.

The floor creaked with footsteps from the floor above. Soon a door opened and footfalls sounded on the wooden steps. Someone was coming. Angling her head toward the sound, Hailey saw a blurry shadow of a man, but had difficulty focusing. The room was still spinning as the man moved closer to the girls. Hailey bit off the urge to scream. Her arms and legs still too weak to fight, she pretended to sleep. Maybe he would go away if he thought the girls were sleeping.

But he didn't. He moved so close to her, she could feel his body heat. Her heart froze when he bent down to her.

Slowly, he stroked her hair. "My beautiful Britta. Don't be afraid. This will soon be over."

Chapter 56

Carlos waited until 2:00 a.m. to carry Hailey into the garage and slide her body onto the back seat of his car, next to her friend. Niki was slumped over in the seat, unconscious. Her breathing was so shallow, Hailey had to strain to hear it. Hailey was still pretending to be asleep.

"I know you're awake, Hailey. Cut the act." Carlos slammed the back door, rounded the car, and got into the driver's seat, placing a duffle bag and his handgun in the console. Pressing a button clipped onto the visor, he opened the garage door and backed into the empty street.

"Where are you taking us?" Hailey's tear-smothered voice whispered behind him. A chill ran up her spine. He was going to kill them both. She was sure of it. They could identify him. It was too dangerous for him to let them live. "You're going to kill us, aren't you? We've seen your face."

"Think that worries me? Before this day is done, I'll be so far away, it won't matter who knows my face. Money has a way of erasing memories. Money will enable me to start a new life. Don't worry. This will be over soon, Britta."

"Who is Britta? Why are you calling me that?"

Carlos glanced at her through the rear-view mirror. "You look so much like someone I used to know. Britta was sixteen, beautiful, and full of life, just like you."

"What happened to her?" Asking the question, she feared the answer.

"Britta was a runaway when she met me. I told her I was in love with her, but I wasn't. But she loved me and would do anything I asked her to do, even things that hurt her—things that put her life in jeopardy."

"What do you mean?"

Through the mirror, he shot her a glare. "Aren't you listening, or are you that clueless?"

Hailey stiffened with shock by his sudden change in mood. She must keep him calm to buy time until she could think of a way out. "I'm sorry…"

"I made her a whore. I sold her on Craigslist and Backpage as an escort. I ordered her to do whatever her buyers wanted her to do, and hand over the money they paid her to me. I told her it was for our future. I would have said anything to get her to do what I wanted." His words were laced with guilt, but his tone suggested Britta's fate was her own fault.

Fear knotted inside Hailey as she realized that was what he had planned for Niki and her. There were no modeling jobs. He'd sell their bodies online to strangers, over and over again, as they endured a living nightmare. Money was what mattered to this man. Not their lives.

Where was he taking them? Had he already sold them online and was delivering them to buyers? Panic like she'd never known before welled in her throat as the houses they passed became sparse, as he drove out-of-town. But what town? Where were they? Hailey glanced at the door handle and back at the speedometer. He was driving sixty-miles-per-hour. What were her chances if she jumped out of the car? And how could she leave Niki behind?

Carlos began talking again in such a way that Hailey questioned if he were talking to her, or to himself. "It was Britta and me against the world. Then Juan Ortiz came back to the states from Mexico and took over my territory. The sick sonofabitch had all my girls, including Britta, marked with his tattoo. Property of Juan Ortiz. I'll never forget the look of betrayal on Britta's face when she lifted her skirt to reveal Ortiz's tattoo. She knew I'd lied about building a future with her, and realized she was no more important to me that any of the other girls. I'd lost her to Ortiz, and then later to meth."

Carlos slowed the SUV and turned onto a desolate gravel road that coiled within a thicket of trees. It was so dark, the only glimmer of light was from the car's dashboard. He stopped the vehicle and removed his handgun from the console. Sheer black fright swept through Hailey as Carlos opened the back door and pulled Niki from the car. She eyed the door handle, her heart pounding painfully hard. Niki was unconscious and helpless. How could she leave her with Carlos? Unable to evade, she went still as a cornered animal.

Carlos opened her door, and brandished the gun before her, aiming it at her chest. "Get out." He led her to a ditch at the road's edge. Horrified, she saw Niki curled up in a fetal position below and couldn't tell if she was dead or alive.

"Get on your knees. Face away from me." Carlos commanded.

Goose flesh rippling up her back, Hailey bent down and thought of her mother. If only she could get lost in one of her mom's hugs one more time.

A white bolt of agonizing pain shot through her brain as she slid to the hard ground, and the world turned black.

Chapter 57

His ringtone sounded and Cameron yanked his cell out of his pocket, hoping for word about Hailey. The more time that went by, the less likely they were to find her alive. He had to find her.

"Hey. This is Deputy Sawyer."

Cameron turned on the cell's speaker so that Robynn could hear. "What's going on, Gail? Are you at Carlos Rodriguez's place?"

"Yes, sir, and it's quite a mess."

"Are we talking house cleaning issues?"

"No, the place was ransacked."

"Seriously?"

"Serious as a heart attack. Looks like a tornado hit. Drawers tossed, cabinet doors open, the whole nine yards. If I were a betting woman, I'd put my money on someone other than us is looking for Mr. Carlos Rodriguez."

"Did you call dispatch to send the crime scene technicians? There's a chance we could get fingerprints or DNA from his apartment that could lead us to Hailey and Niki. We also might find evidence that will lead us to the perp that tossed his place."

"Already called. They're here now."

"Good job. Any signs Rodriguez might return?"

"Doubt it. His closet is empty and there are no suitcases to be found. Just heard one of our state troopers found his car at the Indianapolis International Airport. We're calling the airline. I'll let you know if we get a hit on his flight."

Disconnecting the call, he turned to Robynn. "Any theories on who might want to toss his apartment?"

"I think someone is looking for something of value. It could be a damning piece of evidence that connects him to a crime, or it could be money. We know that Carlos is working for Juan Ortiz. It's not a stretch to think he could be skimming money off of Juan's profits. In addition, he knows too much."

"Which would put Carlos in a world of trouble."

"If I was Carlos and I had stolen money from Juan Ortiz, I'd get out of the country."

Cameron shook his head in disappointment. "Which means we lose our most important lead to the girls."

Chapter 58

There was an explosion, as if a bomb had detonated, hurling Hailey into consciousness. Teeth chattering, she was chilled to the bone, and pain exploded at the base of her skull. Water soaked her clothing, and an instant chill flooded her skin with shivers. Her eyelids heavy, she tried to open her eyes. A blast of wind whipped her hair, stinging her face as rain pelted her body. She blinked as water ran into her eyes, blurring her vision, thunder vibrating in the distance. It was dark, the moon and stars blotted out by thick storm clouds. Her heart raced, nearly bursting out of her chest.

Where was she?

Easing her body into a sitting position, she looked around and discovered she was not alone. Niki was lying next to her, curled in a fetal position, looking pale and lifeless. Oh, please, God. She can't be dead. Leaning closer to Niki, Hailey could hear her taking slow, shallow breaths.

"Niki, wake up. We can't stay here. It's storming, and we're not safe out in the open like this. Please wake up, Carlos could come back any minute to kill both of us. Please, Niki."

Pulling Niki's limp body onto her lap, Hailey shook her friend to wake her, but to no avail. Something was very wrong with Niki.

Why couldn't she remember what happened to them? Hailey's memory ended when she entered the back seat of Carlos's car at the mall. The water! He must have put something in the water. She remembered taking a drink, but was unable to recall what happened after that, until she regained consciousness in the basement of Carlos's house. It was as if she had amnesia.

Carlos had drugged them. Of course he had. What better way to get them to do what he wanted? There was a black hole in her memory, and she shuddered to think of what may have happened to Niki and her during that time.

What she *did* remember was how Carlos had loaded them into his car and had driven them out in the middle of who-knows-where. He'd rolled Niki's body into the ditch as if she were garbage he was tossing. The pain lancing through her head made her nauseous. He'd hit her with his gun, and must have placed her next to Niki in the ditch.

But that was then, this was now. The wind picked up and the ditch was filling with rainwater, inching up to Niki's head. She had to drag Niki to a higher level, before she drowned. Towing Nikki out of the ditch and onto the highway's edge was a daunting task, even though Niki was so small. It seemed every time Hailey got a good grip of her arms, Niki slid out of reach.

Finally they reached the road, and Hailey searched both ways for headlights. She had to get help, and soon. Niki's body was so cold to the touch, and her clothes were dripping wet. Her body started to tremble in jerking movements. Hailey took off her cardigan and wrapped it around Niki's shoulders. She hoped that even as damp as the sweater was, it might still bring some warmth to Niki's body.

Driven by urgency, Hailey had to get help before it was too late. Her cell! Her cell phone was in her purse. She could call 9-1-1. But where was her purse? She searched for her purse in the darkness of the ditch, then hunted along the highway, but couldn't find it. Carlos must have kept it, along with any means of communicating to the outside world.

Where was Carlos? Would he come back to finish the job? She was a witness that he overdosed Niki. Why had he hit her with the gun instead of shooting her? Why hadn't he killed her? It made no sense.

The storm continued to rage overhead, lightning piercing the sky, and trees bending in submission. The angry rain pelted her body.

Profile of Fear

Hailey remembered the times her mom talked to her about the dangers of being out in the open during a storm and being struck by lightning. Fear tightened inside her, and she struggled not to panic. If she was going to save their lives, she had to remain in control, think clearly.

Chapter 59

From his office desk, Lt. Patrick Lair threw a Nerf ball into the basket mounted on his closed door. "Two points."

"You said you had something important for me?" asked Robynn.

"It's more like a gift."

Her eyebrows rose inquiringly. "Gift?"

"One of our troopers, Bob Raines, stopped a car on I-65 for a broken tail light. Trooper Raines asked the driver for his license and registration. When he opened the glove compartment, the trooper noticed a fat roll of money and a small handgun in there. Bob then went back to his patrol car, where he checked our state computer system for outstanding violations, and called for backup.

Once the second patrol car arrived, Trooper Raines asked the driver whether he had any drugs or weapons in the car. The driver said that he did not. The officer then asked for and received the driver's permission to search the car.

During the search, the troopers seized five plastic baggies containing cocaine from a grocery bag of diapers in the trunk. He also seized an unregistered handgun and $1,000 from the glove compartment. The driver was placed under arrest and transported to the station."

"Good arrest, but why would you think this was a gift to me?"

"The driver is Diego Santiago, a known associate of Juan Ortiz. He broke down when he was arrested and told the trooper he couldn't be away from his invalid mother. Says he has info about Ortiz he'd like to bargain with."

Robynn's face split into a wide grin. "When can we get him transferred to Shawnee County to be interviewed?"

Chapter 60

With the road snaking ahead of her and only corn fields on either side, Hailey stopped to rest on the grassy shoulder. Her arms and back ached from dragging Niki, and she didn't know how much farther she could go before she collapsed herself. Niki was still unconscious, and Hailey worried she could die if they didn't get help soon.

She'd never felt so alone in her life; she would have given anything to be in the safety of her mother's arms. If she hadn't lied to her mom, she wouldn't be in this situation. She prayed for a second chance.

Above the horizon rose a blurred and red-blood sun. Soon it would be light. The rows of corn made a snapping sound in the wind, and an earthy smell assailed Hailey's nose.

Hailey spotted a pair of headlights down the road, heading toward her. Moving to the middle of the road, she stood waving her arms, praying that the driver would stop to help and not mow her down. But a warning voice whispered in her head. The car rushing toward her could be driven by Carlos, back to finish what he started. Her pulse began to beat erratically. Her mind was a crazy mix of fear and hope. Should she take Niki and dive into the ditch for cover? It was then that a flashing bar of brilliant lights atop the car pierced the early light.

With a screech of brakes, the vehicle stopped and an Indiana State Trooper cautiously emerged from the car, his hand resting on his gun.

"May I help you?" he called out.

Compulsive sobs shaking her body, Hailey ran to him and threw herself into the trooper's arms.

Chapter 61

Hailey awoke in a hospital bed, bound to an IV running from the back of her hand. In the room was a woman in a white lab coat talking quietly with a tall, handsome, blond-haired man with compelling gray eyes. The doctor was a stranger, but the man looked familiar.

Questions bubbled from her mouth. Her voice nothing more than a broken whisper. "Where am I? Where's Niki? Is she okay?"

The man rushed to her side. "Hailey, welcome back. I can't tell you how many people have been looking for you."

"Where am I?"

"You're in Lafayette at I.U. Health Arnett Hospital. One of our troopers found you and your friend on Harrison Road outside of Battle Ground. He brought you two here. You're dehydrated, but the docs are giving you fluids to make you feel better. You're going to be okay, Hailey. You are one lucky girl."

She didn't feel lucky. She hurt all over and felt stupid for being duped. "Where's Niki?"

The man flashed a glance at the doctor. "Niki is here in the hospital, too."

"Is she alive? Carlos gave us some kind of drug to control us. I think he gave Niki too much."

The doctor moved to the foot of her bed. "I'm Dr. Peterson. Do you have any idea what kind of drug he gave you and Niki?"

"No, but I think he put it in the bottles of water he offered us the first night at the mall. The drug made us very dizzy and sleepy. I can't remember much of anything after getting into the back seat of his car."

"Sounds like Rohypnol. It's a potent sedative that may cause drowsiness, confusion, impaired motor skills, dizziness, disorientation, disinhibition, impaired judgment, and reduced levels of consciousness."

"Can things happen to you when you're on this drug that you can't remember?"

Dr. Peterson hesitated, and then said, "Yes, Hailey. That's why I think we should do a rape kit on you."

Hailey closed her eyes, willing herself not to cry. Oh, God. Had she been raped?

The man squeezed her hand to comfort her. "We'll wait until your mother is here."

"Thank you. All I want is to see my mom."

"Your mom has been notified that you're here, and she's on her way. We'll wait until she's here before we do any testing. She can be with you through the process. Sergeants Chase and Burton will be here soon to talk to you, too."

"Is Niki still unconscious?"

After exchanging worried glances with the man, Dr. Peterson said, "Niki has lapsed into a coma. The next couple of days will be touch and go for her."

Hailey felt tears prick her eyes at the thought of losing Niki. "When can I see her?"

"Let's give her some time, Hailey." Dr. Peterson clutched her notepad and hurried from the room.

The man sat in the chair next to her bed. Hailey recognized him. Why couldn't she remember his name? He looked to be around six-feet-two-inches tall with a lean, muscular body, and had a layer of short-cropped hair the color of wheat. She sensed a sadness about him. He was smiling at her, but it was as if smiling didn't come naturally to him.

"Who are you?"

He pulled out his badge and handed it to her. "I apologize. I should have introduced myself before. I'm Detective Justin Andrews with the Indiana State Police. My team has been looking for you since you went missing. The trooper who found you let me know you were here."

"I think I know you."

Justin nodded and softly patted her hand. "You and your mom attended the First Baptist Church outside Morel at the same time I did. In fact, my fiancé, Destiny Cooke, was once your Sunday School Teacher."

"You're Justin Andrews, and I remember Destiny. I am so sorry about what happened to her."

"She was in the wrong place at the wrong time; her life cut short by Evan and Devan Lucas. I still miss her. But let's get back to you."

Hailey nodded. She couldn't imagine losing someone she loved, like her mom. There was nothing more that she wanted than to get lost in one of her mom's hugs. She was being given a second chance to be a better daughter, the kind her mom deserved.

Just then Cameron and Robynn burst into the room, and Cameron rushed to her bedside, gathered her in his arms, and patted her back like he did when she was small.

"Uncle Cam. I'm so glad to see you."

"Not as much as I am to see you alive and well." Cameron indicated the woman standing next to him. "Hailey, this is Sgt. Robynn Burton with the Indiana State Police." It was the way Uncle Cam looked at the woman that let Hailey know they were more than just co-workers.

Justin said his good-byes and left the room. Robynn and Cameron sat in chairs next to Hailey's bed.

Robynn smiled and said, "It's so good to meet you, Hailey. Sgt. Chase has told me so many good things about you. If you feel up to it, we have some questions we'd like to ask you. Your mother has given us permission to talk to you. We need your help to find the man who did this."

Cameron had a file folder in his hand, from which he pulled out a couple of photographs. He handed one of them to Hailey. "Does this man look familiar to you?"

Hailey's eyes went wide with shock. "That's Carlos! He told Niki and me that we could be models. He said he was taking us to a model call-out for jobs."

Profile of Fear

"Do you remember where he took you?"

"No. There is a black hole in my memory. I remember talking with him at the mall and getting into the back seat of his car with Niki. He told us there were cold bottles of water in the back seat. That's the last I remember until I woke up."

"When you woke up, were you in a house or an apartment?" Robynn wanted to know.

"A house. We were held in a basement with our ankles handcuffed to the floor. Do you think you could find the house? There could be other girls held there."

"That's not much to go on, but we'll try," said Robynn. "Do you remember what happened to you while you were being held in the house?"

"No. I can't remember anything from after I sipped the water Carlos had for us in his car. When I woke up, he loaded Niki and me in his car and then dumped us out in the country. The doctor thinks that Niki and I may have been given Rohypnol."

"If some memories come back to you, please let us know right away."

Referring to the photo still in Hailey's hand, Cameron said, "The man in the photo that you recognized is Carlos Rodriguez. He's a criminal who has served time for meth possession and battery. He also had a prior conviction for promoting prostitution. He's running a con and telling young girls that he's a modeling agent and can get them glamorous, high-paying jobs."

"Make that stupid, gullible young girls. Like Niki and me."

"Hailey, don't be so hard on yourself. He's an experienced con artist, and very good at it." Cameron pulled out another photograph and gave it to Hailey. "Carlos works for *this* man. Does he look familiar to you?"

Hailey examined the picture carefully. "Yes, I think so. I felt very dizzy and disoriented when they took me into the house from the car. But I remember that Carlos was angry with this man for being at the house. This man was sitting at a kitchen island and he yelled at Carlos."

Cameron shot a glance to Robynn and slipped the photograph back into his folder. "The man you identified is Juan Ortiz. He's on the FBI's Most Wanted List and is wanted for questioning in a series of murders in Shawnee County."

Robynn broke in. "Because you can identify him, you may be in danger when he finds out you were found alive. We will place both you and your mother in a safe house until he is captured, for your safety."

Chapter 62

Standing before the interview room's one-way mirror, Cameron watched as Robynn entered the room. She sat across from Diego and he nervously eased back in his chair, his hands folded tightly in his lap. He refused to make eye contact with her. She placed an evidence bag containing three smaller plastic bags of a white powder in the middle of the table.

"I'm Sgt. Burton with the Indiana State Police and these are yours. Three grams of meth found in your trunk and an unregistered handgun in your glove box. We're talking about some serious charges, Diego. Class C felony for the drugs alone."

Cameron entered the small room, purposely slamming the door behind him. Diego's body jerked and his face paled. Cameron pulled out a chair beside Robynn and sat down across from him.

"Let me introduce myself. I'm Sgt. Cameron Chase, Shawnee County Sheriff. I'm Becca's father."

The color drained from Diego's face as a soft gasp escaped, making Cameron certain the man knew exactly who he was.

Cameron placed the sketch artist rendering of Diego on the table.

"This guy look familiar?"

Impulsively Diego shook his head and looked down at his hands. He was visibly trembling now. This was the reaction Cameron was going for. The more fearful Diego became, the more likely it was that he would tell them what they needed to know.

"C'mon Diego. That's *you* in the sketch." Cameron shot him a take-no-prisoners look and Diego seemed to shrink in his chair. "It was *my* house you broke into when you tried to abduct *my* baby girl. It was also you who tried to take her from GoodBuys. So now we're talking breaking and entering, but most importantly, attempted kidnapping. How many years in prison do you think he could get, Sgt. Burton?"

"Minimum twenty, and up to fifty years. That's a long time."

Diego looked as if he might get sick. "My mama…"

"What about your mama?"

"She's very sick. Stuck in a wheelchair with M.S. Mama depends on me to take care of her."

"You should have thought of that when you were dealing drugs and trying to kidnap innocent little kids." Cameron snapped.

"I can't be in jail. I have to protect my mother from Juan Ortiz."

"Juan Ortiz? Now you've got my interest. Why would a sick woman in a wheelchair need protection from Mr. Ortiz?"

"If he finds out I talked to you, he will kill her like he killed Julio Garcia's sister. Julio betrayed him so he cut his sister's throat, and wrote a message to Julio with her blood on her bedroom wall. Juan knows where my mama lives. He will do the same to her. Please, I love my mama, I'll do anything to protect her."

"Do you have information about Juan Ortiz?"

"Yes."

"Where can we find him?"

"I don't know where Juan lives or spends his time. He travels from house-to-house, staying with his dealers. Sometimes he sleeps in the office at his restaurants. He contacts me from burner phones and then we meet. At times, he just shows up and looks different every time. Juan disguises his appearance so that he is barely recognizable. He has looked different each time I've seen him. Bald, not bald, thin, pudgy, glasses, no glasses, ball cap, fedora. His clothes range from Goodwill to Armani. He's a chameleon, and that's why you haven't caught him."

"How do you know him?"

Diego hesitated for a moment and then said, "I work for him.

He hired me to find Donda Hicks because he found out she had his kid."

"Why is he so interested in Donda and the kid?" Cameron struggled to stay in control, to sound neutral as he asked about Becca. Emotions would work against him.

"He wanted to kill Donda and give the baby to his mother, Juanita, in Mexico."

"Juanita wants a baby?" Cameron nearly shuddered with disgust. Juanita Ortiz had a record as a child abuser. She'd have to get past him to get anywhere near Becca.

"I overheard a conversation Juan had with his mother. She's staying with the Vega Cartel in Mexico. Miguel Vega is Juanita's lover, and he's much younger than she is. He wants children so she wants her grandchild, Juan's baby, to satisfy him."

"What's in it for Juan if he delivers the kid to her?"

"He's in deep trouble with Miguel Vega because he stole $50,000 from him to come to U.S. His mother is the only thing standing between him and Miguel's paid killers. She promised to smooth things over if she gets his kid."

"Interesting information, but how do we know you're telling the truth?"

"There's more. Juan bragged about the murder of three girls in Indy. He said he'd set the house on fire to cover the crime. Slit their throats. Juan said they got what they deserved for disobeying. How would I know something like that unless Juan had given me the details?"

"Very interesting," said Robynn. "But any good defense attorney would get that thrown out of court. It's hearsay. You haven't given us much to go on with either case."

"Melanie Barrett."

A chill inched up Cameron's spine at the mention of Becca's social worker.

"What about Melanie Barrett?"

"Juan knew that she had Becca's location. He had me follow Melanie Barrett for weeks. She had drinks every Friday at the Vineyard Wine Bar on Main Street. Juan met her at the bar and romanced her."

"What do you know about her murder?"

"I know that Juan planned a romantic picnic for Melanie on Sunday, the day she was murdered. When I found out later what had happened to her, I knew Juan had killed her. It was the way he ended her life. All the cuts on her body. Juan's favorite killing tool is his knife." Diego guiltily hung his head. "It's my fault she was killed. I'm the one who found her and gave her up to Juan."

"Will you testify to this in court, Diego?"

"Yes, as long as you keep my mama safe."

Cameron glanced at Robynn. "We'll try our best."

"There's one more thing." Diego began. "I didn't kidnap the little girl because I was too worried about what Juan Ortiz might do to her. I wanted nothing to do with it, but he threatened my mother. He gave me no choice."

"You had a choice. You could have reported this to law enforcement. You had a choice, but you chose the wrong one."

Chapter 63

By the time Mollie entered Hailey's hospital room, her daughter was fast asleep. She dropped down in the chair beside the bed, caressing Hailey's hand while she slept. As tears welled in her eyes, she stared at the child she brought into the world.

Her mind sifted through the memories of every moment she had with her daughter as she was growing up, from the moment she gave birth, to the day she got her learner's permit to drive. Quickly wiping a tear streaming down her cheek, Mollie didn't want Hailey to see she was crying. Hailey would be upset enough, and she didn't want to add to it. Her daughter needed her to be strong so that she would heal and forget the awful things that may have happened to her. In the meantime, she would be at Hailey's side during the rape examination, every step of the way.

Mollie kissed Hailey's slender hand, and when she looked up, her daughter was awake and reaching for her. "Mom, I'm so sorry. This is all my fault."

Mollie sat on the bed, pulling her daughter into her arms and held her close. "It's over, honey. You're safe and that's all that matters."

"Nikki is here."

"I know, honey. The good news is that she woke up and is talking. She has a long road to recovery, but the doctors think she'll be fine."

Hailey sighed with relief.

"All I could think about was getting home and telling you

how much I loved you." Hailey tightened her arms around her mother's neck. "I do love you, Mom. I may not act like it sometimes, but I love you so much."

"I found out how miserable my life would be without you. Looking for you and not being able to find you was torture." Mollie stroked Hailey's hair. "The doctor told me about doing the rape kit. If you want me, I'll be there every step of the way with you."

Sighing with relief, Hailey held her mother's hand. "Thank you, Mom."

"Honey, did the man rape you?"

"Mom, I can't remember what happened. I don't know if Carlos raped me or not."

"The doctor told me that you may have been drugged with Rohypnol."

"I think it was in the water he gave us."

"At any rate, I think the rape examination is a good idea. Dr. Peterson said she'd come get us within the hour."

"I'm scared. Don't leave me." Hailey looked so young and frail.

"I'll be there with you holding your hand. Not going anywhere."

Mollie helped Hailey adjust the head of the bed so she was in a sitting position, and then she straightened the sheets and blanket.

"Does Bryan know that I am here?"

Surprised that Hailey would ask about him, she tilted her head. "He knows. Bryan's been worried sick about you. We made missing posters with your photograph. Bryan wallpapered the town with them. He's waiting outside in the hallway."

"Please ask him to come in. There is something I need to say."

Mollie went into the hallway, nodded at the deputy posted outside Hailey's door, and called for Bryan to join her inside. Once in the room, Bryan's face beamed as he went to Hailey's bedside.

"I can't tell you how good it is to see you."

"Hello, Dr. Pittman."

"Please call me Bryan. Dr. Pittman sounds way too stuffy."

"I want you to know that I want you and Mom to be happy. I know you love each other. It's okay with me. She was lucky to find you."

"Does that mean I can start coming to your band performances?"

Hailey pretended to grimace, then broke out in a big smile. "Yes."

"How about your soccer games? I could be the guy cheering the loudest in the bleachers."

Nodding, Hailey let out a giggle, and Mollie didn't think her heart could take much more. The two people she loved most were laughing together in this room. Maybe they could be a family after all. Perhaps she'd get her happily ever after.

Bryan removed a small box from his suit jacket and handed it to Hailey.

"What is this?" She asked.

"Guess you'll have to open it to find out." Bryan said with a smile.

Peeling the wrapping away revealed a brand-new iPhone. Hailey's jaw dropped open and she stared wide-eyed for two full seconds. "You got me a new cell?"

"I heard you might be needing one."

Chapter 64

Bryan's lake house was a wonderful reprieve from their dark days of searching for Juan Ortiz. It would have been easy for Robynn and Cameron to think they were on vacation instead of providing a safe house for an endangered little girl.

Becca giggled as Godiva barked at a family of ducks that floated lazily near the shoreline. Cameron and Robynn sat at a picnic table, watching hotdogs and hamburgers sizzle on the grill. Across the lake some young kids were playing at the water's edge; a group of older kids in deeper water were swimming and splashing each other. Digging her fingers into an ice chest for a bottle of water, Robynn snagged one and handed it to Cameron, who was smoothing a coat of sunscreen on Becca's little arms.

"That call I took a while ago was Gabe. He talked to Mollie. Hailey wasn't raped by Carlos Rodriguez."

"I'm so relieved."

"There's something else. He found Lea Essick."

"Isn't she one of the girls that disappeared from the mall a month or so ago? Did he find her alive?"

Cameron nodded. "She's alive. He found her during an Internet search on Backpage. There was a photo of her scantily dressed under the heading 'Casual Encounters.' The ad described her as young, with a desire to meet dirty old men."

"How did he know it was really Lea?"

"Her mother identified her. Lea has a birthmark in the shape of a heart on her shoulder. You could see it in the photo."

"How did he get to her?"

"Gabe answered the ad and made a 'date' to meet with her at a Hampton Inn off I-74. At first, Lea wouldn't answer to her real name or answer any of his questions. Her traffickers had shown her a photo of her mother and threatened to kill them both if she ever tried to get away. When he showed her his private investigator ID and told her that her mother had hired him, she broke down."

"That poor girl."

"Gabe said she identified Carlos Rodriguez as the man who abducted her from the mall. She also said that she'd seen Juan Ortiz as recently as two days ago, when he announced to the girls he was taking over Carlos's business."

"Another possible witness for the prosecution."

"Gabe returned Lea to her mother, but he said it was going to be a long road for both of them to heal after that kind of experience."

Robynn gestured with her head to the hot dogs and hamburgers on the grill. "Looks like they're almost done."

Cameron flipped the meats and then headed toward the kitchen inside. "I'll get the potato salad, condiments, and that amazing chocolate cake you made."

"I'll help."

Robynn had opened the refrigerator door when she heard a scream, crying, and then loud barking. Becca!

She ran outside to find that Becca was yelling at Godiva. Each step the little girl took toward the lake, Godiva pushed her down to the ground. They were nearly a foot away from the water.

"Becca!" Robynn screamed as she hurried to the water's edge. Reaching Becca, she lifted the little girl until her feet dangled helplessly above the ground.

Cameron rushed to her side. "What happened?"

Tears flowed hot and humiliating down Robynn's face. "It's my fault. What was I thinking going inside the house when a toddler was this close to water? I am so sorry."

Cameron arms encircled them both in a hug. "Hey, everyone is okay."

"She wouldn't have been okay if Godiva hadn't prevented her from getting to the water. The dog saved her life."

Chapter 65

That night, Robynn's bedroom was next to Cameron's and it was all he could do to keep himself from breaking down her door. He'd never wanted a woman like he wanted her—in his bed, and involved in every aspect of his life.

His cell phone sounded. It was Robynn.

"What if I told you that the most I can handle right now is to be held?"

"I'd tell you to unlock the door. I'd ask you to trust me." He arose from his bed and moved to Robynn's door, his heart beating out of his chest. Cameron whispered a prayer for her to gain the strength she needed to lay down her barriers and trust him, let him love her.

For a minute, he thought she'd backed out, until he heard the click of the lock. The door slowly opened, and soon Robynn stood before him wearing an oversized Indiana State Police T-shirt. Her eyes were huge with fatigue, and he wondered when the last time was that she slept through the night.

Leaning against the frame of the door, he wore only boxer shorts and a slow, sexy smile that uniquely belonged to Cameron Chase. His gaze slid down her body before rising to meet her eyes. As he stared down at her, she could feel the heat sizzling in his dark brown eyes. But he just gazed at her for the longest time before he reached out to touch her hair, just the lightest stroke, and it was her undoing.

Robynn wasn't cold, but she began to tremble, and crossed her arms over her breasts. Closing her eyes, she drew in a slow, calming breath. Before she could exhale, she felt his strong arms encircle her body, making her feel things she'd thought impossible to ever feel again. Loosening her arms, she wound them around his waist to press her body closer to his, and the world melted away. Effortlessly, he scooped her up, and gently placed her on the bed. Lying down beside her, he pulled her closer until her head was on his chest and one leg was thrown across his hip.

This was when he would initiate sex. She was sure of it. He had to be as turned on as she was. Most men would, but he didn't. Instead he lightly stroked her arm and kissed the top of her head. Reaching for her hand, his fingers intertwined with hers, sending shivers up her arm.

"I know a thing or two about loss, Robynn." His low voice echoed through her like a lingering caress. "I know what it's like to be only a child and lose both parents. That young, you're not quite old enough to understand the finality of death. 'Mommy and Daddy are in heaven' means nothing to a child, who waits for them to come home like they always did."

Robynn closed her eyes, willing herself not to cry. She snuggled closer to him and realized there was so much more to this man than a handsome face.

"Losing Mom was tougher than losing Dad. I was still a child, but old enough to understand she wouldn't be there to chase the monsters from under my bed, or out of my closet. She wouldn't be there at bedtime when I kneeled to say my prayers. And how I envied the other kids who had mommies to dry their tears when they hurt themselves, and cuddle them after a nightmare woke them screaming out of a sound sleep.

"I'm not saying that Brody didn't do his best. I'm saying that I've had a close and personal experience with loss. It can eat at your soul until nothing's left, if you let it."

She swallowed hard, nodded, not trusting her voice.

"I didn't talk about it with anyone else, either."

"I just can't." Robynn clenched her teeth against the wave of hopeless, bitter pain. She didn't know if she was strong enough to relive the memories and pain of losing her husband, her detective, Alex Easton, and then almost losing her daughter to a hit and run. And today she would have been responsible for losing Becca if she'd fallen into the lake.

"It's okay. I'll be here for as long as it takes." He rolled her on her side and curled around her body like a warm glove, his hard chest against her back, his arms wrapped around her. "You need sleep, Robynn, the kind of sleep that makes tomorrow a better place to be. It will get better. I promise."

Soon she heard his soft breathing as he eased into slumber. His spicy, masculine scent surrounded her, making her feel safe and warm. Robynn closed her eyes, curled her fingers around his arm, and fell into the deepest sleep she'd had for a long, long time.

Chapter 66

The next morning, Cameron cooked cheesy scrambled eggs, Becca's favorite, while Robynn dressed his little girl in a yellow checked dress with a white pinafore. Godiva sat at Cameron's feet, waiting for a morsel of egg to come her way. Picking up Becca, holding her to her chest, Robynn moved to where Cameron was cooking at the stove and kissed him lightly on the cheek. He smiled, turned, and pulled them both into a group hug.

"Anyone up for some cheesy eggs, toast, and orange juice? Gabe and Kaitlyn should be here any minute to start their shift. Hope I made enough for everyone." He filled their plates while Robynn adjusted Becca in her high chair.

Robynn glanced at the skillet-full of food and laughed. "I think you've made enough to feed a small army. I vote for coffee, and keep it coming." Robynn sleepily rubbed her eyes and sat down at the table. She handed Becca's sippy cup to her while Cameron poured some dog kibble into Godiva's bowl.

Cameron set their plates of food before them, and then filled Robynn's cup to the brim with the hot brew. He fell into his chair and reached for his cell. There was a text from Henry Stephens at the jail.

"Message from the jail. Diego attempted suicide last night and was put on suicide watch—still in solitary away from other prisoners. It seems a man came to the jail yesterday asking about him, but was told he was not there, just as I instructed. Diego heard about the visitor and was hysterical. He kept repeating that

Juan Ortiz would kill his mother. They had to give him a sedative to calm him."

"Is his mother still at the safe house on Washington Street?"

"Safe and sound, but he doesn't know that."

"Now that he's had time to stew a bit, perhaps he has more information to give us."

"A definite possibility." Cameron shoveled in his eggs and gulped his coffee down as he simultaneously helped Becca with her food and sippy cup.

"Robynn, I have an idea. It will require a lot of coordination and there's an element of danger, in addition to an extraordinary amount of trust I'll need to give to a pint-sized petty criminal I barely know."

"Okay, you've got my attention." Robynn leaned forward in her chair. "Tell me about it."

"It will be dangerous. If you don't want to be involved, I'll understand."

"Seriously? I'm already involved and I want to be—resolving this situation, and falling in love with you. Where do I sign up?"

Cameron stared at her with surprise, she stared back in challenge. The moment he'd been waiting for had arrived. Robynn loved him and he loved her right back.

Chapter 67

Trembling, Diego gripped the steering wheel until his knuckles turned white. His breath burst in and out as he waited for Juan. Nervously, he fingered the knife he'd strapped to his ankle. There were two ways Sgt. Chase's plan could go, and one of them could get both him and his mother killed. Juan Ortiz would kill his mother first, cutting her into pieces, and make him watch.

Pushing that image to the back of his mind, Diego took a deep breath, willing himself to calm down before Juan Ortiz arrived. The man could sense fear a mile away. He'd convinced Sgt. Chase it was too dangerous for him to wear a wire, so he was on his own. He wondered how fast the cop in the unmarked car at the corner could get to him if he needed help. If he wasn't convincing, he had no doubt he would die.

Soon Juan pulled up to the convenience store driving an old Dodge Dart and made his way to Diego's vehicle. There was no mistaking the pissed-off expression on his face and Diego's heartbeat raced, nearly exploding out of his chest.

Juan jumped into the car, slamming the door behind him. "Where the hell have you been? Why haven't you answered my calls?"

"Had car trouble and had to pull off the Interstate to get it fixed. Took days."

"Where's my supply?"

Diego withdrew three plastic bags filled with meth from the

glove box and handed them to Juan, who slipped them in his pocket.

Still suspicious, Juan eyed Diego. "That doesn't explain why you haven't answered my calls."

"I found where they're hiding your kid."

"What?!"

"I kept an eye on the main house and followed the blond-haired woman to a house on Shadow Lake. She's living there with the kid."

Removing a folded rough sketch he'd drawn of a map of the property, he handed it to Juan. "Here's the house. The back faces the lake and three sides of the house are surrounded by a trees."

Pointing to a spot on the map, he said, "I have this all planned out. We put my cousin's boat in across the lake from the house. When we get to the shore, we dock it right here in these trees so we can slip through the woods to get to the house. I've disconnected the house's motion activated floodlights, so it's not likely we'll be seen.

"Who's guarding the house?"

"Just one woman inside, and she sleeps in the downstairs bedroom at the back of the house."

"Just the woman. Where are the guards?"

"No guards. This place is in the middle of nowhere, very difficult to find. I would never have found it if I hadn't followed the woman."

"What about my kid?"

"Her room's upstairs. It faces the front of the house. I've seen her through the window. At night, there's a dim light glowing in her room. The plan's simple, Boss. Avoid the woman's bedroom on the first floor, climb the stairs, I grab the kid, and escape. Easy."

"Not so fast. You're not going for my kid. I'll do that myself. You've screwed up one too many times. You'll wait by the boat."

"But, Boss—"

"Shut up. I have to make a call."

Juan push a speed dial number that Diego guessed was to Juanita Ortiz in Mexico and settled back in his seat. He seemed pleased with Diego's plan.

"Juanita, get a flight to Indianapolis. Let me know the day and time. I'll hand over your granddaughter and you will give me a carry-on bag of $100,000 with the promise that Miguel Vega calls off his killers. Do you understand?"

Chapter 68

The row boat glided quietly over the water. Close to shore, thick tree trunks and overhanging limbs came into view, along with a dark path that snaked through the woods. Diego pulled the boat onto the shore and helped Juan get out.

"I can do this, Boss. Let me go get your kid."

"I said no. Shut the fuck up. Stay here and be ready to go when I come back with Becca. You're a screw-up, Diego, and you're lucky I haven't slit your damn throat. If I come back empty-handed, I may do just that."

Juan Ortiz moved into the woods like a panther, watching, stalking, and waiting. He had the fluid, long-legged gait of the predator he was. He focused on his prey, the innocent little girl inside the house. Holding a flashlight in one hand, he outstretched his arm to ward off unseen obstacles like tree branches, and soon he reached a clearing, the house just up ahead.

As soon as Juan was out of sight, Diego took out his phone and sent a text. He made the sign of the cross, said a prayer, and sat on a rock near the shore.

By the time Juan reached the front porch, he already had his lock pick tools out and swiftly unlocked the door. Creeping inside, he froze until his eyes adjusted to a dim light in the room. The sound of the air conditioning softly hummed as he stood in a spacious living and dining area that led to a kitchen. Scanning the room, he located the stairs to his left and began the climb upstairs.

There were several rooms on the second level, but only one with the door open, a dim light sifting out into the hallway. Peeking around a corner, he saw a small child with long, blond hair sitting with her back to him at a small desk covered with children's books and toys in front of a window. His little one was awake.

"Becca." He whispered. The child had no response so he moved a step closer. "Becca?" He repeated, and still no reaction. Did his child have a hearing problem? Stroking her hair, he leaned closer. Her head slammed onto the desk like rock. "What the hell?" It was a doll.

Cameron burst from the closet and launched himself into Juan's body, slamming him hard against the wall. Juan recovered, sprung to his feet and with a well-placed kick, knocked the weight-bearing leg out from under Cameron and he went down. Robynn was a flash before Juan's eyes as she sent a kick to his groin, and pulled out her weapon as he moaned with pain.

Robynn shouted, "Police! Freeze!"

Juan ignored her, lowered his right shoulder and charged, sending the gun flying and slamming Robynn against a crib. By the time Cameron managed to struggle to his feet, Juan had swiped at his ribs with a lethal-looking knife. The front of his shirt reddening with a gush of blood, Cameron kicked the knife out of Juan's hand.

Juan rushed into the hallway with Robynn close behind. She planted her foot in the middle of his back and gave him a solid shove down the stairs. His body tumbled like a rag doll, ripping flesh, tearing muscle, and breaking bones.

He landed in a heap at the bottom of the stairs, with Carly and Brody waiting for him. He struggled to get up, but Carly pressed her booted foot hard on his chest while Brody flicked on the light.

"Hello, Juan," said Carly. "Remember me?"

Epilogue

One Year Later

As celebrations go, this was the happiest in Chase family history. All the ugliness in their past had been erased by months of joy.

Fingering his wedding ring, Cameron thought about Robynn and had no desire to be anywhere but right here at this very moment. Filled with love, he watched the arrival of their guests. First to arrive were Michael and Anne Brandt along with their twins, Michael Jr. and Melissa. Next came Lane and Frankie Hanson with their children, Ashley and Tim. Sheriff Tim Brennan with his wife Megan arrived and quickly gathered their grandchildren into their arms.

Gabe set out the last of the folding chairs under the tent, while Robynn and Kaitlyn were upstairs dressing Becca and putting finishing touches on her long hair. In a lavender floral dress, Ellie chirped with amusement as she played fetch with Godiva in the yard. Brody and Carly, in their Sunday best, dodged balloons and streamers as they brought out the sheet cake and punch bowl.

Michael pulled Cameron aside. "I was talking to a judge buddy of mine the other day."

"Is that right?"

"I told him how you captured an FBI Most Wanted fugitive and foiled a kidnapping using a resuscitation doll. I still laugh when I think about it. Talk about a brilliant plan."

Profile of Fear

A broad smile creased Cameron's face. "We're just glad it worked. Juan Ortiz's trial comes up next month, and I'm hoping for a life term, locked away where he can keep his misery to himself."

"What about his mother, Juanita?"

"We were happy to give her a ride from the airport straight to jail. She is also awaiting trial."

"To change the subject, Anne and I are honored to be here today for your vows and celebration. Most people are satisfied with signing the paperwork with a judge. Glad you and Robynn went the extra step."

Robynn—with the girls in hand—motioned Cameron to step forward to start the adoption ceremony. As their guests watched from their seats, they formed a circle, held hands. Each had something to say.

Cameron spoke first. "We invited all of you here today to join our celebration."

He turned to the girls. "We are so happy that you are our daughters, Ellie and Becca. We promise to do our best to be good parents and keep you safe and protect you. We will be here to listen to you."

Robynn cleared her throat and chased away a tear streaming down her face, then began. "We will be here to guide you when life is hard or confusing. We will cheer you on and celebrate your victories. We will learn from the love that God has for His children, and we will do our best to love you that same way."

Ellie pulled Becca to her side and urged her to speak.

"We are happy you are our mommy and daddy," said Becca.

"We promise to always be a part of this family," Ellie added.

Kaitlyn rushed to the front with her camera to get a shot of the two little girls as they turned around to face their guests. Each had a sign hanging around her neck that read: "I belong to the Chase Family, and they belong to me."

The Profile Series by Alexa Grace

Profile of Evil

Carly Stone is a brilliant FBI agent who's seen more than her share of evil. Leaving the agency, she becomes a consultant for Indiana County Sheriff Brody Chase, who needs her profiling skills to catch an online sex predator who is luring preteen girls to their death in his community.

A life hangs in the balance, and the two rushes stop the most terrifying killer of their careers—and time is running out.

Profile of Terror

Social media sites are the playground for twin sexual predators and are the last stops for three young women. When an ex-girlfriend goes missing, Private Investigator Gabe Chase is obsessed with finding her. Once her lifeless body is discovered, her gorgeous and accusing older sister is the distraction Gabe doesn't need as the body count increases and he hunts down the killers.

Profile of Retribution

For their parents, the nightmare didn't stop after Evan and Devan Lucas snuffed out the lives of seven victims for fun. It was just beginning. At a support group, the families of the women murdered by the Lucas twins gather to tell their stories, share their anger and grief, as they move toward a new normal.

For one member of the group, an obsession for payback drove his days and nights. He pledged to make Bradley and Tisha Lucas pay for the crimes of their sons. It was a pledge he was determined to keep. He'd make them suffer, just as their sons' victims had. Those who spawn monsters shall be judged, shall be condemned. Retribution would be his.

Other Books by Alexa Grace

From *USA TODAY* Bestselling Author Alexa Grace, *The Deadly Series*, four books with non-stop suspense and a healthy dose of toe-curling passion will have you holding your breath from the first page to the last.

Deadly Offerings (Book One)
Anne Mason thinks she'll be safe living in the Midwest living on a wind farm left to her by her ex's mother. She may be dead wrong. Someone is dumping bodies in her corn field and telling Anne they are gifts—for her! And how can she be falling in love with the hot attorney who represented her ex-husband in their divorce proceedings?

Deadly Deception (Book Two)
Enter the disturbing world of illegal adoptions, baby trafficking and murder with new detective Lane Hansen and private investigator Frankie Douglas. Going undercover as husband and wife, Lane and Frankie struggle to keep their relationship strictly professional as their sizzling passion threatens to burn out of control. Can they keep passion in control long enough to take down two murderers?

Deadly Relations (Book Three)
Detective Jennifer Brennan, still haunted by her abduction five years before, devotes her life to serve and protect others. Love is the last thing on her mind, but will it find her after three young women go missing and are found murdered on her watch and she vows to find the killer—or die trying.

Deadly Holiday (Book Four)
If you liked *Deadly Offerings, Deadly Deception* and *Deadly Relations*, you'll LOVE this nail-biting, holiday-themed novella where the characters return to search for a lost boy, fight breast cancer, deal with the personal financial impact of a bad economy, and seek a Christmas miracle.

Alexa Grace's Deadly Boxed Set
With more than 1,000 five-star reviews, it's time for you to discover *the three Deadly Series books: Deadly Offerings, Deadly Deception* and *Deadly Relations.*

For more information, go to www.authoralexagrace.com

About Alexa Grace

Alexa Grace is the *USA TODAY* bestselling author of riveting romantic suspense novels including the *Deadly* Series and the *Profile* Series.

Alexa's journeys into suspense are accurate police procedurals with a healthy dose of passion. A voracious reader, she has been influenced by writers ranging from James Patterson to Lisa Gardner to Nora Roberts.

Her books, *Deadly Offerings* and *Profile of Evil*, have been recognized by *RT Book Reviews* as Top Picks. *Profile of Terror* was awarded Best Romantic Suspense of 2014 by the Little Shop of Readers Reviewers Choice.

Alexa Grace earned a bachelor's degree in Communication and a Master's degree in Education from Indiana State University. Before becoming a full-time author, she worked as a corporate training director.

An Indiana native, Alexa divides her time between Indiana and Florida. She has a daughter and four Miniature Schnauzers, three of which are rescues. As a writer, she is fueled by Starbucks lattes, chocolate and communicating with her street team and readers.

You can visit her website at – http://authoralexagrace.com

Subscribe to her newsletter at – http://eepurl.com/sJ-Df

Friend her on Facebook – AuthorAlexaGrace

Tweet her – @AlexaGrace2

Join her street team on Facebook at https://www.facebook.com/AlexaGraceStreetTeam

Made in the USA
San Bernardino, CA
17 June 2016